"I don't l
and this is my .... Carlos
stance and h .... were proprietary and it
sounded like he was staking a claim to Kate. It had a
definite "hands off" tone to it.

Sam raised his eyebrow and tilted his head ever so
slightly as if listening for the secondary message
Ramirez was conveying. "Sam Slater." He extended his
hand to Ramirez to shake. He then turned to Kate and
took her hand in his, gently, almost reverently. "Ms.
Hunter, it is a pleasure."

"Hello, Mr. Slater." Even at five feet eight inches
tall, and wearing heels, Kate had to look up at him. He
watched as her eyes scanned his face. He kept his gaze
direct, expressing genuine interest. His smile reached
his hazel eyes when he turned to look at her. "Weren't
you the gentleman helping to hang some of the artwork
on Saturday afternoon?" she asked, smiling back.

"Guilty as charged." He was still holding her hand.
She tugged her hand from his grasp, then took a small
sip of champagne. Sam's gaze fixed on her. Carlos
might not even be there as far as he was concerned. The
room had shrunk to a small 3-foot diameter containing
only him and Kate.

Praise

To Stephanie
A fun evening
& great intro
new friends!

Art from Darkness

by

CA Humer

CA Humer

Art from Darkness

Cover Art by *Kim Mendoza*

The Wild Rose Press, Inc.
PO Box 708
Adams Basin, NY 14410-0708
Visit us at www.thewildrosepress.com

Publishing History
First Edition, 2023
Trade Paperback ISBN 978-1-5092-5170-4
Digital ISBN 978-1-5092-5171-1

Published in the United States of America

Dedication

For Lynn, Emily and Sue. True friends and honest
critics. We need both in our lives.

Prologue

House GOP Website April 20, 2022

Since Jack Sinclair took office and started implementing his radical open border policies, 42 people on the terrorist watchlist have been apprehended attempting to illegally enter the United States through our southern border.

Even more disturbing is that earlier this week, White House Press Secretary Jeff Jakubowski could not guarantee that none of the *over* two thousand illegal immigrants a day who avoid US Customs and Border Protection (CBP) capture entering our southern border were on the terror watch list.

****

Afghanistan—four years earlier…

The Humvee rocketed out of the compound on the heels of the dusty Corolla. Sam wanted nothing more than to pull the little shit out of the car and beat him to a pulp. Killing him would be stupid, but he'd earned a good hiding. What the hell did the snot-nosed kid think he was doing? Taking a sharp left, the car headed toward the marketplace, hoping the crowds and more narrow streets would prevent the larger vehicle from pursuing. Sam read the kid's mind and sped up to close the distance and kissed the rear bumper of the Corolla. Taking evasive action, the Toyota careened around the corner toward the school. Sam had lost some ground but had the objective in his sights. Riding shotgun, Jake tracked the car. Pointing to the side street, Jake called out where the car had disappeared. Sam changed his path. A tradesman pulling a handcart filled with fruits and vegetables came out of the alley. All Sam saw was the panicked look on the man's face as the Humvee swung wide to avoid hitting him and the cart. Sam careened around the corner, narrowly missing the old man, scanning ahead for the car.

The Corolla was getting away.

A group of schoolgirls stopped along the side of the road, pointing at the car as it made its mad dash, kicking up dust. Sam increased speed. Suddenly, everything went into slow motion. The detonation lifted the Humvee onto its two right wheels. Sam felt weightless as the vehicle lifted, then crashed to the ground. It threw Jake from his perch and rolled the Humvee onto its side, trapping Sam beneath. Gunfire erupted from what felt like a dozen different directions. Jake laid down covering fire and sprinted to Sam, dragging him out of the vehicle and behind a brick wall where the two were pinned. They hunkered down and used the radio to call for backup. Sam was busted up pretty badly from the crash and had been shot. Jake had taken a couple of rounds to the back and shoulder, but he could still pull the trigger. Jake and Sam would survive.

The girls walking home from school weren't as lucky. Sam had failed once again.

Chapter 1

Present Day…

Sam jolted awake in a cold sweat, knowing he had failed—failed to protect. It came with rain. Last night had started with a soft drizzle that built into a lashing, thunderous downpour. It drowned out his calls and erased the tracks. He couldn't move, couldn't see or hear. Helpless to stop it, Sam never knew what he was supposed to stop. Failure to protect…but protect what? Whom? In the past, when Sam failed on a mission, they were soldiers. They knew the risk, but there was one that haunted him because she didn't. Her world had still been full of love and wonder. He'd failed her and God had failed them both.

Sitting on the edge of the bed, he ran a hand through sweat-soaked hair, breathing to calm his racing heart. Scrubbing his hands over his face, Sam closed his eyes to banish the visuals and smells that accompanied the dream–blood, death, failure. Padding barefoot through the dark house, he grabbed a bottle of cold water and drank, trying to erase it all. It's over–it's only a dream, he kept repeating to himself. It was an all too familiar mantra.

He stood looking out the window, thinking of the light drizzle that had started when he went to bed. Lacing his fingers at the back of his head, Sam pressed his head forward and rolled it back and forth, stretching the taut muscles in his neck and shoulders. Sam drew in a deep, cleansing breath and blew out a deep sigh. God, you'd think he would have expected it when the weatherman had predicted severe storms. Now all Sam could hear was the rattle of the window panes when the thunder crashed against the glass and the walls of his heart. He watched the lightning blaze across the sky and the wind whip through the trees, threatening to break the blades of the silly, whirly gig his sister had given him for the garden. The sound reminded him of his helplessness and failure, threatening to drive him crazy. As the storm and the pounding in his heart and head died down, the sky lightened.

Changing into running shorts, Sam set out for the usual run, hoping to clear his head. As his footsteps took him further from the pain and memory, he felt better. Maybe numb was a more accurate word. Sam added an extra two miles to the usual three just to be on the safe side. Work and physical effort were the best antidotes for the dream. Falling into bed exhausted was the best way to deal with the darkness. Rounding the corner toward home, he slowed to a walk and only felt a slight tug in his knee, climbing the stairs to the porch.

Unlocking the front door, Sam stepped into what, for most people, would have been a disaster zone, but for him was peace and purpose. Returning home to Fort Worth following his transfer four months earlier to the Southwest office of the Department of Homeland Security, Sam reacquainted himself with his old stomping grounds with the help of Emily, his sister. Working in HSI, the Homeland Security Investigations division, Sam was collaborating with Immigration and

Customs Enforcement, investigating weapons and drug smuggling. Ever since the administration had relaxed its position on border crossing, the flood of illegal immigrants, along with drug and human trafficking, had escalated tenfold. Sam was working to curb that trend. It kept his mind occupied. There was a genuine threat of terrorists using the mass confusion to sneak over the border to perpetrate the next 9/11 type attack. They charged Sam with helping to find the bad guys before they could succeed.

The 1931 craftsman bungalow Sam purchased when he first moved to town was in sad shape, but it filled Sam's empty hours when not working. The Magnolia area was going through a re-gentrification, but there were still bargains to be had if you wanted to put in the sweat equity. Sam had the time and talent and needed the mind-numbing work of refurbishing the old place. Grabbing a bottle of water, he went out back to the garden to cool down and review today's 'to-do' list. He breathed in the scent of damp earth and sweet alyssum blooming along the shrub beds flanking the concrete garden walls. This was his oasis from all that troubled him. Cutting down the jungle of weeds and junk trees that had taken over the house when it was left to go to rack and ruin, he'd unearthed a ridiculous number of old tires and broken bottles. Clearing out the mess, he installed new landscaping and a fountain. It was very reminiscent of the walled garden he enjoyed when stationed in Kandahar, minus the bullet holes, Sam recalled, with a slight shake of his head. It brought him hours of peace and tranquility after a long day at HSI, or working on the house. The birds and butterflies were finding the water and the plants intentionally selected to attract them.

Of course, modern conveniences like indoor plumbing and hot water were high on Sam's list of bare necessities. The only bath was on the first floor. Replacing the dated and nasty toilet and sink was a start, but until something was done about the shower, he'd have to continue using the gym's facilities to clean up. It freshly motivated Sam to tackle the shower in what would eventually be the guest bath. He'd already installed the new pan and waterproof barrier. Today's work list included starting on the tile.

Returning to the kitchen, Sam grabbed a breakfast bar, turned on some classic rock and roll, and headed to the construction zone, last night's dream fully encased in the little concrete bunker in his brain until the next time.

****

Emily used her hip to push open the door. "Sam? Hey, are you home? Jiminy Cricket, do you ever lock your doors?" It was a little after 12:15, and knowing her brother as she did, Emily knew he wouldn't think about breaking for lunch. She put the barbeque on the kitchen counter. "I will be so glad when you get those darn stone countertops installed. What a mess..." she muttered, wiping at the construction dust, her pert little nose turned up in girlie disgust. "He sure isn't Mr. Clean." Emily walked toward the bedroom. "Hey, big brother! Are you deaf?"

Sam cranked down the volume on a Stones classic, bobbing his head as he continued to hear it play in his head. "Heck no. Just admiring my handiwork. What do you think?" Sam asked as he stepped out of the walk-in shower and gestured like a Price is Right model.

Emily leaned against the doorjamb and gave it a critical eye. He had just completed installing the tile on the walls. "Sam Slater—this is amazing. Wow! Where did you come up with this idea? It's beautiful."

"Jeez, I can tell you don't like it." He laughed. "Actually, I remember seeing a waterfall that fell into a pool on the patio of a house in Kandahar. It was so, I don't know, cooling, peaceful, calming. The sun lit up the courtyard and sparkled in the water. I was trying to recreate the colors and flow by doing the glass tile in a vertical pattern of blue and sea green to mimic the reflections of the fountain water. I'm pretty pleased with it. Obviously, you think it's good too."

"Good doesn't begin to describe it. Brother, sometimes you surprise me. Here I think you're some rough, uncouth guy with a legal geek brain and then you come up with this artsy-fartsy side of your personality. You didn't learn this in the SEALs. Maybe it's brain damage from that IED." Emily jumped back as Sam reached out to thump her on the noggin for that verbal jab. "Ha, missed me! Hey, I brought barbeque. You ready for a lunch break?"

"Absolutely. Give me a sec to wash my hands. Why don't you grab a couple of sodas from the fridge?"

"Sounds good. Oh, by the way, I have an ulterior motive for my visit and this great barbeque. Not only did I need a break after my morning at the gallery, but I also need to ask for a favor," Emily called back as she made her way to the kitchen.

"Really? What a surprise." Sam smiled while washing his hands. Grabbing the ice-cold coke Emily handed him, he took a long swallow. "Hmm, that hits the spot. So, what's up?"

While Emily started in on the litany of problems and other challenges she was encountering at the gallery, Sam grabbed some paper plates and towels. Emily dished out the food and, while they ate, shared the latest news about the exhibit and the last-minute tasks that needed doing. She was very particular and didn't trust just anyone with her vision. Sam got that. Popping the last bit of barbeque into her mouth and wiping her hands, Emily tilted her head, thinking.

"Sam, can you spare some time and come help me hang the last few pieces of art?"

"Sure, you want to do it this afternoon? I need to let the tile cure before I grout it, so I have the time."

"Oh, that would be great if you're okay working around an interview I'm giving to a reporter. She does features for several local and state publications and is going to write an article about the preview event and the show. Larry arranged it."

"Just point me to where you want them hung. I'll stay out of the way."

"Thanks a bunch. Go get cleaned up and I'll 'Do the Dishes'" Emily made air quote signs and dropped the paper plates in the trash.

"Dang. You're really domestic." Sam laughed as she smacked him on the cheek playfully, followed by a hug, and left for the gallery. He thought about how hard she had been working on this new project of hers. Since her fiancé, Greg, had been killed in Afghanistan; Emily had been volunteering and working hard to support the returning veterans. Discovering that several of the wounded warriors in the area were also very talented artists, she wrote up her vision and pitched the idea to her boss, Larry McGill, the owner of McGill Gallery.

Sam remembered how Emily had mimicked Larry's coquettish glance and sultry voice. "I love the idea–so masculine and if they don't ask, I won't tell".

Emily gave a perfect imitation of the little chuckle Larry used when flirting. He was a teddy bear of a guy that loved everyone, and Larry meant everyone. Flamboyant to a fault, Larry wore polka-dot bow ties and plaid vests. He made the women feel like the Queen of Sheba and the men like Tom Selleck. Larry was happy with either. He gave Emily carte blanche to find the artists and produce the show. Sam recalled how Emily had thrown herself into it with complete abandon. This was her way of promoting the new gallery and supporting the returning vets by featuring their artwork. These artists had served honorably in the military and sacrificed. Emily wanted to do something for them. When Sam considered that besides Greg, they had lost their younger brother, Paul, while he was working with the Afghan forces to fight the Taliban, Sam couldn't fault her motives. Many more of our heroes had come back less than whole. Stuffing a change of clothes into his duffle bag, he recalled how Emily had pestered him on more than one occasion.

"Sam, why don't you reconsider my suggestion that you put together a collage for the show? After all, you're not exactly whole either. Of course, maybe a finger painting would be more your speed."

"Aren't you too funny" he'd told her, thumping her on the head, but she was right and one of only two people that really knew about his dreams and demons. Even though Emily was sometimes a pain in the backside–especially with this art stuff, he admired her heart and tenacity. He'd help her with her few last details and even attend the big event. It was a dress-up affair and though jeans were his usual attire since moving here, he'd see what he could drag out of mothballs. With luck, he'd have a fully functioning shower by Wednesday and be able to take a real shower in his own home for the gallery preview party.

****

Sam cleaned up his work, double checked his duffle bag and toolbox. He ran by the gym for a quick shower and headed to the gallery on 7th Street near the old Montgomery Ward building. Someone had finally turned the old department store into a mixed-use retail space with lofts and high-dollar condos above. Sam envisioned doing that before he'd left for the SEALs. Driving by, he watched the buzz and busyness of the people shopping or enjoying the sunshine and a meal at the alfresco restaurants. All the shops were high-end boutiques, with some condos selling in the one million plus range. Oh well. Timing was everything. It was a trendy and perfect place to host a posh event for the Fort Worth upper crust.

Sam parked his jeep Gladiator and was grabbing the toolbox from the back when a Honda mini-roadster pulled into the parking space beside Emily's Ford Focus. A nicely shaped leg exited the driver's door, followed by a tall, blond-haired beauty that took Sam's breath away. She wore a stylish pencil skirt with a slit up the front side, which accentuated her long legs and a simple fitted long-sleeved white shirt. Her hair was pulled back into a lazy ponytail with tendrils escaping to frame her face. He couldn't see her eyes because she was wearing Hollywood actress-size sunglasses. She locked up the car and, much to Sam's surprise, walked to the front door of the gallery. Whoa, Nellie, Sam thought. *Is this the reporter? Okay, just play it cool, Slater. You've seen beautiful women before; even dated a few. Don't go stupid on me.*

Sam reached the door just as the reporter was pulling it open. He caught the handle and held it while she passed through. Tugging off her sunglasses, she shot him a dazzling smile over her shoulder. Sam felt a tightening in his gut when they locked eyes. Hers were the color of lapis lazuli. He felt the impact of her glance slam into him like the recoil of an AR15 on automatic. Holding his breath for a millisecond, he slowly exhaled.

Nodding to her, he stepped off to the side of the foyer. About a dozen paintings were leaning against various display walls. *Last few pieces? Looks like half the artwork.* Thankfully, the few sculptures and other "mediums" to be displayed were in place already. It was a big show. The opening preview night on Wednesday was going to be a huge deal—one that a lot of high-profile people were going to be attending. Emily had every right to feel nervous. It would open doors for her and the veterans in a lot of ways.

Sam caught Emily's eye. She excused herself from the reporter and walked over to him. "And I always thought an Art Appreciation major was a waste of time," Sam joked when she greeted him. "Hey, who is the reporter?"

"Art Appreciation major–HA HA–thanks a lot, funny man!" Emily followed Sam's gaze. "Ah, yes. That, my drooling brother, is Kate Hunter. She freelances for local papers, Texas Quarterly, and several other publications. She's interviewing me about the show and preview night. This is a real coup to get her to do an interview and see some of the art early. She'll also be covering the Preview on Wednesday night and then writing a follow-up piece to announce the Saturday opening to the public. I'm stoked, and have to keep reminding Larry to breathe. He is practically hyperventilating with excitement. Anyone who is loaded with money or politically ambitious will be there, so it could be on the front page and the society pages. It will be so classy we'll have to mind our p's and q's." Emily winked.

"Sounds like it will be very fancy." Seeing Emily's 'mom' face, he held up both hands in mock surrender. "Don't worry, I'll wash behind my ears and put on clean underwear for the event."

"You better!" Emily snorted a laugh and punched him in the arm.

Looking around, Sam gestured at all the artwork leaning against the walls. "Looks like a lot of paintings are still to be hung. Do you trust simple ol' me to hang them or do I need supervision?"

"Oh, Sam, you always need supervision, but I'm way ahead of you, brother. I set them against the display wall where to mount and placed a post-it on each painting with height, etcetera instructions. If you can't read my mind, just holler," Emily said over her shoulder as she walked back to Kate.

Sam hooked on his tool belt and set to work. He took after their dad. See the job–do the job. Not that he didn't have vision; it was just linearly focused. Emily took after their mom and was the total opposite. She was the artistic one. Dark-haired and petite with perceptive green eyes; Emily was the energizer bunny with a heart of gold, working hard to see the best in people but had an unerring sixth sense for judging character. She called it her secret radar, and it could penetrate through the most hardened armor plate and practiced deception.

After Paul, their younger brother, and Greg, her fiancé, had died in Afghanistan, Emily had closed herself off, surrounding herself with her artwork. She learned quickly crafting works of art wasn't her strong suit and embraced the old philosophy, 'those that can, do; and those that can't, teach'. Emily, Sam thought, was exceptional in that regard. She nurtured budding artists, helped them to build a following using social media, and eventually landed this job with Larry at the McGill Gallery. He was enormously proud of her, but protective, too. Greg's death had hurt her deeply. Sam knew she still wore her engagement ring on a chain around her neck. He'd watched her rub it along her cheek and across her lips while she stared off into space with sad eyes. He worried about how long she'd continue to mourn.

Sam picked up the post-it note on the first painting. LOC—left of center, ROC—right of center, AFF—above finished floor, shit, even TSU—'this side up'. She had left nothing to chance. He snorted, earning a 'mom' look from Emily before she turned back to Kate.

Sam laughed when he read the typical OCD style instructions Emily was wont to provide attached to each painting, but he carefully measured the height above the finished floor, distance from left to right, etcetera. Problem was, Sam was distracted every time he glanced at Emily and the reporter. Emily was a perfect hostess and made the reporter—*What was her name again? Oh, yeah, Kate Hunter*—relaxed. There was peach tea and comfortable seating at the front of the gallery, where the two women chatted easily about this and that. Sam listened as Kate asked a general question about a particular piece of art, allowing Emily to expand on the topic, and giving it depth and substance. Every so often, Sam could hear Emily laughing at something Kate said. He also caught the reporter glancing at him several times. Kate was confident and good at disarming her subject quickly and effectively. He could have used her talent when interrogating the Taliban. After a while, Kate turned the focus of the interview on Emily.

"Not every gallery would take a risk on unknown artists. Can you explain your motivation for featuring this work, these artists?"

"As you know, Kate, my fiancé and brother lost their lives in Afghanistan. The artists featured in this show are veterans. We owe them so much. Each individual sacrificed for this country. Many suffered physical injuries or have fought their way back from the dark abyss of depression. Their work reflects the deep emotions that only facing death can create. Yet they create beauty. There is solace in their work for them and the viewer. All are very talented and deserve an opportunity to showcase their art. I am proud to offer them that."

Thirty minutes later, Sam heard the front door open, then close. Emily approached and stood at his side, admiring his work. "You follow instructions well", she observed. "It must be all that military training."

"More likely experience following your orders in order to stay alive. I'm sure you'd kill me if I did this wrong."

"That's an affirmative, sailor. Seriously, everything looks good, Sam. Let me help you finish up the rest of these. Then, if you're not too beat from all this hard work and have the time, I'll give you the nickel tour. It'll give you an advantage at the preview on Wednesday night, in case you see anyone you'd like to impress with inside information." Emily looked at Sam with raised eyebrows. She must have caught his interest in Kate or Kate's gaze wandering in his direction during the interview. *Don't play matchmaker, sis.* Sam was willing to admit he didn't have any social life. He spent too much time on the job and the house but hell, it had only been four months. And Emily was one to talk. She spent all her time focusing on the show. *Maybe we both need time to heal, kiddo.*

****

Tuesday morning, Emily was sitting on the front porch of Sam's house with the paper in her hand, waiting for him to return from his morning run. She was tapping her foot and drumming out a tattoo on the arm of her chair, impatient with excitement. When he turned the corner, she jumped up, bouncing on the balls of her feet. A smile brightened her face and lit up her eyes.

"Oh, Sam, did you see it? What a wonderful article! Kate really nailed the essence of the show, the energy of the work. She is amazing. I called her and invited her to lunch to thank her. Such an excellent writer. I like her. She's bright and well educated, interested in a lot of different things. What about you?"

"Me? Oh, I'm interested in a lot of things and I think I'm pretty bright and well-educated. A kind of renaissance man." Grinning, Sam goaded Emily. He knew full well her meaning and refused to rise to the bait. Emily was up to her usual attempt at matchmaking. He'd seen it plenty in the last couple of months.

Emily stuck her tongue out like a juvenile. "You are such an idiot! I meant about Kate? Do you like her?"

"I don't know. I didn't spend thirty minutes talking to her like you did. She isn't too hard to look at, if that's what you mean." Opening the door, they entered walking through to the kitchen. Sam grabbed a bottle of water for himself and poured coffee for Emily. He relaxed against the kitchen sink with arms crossed loosely across his chest, while Emily continued her not-too-subtle pitch.

Taking the coffee from Sam, she smiled innocently at him. "Why don't you join us? We're going to Gretchen's. I know how you like their food."

Sam hesitated, put down his bottled water, and turned to stare out into the backyard. Sam pursed his lips and shook his head. "Being a bit obvious, aren't you? Don't you think it would seem just a little suspicious if I mysteriously showed up? No, I don't think it's a good idea. Look, Emily, I appreciate your reconnecting me with the old gang, helping me settle back into Fort Worth, but things have changed. I enjoy my work with Homeland Security and I feel like I'm putting down some roots, but I'm not who you knew before. Things changed—I changed. I'm not ready to risk failing someone I care for. You know that. But, I promise, I can and will meet someone someday. I can do it without your help. Besides, I'm sure she's already seeing someone." Sam hoped it wasn't the case, but someone as attractive as Kate, was probably in a relationship. Of course, maybe it wouldn't hurt to ask her out. All she could say was no.

Sam scooted Emily out the door and then settled into his makeshift office at the house, checking emails before leaving for Homeland Security headquarters. He ran through the information uncovered so far on the weapons flooding into the country from Mexico. The alarming number of shipments that had made it to Chicago, Atlanta, and Baltimore blossomed before his eyes. Mass shootings were on the rise and the local law enforcement agencies were up to their asses fighting off the BLM and defunding the police issues. Sam had a meeting with his boss, Commander Collins, later that afternoon to review the evidence the team had gathered to date and the next step in the investigation. He combed through the data the American Immigration Council was publishing. The numbers were staggering.

Rubbing at the headache building behind his eyes, Sam leaned back in the chair and stretched. He brought both hands down behind his head and blew out a frustrated breath. Hell, he thought, back as early as 2000, the Border Patrol recorded 1.7 million apprehensions. Still, the Department of Homeland Security estimated an additional 2.1 million successfully made unlawful entry. The number of single adults coming to the border seeking entry to the US was rocketing. Just in the first six months of 2021, it had increased by almost sixty-five percent And although the large majority of the people arriving at the border in the first half of the year were from Mexico, Guatemala, Honduras, and El Salvador, by the end of the year an increasingly large portion came from other countries in the Western Hemisphere like Venezuela, Nicaragua, Cuba, Haiti, and Columbia. This was like looking for a needle in a haystack. He created the graphs and pie charts to impress Collins and closed up the lap top hoping his one tenuous lead would yield a direct connection.

****

Sam pulled into his usual spot at headquarters. It was on the back side of the parking lot and under an oak tree that helped shade his jeep from the brutal Texas sun in the late afternoon. There was always the chance of bird shit from the grackles, but in one-hundred-plus degree weather, the risk was worth it. He walked briskly to the commander's office. Collins motioned Sam in and to a chair. Finishing up the documents in front of him, Collins turned an expectant eye toward Sam.

"Slater, good to see you. I hope you have some progress to report. I specifically requested your transfer here to follow up on the source of all these weapon shipments and to close it down."

"Yes, sir, and I'm glad you did. After tracking various leads from Florida to Venezuela, it's a logical next step to come to Fort Worth to continue the hunt. I have the figures you requested and some ideas on how to proceed." Sam pulled out the file and handed it over. He sat back in the chair and gave the commander time to review everything he'd put together.

Collins' desk chair squeaked as he rocked back and forth, paging through the neatly bound report. He had reviewed Sam's recruitment file with the same attention to detail. Collins believed Sam's ability to identify and intercept terrorist cells, tracking and killing them as necessary, was an asset. When Sam's tour of duty and enlistment with the SEALs was over, the feds had snapped him up. Being shot and screwing up his knee in the field didn't seem to matter to Homeland Security and the other 'injury'–the one Sam never talked about–hadn't come up in the interview process.

"This is good, Sam. You have a unique talent for ferreting out information, but how are we going to bring that bastard in? Where is the proof we need? Carlos Ramirez is a prominent politico. Your law degree needs to come up with a legal way to tie him to the weapons smuggling."

Sam shifted uncomfortably in his chair under Collin's hard scrutiny. Collins' expectations were high. Sam knew he had been a high-profile and desirable recruit for Homeland Security and the man Collins wanted to lead the Fort Worth investigation. Sam respected him, but the bottom line was that Collins really didn't care about all the BS. Collins wanted results.

"Ramirez is well insulated, Commander—iron-clad alibis, no phone or computer records we can tie directly to the cartel. Even with the Patriot Act, I can't get the intel; at least not timely enough to get the results we want. I've had him under surveillance for the last month. He works at the consulate in Dallas and lives on site at the private residence of the Consulate Compound in Fort Worth. I've included photos of his recent activities and known associates. Nothing leads directly to weapons smuggling. There is an upcoming social event where I have teams embedded. I'll be attending as a guest. It promises to include several guests with connections to the import/export business and large financial organizations who we suspect may be funding the operations. I hope to garner more info."

Collins leaned forward and laid the file on his desk. "Let's hope so, Slater, let's hope so."

Chapter 2

Sam arrived thirty minutes early to the preview on Wednesday evening. He needed to check on his team to make sure they were in place and confirm the listening devices planted when hanging the pictures on Saturday were in working order. The catering truck would monitor everything to see if there were any enlightening conversations. Sam thought he'd also help Emily take care of last-minute items and try to calm any nerves she had about the big event. It surprised him to see her serenely strolling about the gallery, touching surface areas to check for dust. *OCD as ever.* He chuckled. With the recommendation of Sam, Emily had hired Aalem Siddiqi, a recent Afghani immigrant, to cater the event. Sam had a unique relationship with Aalem that Emily found puzzling.

"Sam, if I didn't know better, I'd think Aalem works for you instead of me. He is so respectful to you, like you're his commanding officer. Did you guys work together in Afghanistan?"

Sam sampled one of the hors d'oeuvres before replying, "Hmmm, that's good." He grabbed a napkin. "There were a lot of locals we worked with over there. Aalem might have been in the mix. He's from Kandahar."

"Well, for what it's worth, I think he is fabulous, and thank you for suggesting I hire him. Everything looks and tastes wonderful. I still think you're holding something back." Emily knew Sam worked for Homeland Security and was investigating criminal activities.

Sam watched as she continued to circle the room, making last-minute tweaks to the displays. He exchanged quick looks with Aalem. Everything was under control. Aalem's family had run a catering company in Kandahar while he scouted and worked as a translator for Sam's unit. His brother, Hamad, immigrated to the States with Aalem and ran the catering part of the business while Aalem continued his work with Sam. There were mini bites of spanakopita, puff pastry filled with mushrooms, salmon or chicken pate, cream cheese stuffed grape tomatoes, mini crostini with herb cheese, lamb tarts and dainty little kebobs. Everything was easy to consume in one or two bites, allowing the guests to hold their drinks and look at the artwork. Aalem had placed fragrant floral arrangements of ginger and jasmine around the room in ways that didn't distract from the exhibit but added a heady perfume to the air. There was the sound of water from small fountains discreetly positioned throughout. It was like walking into a garden in some exotic land.

Sam turned to see Emily watching him with her sixth sense, squinty-eyed radar expression. He could see her wheels turning as she approached him.

"Okay, you're not fooling me, Sam Slater. I'm even more convinced there is a connection between you and Aalem that goes deeper than a caterer you just 'happen' to know. This atmosphere, the flowers, the scents, the fountains–it's exactly like your backyard. It has the same quiet, soul-soothing quality about it."

Emily poked him in the chest. "I have things to do right now but we're going to talk later, brother." Emily huffed and turned her focus to the impending arrival of guests.

At precisely 7 p.m., the doors opened. Emily was there to greet each guest and introduce them to Larry. Mavis Baldwin, one of the scions of Fort Worth society, entered at 7:20. She always made a grand entrance. She came from money and married money, outlived two husbands, and had a daughter that had moved to New York after some rather unpleasant and sordid stories about her and some man circulated about town. Her daughter didn't grace Texas with her presence any longer. Rumor had it Mavis had had an affair with the governor. It was her money that helped get him elected. When she showed up, you could count on the rest of the high society wannabes attending and lots of money flowing. Larry recognized a cash cow when he saw one and immediately latched on to Mavis, fawning over her.

"Mavis, darling, let me look at you. Is that a Mac Duggal? Ooh, your style puts every other woman in the room to shame. You are glowing, absolutely glowing…" Larry's voice faded out while escorting her around the room, pointing out the more expensive pieces of art.

Emily was in her element—greeting and shmoozing everyone. She remembered names and something personal about each individual. She expertly funneled the guests in one direction or another, inviting them to have refreshments and enjoy the show. With an eye on balance, she avoided overcrowding at any display. Emily knew how to manage her traffic.

Another talent inherited from her mother. The Gallery staff was knowledgeable about each piece and made themselves available for questions and offers to purchase. Sam had selected a position off to the side with his back to the wall. He monitored everything. His stance was casual and relaxed until he saw Kate walk through the doors. She was hard to miss in a deep red wrap dress that clung to her slim figure perfectly. It hit just below her knees and in her Louboutin bone-colored pumps; it looked like her legs went all the way up. The V-neck line drew the eye to just enough cleavage to be enticing, yet tasteful. Sam enjoyed the view. Greeting Emily warmly, she allowed herself to be directed toward the mosaics on display–a sample of custom artwork that could be commissioned and personalized for the individual client. It was something Sam loved. He sensed Kate felt a connection with the artwork as well.

Putting his drink on the tray of a passing waiter, Sam was making his way over to Kate when Carlos Ramirez, the attaché to the Mexican consulate, greeted her like they were old friends with a big smile and a kiss on each cheek. It was very European and very nauseating. Too personal to Sam's way of thinking.

What the hell? Carlos was not only a person of interest in Sam's investigation into drug and weapons smuggling, but also a known raconteur. He was a dangerous man, even though every single woman in Fort Worth found him irresistible and had tried to land him. Was he more than a friend to Kate? Carlos took two flutes of champagne from a passing waiter and handed one to Kate. He touched her hand a little too long from Sam's point of view, then took her by the elbow to guide her around the room. They moved toward a large oil painting of a desert sunset. Ramirez was speaking into her ear and gesturing. Was he sharing his interpretation of the subject? *Crap. What a douche.* He watched Kate listen attentively and occasionally smile at something Carlos said.

Talking discreetly into his earpiece, he touched base with his team in the van listening in. "Ramirez is speaking with Kate Hunter. She is a reporter and nothing has come up indicating she is a contact. He is probably just making a move on her. Let me know if he says anything interesting."

Sam watched Ramirez doing his best to impress Kate. It appeared to be working. Even though Sam had no claim on the woman, he couldn't stop muttering under his breath. "Oh, hell no! She isn't that shallow to fall for Ramirez's slick style. At least I hope not. Well," —he shrugged— "it's her choice and none of my business."

Watching and listening to their prime suspect and others who might have a hand in the action had advantages. Sam turned back toward the catering station to speak with Aalem. The evening's guests included an investment banker with ties to Halliburton, NOV and Baker Hughes. The banker was hosting an informal meet and greet of his clients with several Middle Eastern oil magnets hoping to fund new explorations. He had brought his guests and their entourage to the gallery preview. Sam instructed Aalem and his waiters to keep an eye and ear out for any new intel they might pick up during the evening. Ramirez was known for passing instructions and information at innocuous social functions like this. Sam scheduled a meeting with Aalem for later to discuss anything they learned about the terrorist threat. During their exchange, Sam noticed Aalem straighten and give a bow to someone. Sam turned to see Carlos and Kate standing behind him.

Ramirez complimented Aalem on his work. "You have done an amazing job catering this event. May I have one of your cards? I would like to recommend you to the wife of the consulate. She hosts many charity events and is always looking for a good catering company."

"Certainly, sir. I won't be but a moment." Aalem exchanged looks with Sam and turned toward the room where his staff was working, to get a business card. This left Sam face-to-face with Ramirez and Kate.

"I don't believe we have met. I am Carlos Ramirez, and this is my good friend, Ms. Kate Hunter." Carlos' stance and haughty look were proprietary and it sounded like he was staking a claim to Kate. It had a definite "hands off" tone to it.

Sam raised his eyebrow and tilted his head ever so slightly as if listening for the secondary message Ramirez was conveying. "Sam Slater." He extended his hand to Ramirez to shake. He then turned to Kate and took her hand in his, gently, almost reverently. "Ms. Hunter, it is a pleasure."

"Hello, Mr. Slater." Even at five feet eight inches tall, and wearing heels, Kate had to look up at him. He watched as her eyes scanned his face. He kept his gaze direct, expressing genuine interest. His smile reached his hazel eyes when he turned to look at her. "Weren't you the gentleman helping to hang some of the artwork on Saturday afternoon?" she asked, smiling back.

"Guilty as charged." He was still holding her hand. She tugged her hand from his grasp, then took a small sip of champagne. Sam's gaze fixed on her. Carlos might not even be there as far as he was concerned. The room had shrunk to a small 3-foot diameter containing only him and Kate.

Breaking into his and Kate's moment, Ramirez attempted to draw attention back to him. *The self-centered SOB*, Sam thought.

"Oh, is that what you do, Mr. Slater? Are you a handyman for the gallery? How interesting, and now you clean up and come to the show. Is that in case there are any quick repairs needed, or perhaps a painting falls off the wall?" Carlos sniggered at his joke. His tone was disdainful.

Sam almost choked on his drink at the not-too-subtle insult. The only visible hint of his annoyance was a slight clenching of his jaw. Cutting his eyes to Ramirez, he replied quietly, "Only when my sister requests it from me. I'm Emily Slater's brother. Actually, I'm an attorney, Mr. Ramirez. I trust you don't hold lawyers with the same contempt as you appear to hold handymen." With that, Sam turned to Kate, took her hand once again. "It has indeed been a pleasure, Ms. Hunter. I hope we meet again." He walked away with no acknowledgement to Ramirez.

Kate's gaze followed Sam as he walked away. When she'd first seen him on Saturday, she'd found him attractive. Kate remembered her gaze wandering to him while she and Emily had discussed the artists and their respective works. She had thought he must do a lot of work for the gallery, since Emily had just left him to his own devices. Kate was no stranger to a fine physique. She'd worked in the fashion industry for a couple of years while in college and saw enough male models to know the proper proportions to fill out a suit in the right way. A lot of the models were full of themselves, but she hadn't thought this guy was. He'd radiated "man". Kate hadn't been able to keep her eyes from drifting toward Sam now and again. He was tall, with short sandy-colored hair. His legs were long, in just the right proportion to his upper body, which was topped by broad shoulders. She recalled how the faded jeans fit his trim hips like a glove and did a nice job molding to his front. He'd had the sleeves of his blue chambray shirt rolled up, revealing golden arm hair on tanned forearms, and a watch that looked like military issue. His work boots were worn but of good quality. No, she remembered thinking, he didn't have a body builder physique but one rather more like a big cat, long sinewy muscles rippling just under the skin, the kind of strength that would envelope and conquer a woman if she wasn't careful.

Now, on closer inspection, she noted his face was imperfectly handsome rather than pretty. His firm jaw line and cleft chin gave an impression of confidence and determination. His nose was slightly crooked, and he had a small crescent-shaped scar just above his left cheekbone. When he'd taken her hand in his and gazed at her with his inquisitive hazel eyes, a flame ignited in her core, coursing through her body, robbing the room of oxygen. She grew breathless as the heat spread through her. Kate threw back the rest of her champagne. How did a man she barely knew do that? Wow! When she felt Carlos' eyes on her, she looked down quickly, composing herself. Turning her gaze up to Carlos, she watched him motion to his—what? Bodyguard? Whoever he was to Carlos, the man brought them two fresh flutes of champagne.

Taking the proffered glass, Kate shook her head. "What an interesting man. Do you know him?" she asked, keenly aware of Carlos' stiff posture and belligerent expression. She thought the entire exchange between them was odd, almost aggressive, like two rutting bucks facing off. She felt both powerful and embarrassed.

Carlos smiled, and shrugged it off. "I don't know him personally, but I know his kind. They are handy with a hammer but rarely an intellectual match to a woman of your depth and culture." Taking Kate by the elbow, he expertly guided her to other groups of influential guests in the room. He was charming and introduced Kate to the noteworthy attendees she had hoped to meet and talk with about the show. It fit perfectly with her work assignment, so she enjoyed the evening and the company of Carlos. When an environmental engineer from the university engaged her in a conversation about her recent article on the Edwards Aquifer, Carlos briefly stepped away to speak to one of his staff from the consulate. Otherwise, he rarely left her side. When it came time to say goodnight, Carlos stayed with Kate while the valet retrieved her car.

"I am so happy we had a chance to get to know each other better, Kate. The brief time we spent together when you interviewed me was very enjoyable, and tonight was even more so. I hate to say goodnight." He pulled her hand through his arm and leaned into her, his breath tickling her ear as he spoke. "May I take you to lunch tomorrow?"

Kate looked up at Carlos and smiled. "I'd enjoy that very much." Her car being delivered interrupted further conversation until Carlos, handing the valet a ten-dollar tip, helped Kate into the vehicle himself. "Is twelve-thirty convenient? I'll pick you up."

"That works for me. I'll text my address. It's on Willow Dr."

"Yes, I know. I'll see you tomorrow." Carlos smiled and closed her car door, sending Kate safely on her way.

It was a short drive back home and Kate was getting ready for bed while reviewing the evening before she even thought to herself. *'Yes, I know?' Know what? Where I live? How did he know that?* It was very romantic or very creepy. She wasn't sure which. Shaking her head, she focused instead on the comments she'd heard from the guests earlier in the evening, making notes for the follow-up article she would write on the gallery show opening.

Chapter 3

He saw the text and swore out loud. The stupid fuck! What did he expect to happen? He would have to deal with this minor inconvenience and it would put him behind schedule, which pissed him off even more. He took the next exit, drove through the gate of the razor-wire fence into a weed-strewn crumbling parking lot. Cortino was on him the minute he stepped out of the car.

"I thought you said your guys knew what the hell they were doing? The border patrol busted the god-damn courier. He's sitting in a jail in Del Rio, probably puking up every detail of the deal right now." Cortino poked Carlos in the chest, punctuating every other syllable of his diatribe. "I'm out hundreds of thousands and you're going to replace that product at your own expense. You got that '*amigo*'?"

Carlos took Cortino's extended finger in his hand and deliberately moved it away. "Shall we take this conversation inside?" Carlos led the way into the garage. Flicking a speck of dust from his suit, he turned contempt-filled eyes toward Cortino. He hated dealing with morons. Sadly, Robert Cortino was the younger son of a long-standing client from up east and required special handling. Otherwise, Carlos thought, he'd be dead.

Carlos explained in a way that any imbecile would

understand. "This is most unfortunate, Mr. Cortino. But you may rest assured, my courier isn't puking up anything of importance." Carlos sat on the edge of the desk and calmly watched Cortino pace. His pupils were pinpoints; his face shiny with perspiration. The greasy hair was coming undone from his man bun, and Carlos could smell the stale sweat evidenced by the stains circling the armpits of his shirt. Obviously, the man enjoyed the product he sold as much as the profits his family made from it. Carlos shook his head. It was such a shame that this excuse for a son was dishonoring his father, a man for whom Carlos had a great deal of respect. Ah, well, stupid is as stupid does and Robert Cortino was stupid.

Cortino kicked a trash can across the room and spewed every coarse adjective he knew. "Your fucking wet back swam across the Rio Grande with a kilo of bird on an inner tube. The border patrol could have been deaf and blind and still busted him. Is this the delivery system you have in place? My father says your brothers run a solid organization. What the hell's wrong with you?" Carlos felt the spray of spittle as Cortino pushed into his face. "Are you the retard of the family?"

Running out of patience, Carlos shot up and grabbed Cortino by his shirt, pushing him up against the wall. "He knows nothing important." Carlos gave Cortino a shove and stepped back. Pulling a fine linen handkerchief from his pocket, he wiped his face and hands. "I run an extremely compartmentalized operation. All that courier knows is that he received a package of unknown items, the quality of which questionable, and is to deliver it to an address that is untraceable to either your organization or mine for which he will receive generous compensation upon his return. In the meantime, the twenty kilos you requested are en route to our pre-arranged destination and conveniently slipped under the border patrol's nose."

Carlos spat at Cortino's feet and walked to the door. Before slamming it behind him, he turned back, drilling Cortino with one last look. "One of my reasons for compartmentalization is never having to deal with scum like you, Mr. Cortino. You are an idiot and if my family did not hold your father in such high regard, you'd be dealing penny packs out of the trunk of your car snorting as much as you sell. Never contact me again, 'amigo'."

Carlos tamped down the anger he felt at Cortino's idiocy. Dealing with the dumb fuck was one of the irritating inconveniences he'd have to deal with until the family could achieve their goals. The cartel was the foundation for building all the power in Mexico. Carlos' father had raised three sons with specific plans for each. Ric, the eldest, would take over the operation of the Cartel when his father stepped down. Eduardo, a financial genius, would run the banking portion of the business and eventually be Secretary of the Treasury when Carlos, the most handsome and polished, was elected President. Carlos swallowed his anger when he imagined living in the Presidential Palace, enjoying all the control and power the position afforded. He would be glad when his time as an attaché was over. It was a tedious role required to build the political contacts he'd eventually use to further his ambitions. The other goal was to find an American wife, one that would advance his bid for the presidency. She would need to be beautiful, intelligent, and a perfect ornament during the campaign rallies and subsequent social functions. She'd be his helpmate, supporting relations with the American politicians he'd be using to build the family empire. He was confident he had found the right woman in Kate Hunter.

Carlos turned the corner onto Willow Drive and pulled to the curb in front of Kate's house. He checked his hair in the mirror and straightened his tie. When he climbed out of the car, he took a moment to look around. He walked up to the front door, admiring the neatly trimmed beds along the porch. She had a Mexican landscape company. One he'd conveniently placed to gather information about her. Ringing the bell, he took one last look at his reflection in the glass. Hers was a charming home, just as his men had reported. Small, almost doll house in appearance, in a very well-kept, trendy area of Fort Worth. She rented rather than owned, was well-liked by her neighbors, but rarely called attention to herself. There were pots with colorful flowers of the season decorating the porch and a wine cork wreath hanging on the front door. The door mat said 'Good friends bring wine'. He made a note to remember that and rang the bell.

When she answered, he grinned and, holding out his empty hands, glanced down at her door mat. "Would I be forgiven if I bring two bottles next time I visit?"

Kate gave him a puzzled look, and when realization popped into her face, laughed at his joke. "Hmmm, don't know. Depends on what kind of wine you bring. Two-buck Chuck? I'd probably have to give serious consideration to letting you off the hook." They laughed over the joke while Kate locked her door and they walked to the car. Carlos held her hand as she settled into his Mercedes and, once buckled in, they drove off.

Kate was an enigma; a woman of intelligence and intuition. Her articles were accurate in fact and sensitive to feelings. She could converse on everything from history to architecture to fine cuisine. When she had requested an interview with Carlos to discuss Mexico's position on the immigration challenges faced by his government and the crisis at the border, he discovered she was a woman that excited a man's mind and his body.

Carlos snuck a look at Kate as he maneuvered through the streets of Fort Worth to a little restaurant he favored for lunch. American women were too often vacuous, impressed only with physical looks and money, especially money. Carlos was introduced to the upper crust of the city upon his arrival in Fort Worth. He became a sought-after dinner guest. Each mother hoped their debutante daughters would catch the eye of the rich, debonair attaché. Oh, he'd enjoyed most of the single Fort Worth society women in his bed. They served as short-term entertainment, but he soon grew bored with them. But Kate Hunter could be different. Someone like Kate could help him achieve his political goals. That's not to say he did not desire her. He had made it a priority to learn more about her. Lunch was merely the first step to building a relationship with a woman he felt would bring him great pleasure. He had initiated step one in his plan.

"Senior Ramirez. It is an honor to have you with us this afternoon. I have your table ready and the wine chilling as requested." Enrique led them to a quiet corner, where Carlos pulled out Kate's chair and the waiter placed her napkin on her lap. Settling himself, he watched the waiter open the wine, presenting the cork for his approval. He took a small sip and gave a nod of approval. After the waiter returned the bottle to the wine bucket, he discretely stepped away. Carlos took Kate's hands in his. "May I order for you? I am especially fond of their mushroom soup and the Chicken Forestier is a light entrée, not too filling. I think you will enjoy both."

Carlos was schooled in proper etiquette, and his manners were exemplary. He prided himself on every detail and decision-making. It was all very European. The dossier his men had compiled on Kate told him she had been raised to expect no less from a gentleman. He also had made sure to be punctual, another of her expectations.

"I hope I didn't come too early to pick you up. I was looking forward to seeing you again and may have misjudged my arrival time."

"Oh, not at all. I know it sounds silly, but being late is one of my pet peeves. Punctuality is a sign of respect. I remember my dad always joking with me. He'd quote an old TV show where the character said it was better to be three hours early than even three seconds late. I actually think the line was stolen from Shakespeare."

"I think it is refreshing to meet a woman who is on time for a date. So often there is the last-minute fussing with the dress, the hair. Well, I have cousins, so I can attest to waiting more often than not to leave for church or a family dinner. Do you have family, Kate?"

As they talked about easy and small things, Carlos studied the woman he wanted in his bed and potentially by his side. His assistant was a thorough researcher and Carlos had made it his business to get to know as much about her as possible. To hear her small laughs and watch her wistful smiles as she shared precious memories, made it more meaningful, more poignant. If she was to be the first lady of the president of Mexico and pass muster for his mother, she must have a proper pedigree.

The wait staff brought lunch, poured wine, and made themselves virtually invisible while Carlos guided the conversation. He asked questions about Kate and she talked. Where was she from, where did she go to school, what brought her to Fort Worth? Had she been a journalist for long? Did she come from a big family? With unerring smoothness, Carlos knew exactly what questions to ask, when to give encouraging nods or quiet 'hmm's', and when to cover her hand sympathetically or shake his head in astonishment.

"Fort Worth isn't my home. I settled here because it is centrally located and I can travel conveniently for my work. Texas is also a political hotbed. There are a lot of interesting articles waiting to be written."

"But without family, aren't you lonely, especially during holidays, times when family is so important?" Carlos reached over to top off Kate's wine, smiling encouragingly at her to continue.

"I've been on my own for so long, Carlos. My folks died in a car accident when I was fifteen years old. I'm not very close to my family anymore. I'm the youngest of three siblings. My brothers were several years older than me and we were not close. When my folks died, I was still at home. I had to be the strong one, the one to take charge and make all the decisions. Following the accident, I handled my parent's funeral arrangements and worked with the attorney to execute the will." Carlos tut-tutted sympathetically, pouring her more wine.

On a sigh, Kate sipped and continued. "I don't know. My brothers either didn't care or were too broken up about losing our folks. I'm not sure which, or if, it even matters now. That was when I learned I had to rely on myself. I rarely see them anymore." She leaned back in her chair, closing her eyes to compose herself, and pressed her napkin to her mouth. Carlos laid his hand over hers, softly running his thumb over her knuckles. He felt her eyes studying him as he toyed with her hand, turning it so the palm faced up, twining his fingers with hers. It was a practiced move that was both sweet and supportive all at the same time. Carlos sensed Kate was drawn to gentleness, overlayed with subtle power and domination. Carlos felt her pulse race with arousal.

She sighed in surrender. Sadly, Kate found the men she had dated previously were like her brothers, wishy-washy, unable to make a decision, weak. It was refreshing to have someone take control and decide on her behalf. Kate had only slept with one man in her life. It had been a schoolgirl crush in college. He had been pretty, but also weak. Maybe she had read too many fairytale romances where the handsome prince swept into the heroine's life, rescuing her from disaster and carrying her off to his castle in the sky, fulfilling her every fantasy. Kate wanted to give herself to someone that was her intellectual and emotional equal. Someone strong-minded and decisive. She was astonished when she wondered what Carlos would be like in bed. When Carlos asked for the check, it surprised her to find it was four already. Where had the time gone?

Carlos stepped around the car to help her out and walked her to the front door. Taking the key from her hand, he unlocked her front door and pushed it open. Another romantic gesture that had Kate's head spinning and her heart tumbling.

Toying with her key chain, Kate watched as Carlos cleared his throat. Raising his shoulders in a self-conscious shrug, he gave her a sheepish grin, like a shy teenager. "You know, I had an ulterior motive in ordering such a light lunch. I was hoping you'd be hungry again soon so we could enjoy each other's company once more. Would it be presumptuous of me to ask you to dinner this evening?"

Kate laughed. "You are a very clever man and I'd enjoy that very much."

"Is eight too early to pick you up? I know it's only a little over three hours from now, but it will be the longest three hours for me to wait to see you again."

"You smooth talker!" Kate's eyes sparkled at his shameless flirtation. "Make it eight-thirty. I have to do *some* work today." Kate laughed and kissed him lightly on the cheek before closing the door.

Carlos walked to his car with an arrogant step. He sat with a satisfied smile as he examined the wax impression he'd made of Kate's house key. It would be adequate to have a copy made later. He placed the wax in a small container and, tossing it in the air like it was a coin he had just flipped, slid it into his pocket. Step two, he thought.

****

Carlos liked to take time with his appearance, especially when the prospect of spending an evening with a beautiful woman and the promise of things to come ran through his mind. He dressed in a soft gray French serge suit and finished it with a butter-yellow Hermes tie.

When Kate opened her door, Carlos watched her eyes begin to simmer as they moved over him. He'd combed his hair back, but a small lock had worked its way loose and fell over his forehead. He knew it made him look reckless. At six feet, Carlos wasn't too much taller than Kate in heels. What he lacked in height, he more than made up for with his bearing and commanding presence. He dwarfed everything and everyone around. His aquiline nose and dark eyes gave him a mysterious and dangerous look. Carlos heard the sharp intake of Kate's breath and read the heat of passion in her eyes as she damped the embers ignited by his bad-boy persona.

Carlos smiled and leaned in to kiss her cheek. Kate preferred scented lotion to perfume, and the fragrance of orange and ginger floated around him. Carlos pressed his cheek to hers and took a moment to breathe in her scent. It was intoxicating.

For dinner, Carlos had selected a small bistro on Lancaster Avenue. The owner knew him personally and placed them at a quiet table in a back corner. While they made small talk, the waiter brought their cocktails.

"I have always enjoyed this restaurant. The décor reminds me of my time in Spain. I spent a semester studying at the University of Salamanca. I fondly remember sitting in the plaza enjoying too much sangria and tapas until all hours of the night. It was a time of carefree youth and adventure. I understand, Kate, you have also traveled to Spain?"

Kate had loved her time spent in Spain and was thrilled to share her impressions of the country and the people. "Life appears so simple there. I think I could get used to siestas and late dinners in the plaza. I have to confess, I never liked anchovies or olives, yet when I had them at a little restaurant in the Plaza Mayor in Madrid, I came to love both."

"Ah, do you speak Spanish then?"

"I'm embarrassed to say only enough to find the *servicios* and order Sangria. I'd like to return someday. There is something very compelling about the Latin approach to life. More relaxed, I think."

"Then I hope you will soon allow me to introduce you to the Mexico where I grew up and my home. It isn't Spain, but I think you would find it equally enjoyable. Our small hacienda in Guadalajara has a lovely courtyard–very reminiscent of a Spanish plaza. The family gathers most evenings to enjoy cocktails and dining under the stars. Here, let me teach you a new phrase in Spanish. *Seria tan facil enamorarme de ti...*"

Kate attempted to repeat the words. Carlos didn't laugh at her. "So, what did I just say? Will I get in trouble if I say it in mixed company?"

"Well, I wouldn't want you to say it to my mother."

Carlos feathered his fingers over her hand, whispering in her ear. His breath fanned the soft hairs on her neck and Kate bent her head shyly. "Perhaps someday you'll say the words to me."

Kate wasn't sure what he'd said, but something

about the look in his eyes made her think it held the promise of heat and excitement.

Carlos leaned back in his chair, keeping a hold of her hand. They talked about an imaginary trip they'd someday make together. Kate shared her experience visiting Fatima in Portugal. Carlos talked about his ambitions to advance in the diplomatic corps and eventually run for political office. "I hope I will find a woman who can stand by my side when that day comes."

Those words lingered in her thoughts during coffee and after-dinner drinks—Cognac for Carlos and Frangelico for Kate. Afterward, Carlos drove to Kate's home via the scenic parkway that ran along the river. He'd opened the moonroof to the cool spring breeze. As it lifted tendrils of Kate's hair around her face, he held her hand to his mouth, trailing light kisses across her knuckles. Kate leaned back, enjoying all the sensations created at that moment. When they arrived at her home, Carlos helped her out of the car, pulled her arm through his, and walked her to the front door. He held Kate's hands and looked into her eyes. Without breaking his gaze, Carlos slowly brought her hands to his mouth, laying a light kiss across the back of each. He turned them over and sensuously kissed the center of each palm, then moved on to kiss the inside of her wrist. It was hypnotic. Kate couldn't look away, couldn't move, couldn't breathe.

Carlos drew her into his arms and, cupping the back of her head, brought his mouth down on hers, for a soft and expectant kiss goodnight, which quickly deepened, leaving her trembling and breathless.

Pulling away, Carlos said, "It's been a perfect day.

I don't want to say goodnight. May I see you again? I have commitments tomorrow, but are you free for dinner Saturday evening?"

Kate was still reeling from the aftermath of his touch but whispered, "I'd like that."

Carlos kissed her once more and, seeing her safely inside the house, drove home. Step three, he thought.

Chapter 4

Emily was on his front porch, pacing, when Sam rounded the corner. He wasn't surprised to see her waiting for him. He had already seen the paper. It featured a section called "The Weekend Guide". The article Kate had written about the gallery opening was prominently displayed on the front page. She had titled it "Art from Darkness", touching on the influence the wounded warrior artists brought to their work. Larry, the owner, had already sold Mavis Baldwin a huge expensive desert scape from the preview and was ecstatic. Emily felt as if all her dreams and ambitions were coming true. Sam knew what she was there for.

"Oh, Sam! Did you see it–the article in the Weekend Guide? Kate hit all the highlights from the preview. She promoted the gallery and the show without it sounding like it was a paid advertisement." Emily was dancing in circles, pumping her fists in the air triumphantly. "It could have a significant impact on the success of the show."

Hugging the newspaper to her chest, she bubbled over with enthusiasm and happiness so typical of Emily. Sam had seen the article on the society page touting Mavis Baldwin's attendance, and recognizing the interest of the Mexican Consulate and other foreign visitors. Kate hadn't mentioned Ramirez specifically in her article, and unfortunately, his team hadn't picked up any clandestine meetings or conversations while he was at the preview, although the guys in the sound van had ribbed him about the exchange they heard between him and Kate. *"She sounds hot. Is romance in the air?"* Sam cowed them with a look. All but Tom, his tech expert, dropped their eyes.

Tom grinned like an idiot and slapped him on the back. *"It's ok, sir. We recognized your subtle interrogation of the female subject. Were you able to learn any state secrets or just the color of her eyes?"*

Sam shook his head then and now, remembering the laughter and comradery of his men. He turned his attention back to his grinning sister.

"It is a good article. Kate Hunter is good at what she does. I agree. It will be a boost to the show. Didn't you say you were having lunch or something with her?"

"I asked, but she was busy. Apparently, the Mexican Consulate, Carlos Ramirez, has been bogarting all her time. He's a hottie, but I've heard rumors. Unsubstantiated, of course, but where there's smoke, you know? I heard he dated Mavis Baldwin's daughter when he first got here and then she up and moves to New York. No rhyme or reason to it, and it was so sudden. Folks won't say anything out loud." Emily shifted her gaze toward the azaleas in the front bed, budding out. "I don't know, Sam. I can't put my finger on it, but I think there is something dark and dangerous about that man. I hope Kate isn't taken in by his smooth sophistication. I'll have a better sense next week when we get together for lunch. The invitation for you to join us is still on the table. I could tell you were interested when you were at the gallery on Sunday, hanging those last-minute paintings for me. I noticed her checking you out as well. Come on, Sam. You're much nicer than that Carlos guy and it's about time you started dating. It's past–it's over. You can't change it. You need to put all that behind you."

Sam's hands fisted, then let loose. He breathed in slowly and deliberately to quiet the pounding of his heart. He frowned, remembering his dad telling them that even when you lose, as long as you learn something, it's a win. Yeah, he'd learned a lot that day in Kandahar. How to not get suckered again and how not to let your heart overcome your head. Still, it galled him that Carlos was making moves on Kate. Hell, what was he thinking? She was a free agent, as far as he could tell. He certainly didn't have any claims on her– hadn't exchanged more than a dozen words but when he'd held her hand at the preview party on Wednesday night and gazed into her eyes, he'd fallen into a clear blue lake with a whirlpool at its center that threatened to take him down. If someone had asked him to paint perfection, it would be her. Sam had seen something in her; something that touched his soul. It infiltrated all the layers, bursting through every barrier he'd erected since Kandahar. He'd been lost. But getting involved meant opening his heart, and opening his heart meant taking a risk of failing someone. His pulse rate jumped again, and beads of sweat dotted his hairline. Emily left him to brood.

Sam continued to brood. Changing into work jeans and a scruffy old t-shirt, he set up his workspace and tools. The door was laid across sawhorses on the front porch. The weather was perfect, and he was losing himself in some good rock and roll, putting the final coat of teal paint on the new front door, when the

Harley pulled to a stop in front of the house. The tall stranger pulled off his helmet and mirrored sunglasses. He ran a hand along a braided ponytail. "That's a pansy ass color for a front door, if you ask me."

Sam's shoulders tensed. He carefully put the paintbrush down and turned. He took two steps toward the stranger. "You should know. You look like a pansy yourself."

"Them's fighting words!" The stranger lunged forward, grabbing Sam in a headlock that quickly turned into a noogie. "Sam Slater, you SOB! How the hell are you?"

Sam pushed off from Jake Edwards and gave the braid a tug. "Better than you, I'd say. What's this? Can't afford a barber?"

"I can–choose not to. Who the hell cares? I'm in construction and it looks like you want to be. What the hell, Sam? Didn't I teach you better? Teal? Jesus. Pansy ass… Where's the beer?" Jake gave a derisive snort and walked past Sam through the house toward the kitchen.

Sam closed up the paint can, dropped the brush into turpentine, and followed him in. Jake found a couple of cold brews front and center on the main shelf of the refrigerator. He was glad to see that some things hadn't changed. Popping the top off his beer, he handed the other one to Sam.

"Jeez, Slater. This place is a disaster. Tell me you have indoor plumbing." Jake walked around the kitchen with its green laminate countertops and construction grade cabinets. He poked around and finally ended up in the guest bath. "Oh yeah, now that's what I'm talking about." He patted Sam on the back. "This is ok. Good grout lines, nice touch with the tile pattern. I guess this blue/greenie stuff is the theme, huh? Well, at least it ain't pink." He clinked his can to Sam's, wrapped an arm around Sam's shoulders, and turned them both back the way they'd come.

"Thank you for your approval. I see you got my distress call. I'm capable, but a lot of this is a two-man job, and I figured you wouldn't argue with free room, board and beer."

"Happy to help. I just finished flipping that place up in Durango. Made a nice little return on my investment and thought I'd take some time to ride the Hill Country roads. Stopping in to see you and drink your beer is a bonus, although you're going to have to buy better stuff than this. Shiner? Seriously?" Jake emptied his can, crushing it one-handed. He tossed it into the trash like Luka Doncic and grabbed a second one. Throwing himself down on the one decent chair Sam had, he propped his feet on the coffee table. "So what have you got yourself into, Slater? And how can I help?"

Sam studied his long-time running buddy. Outside of the long hair, Jake Edwards hadn't changed that much in the few years since they got out of the SEALs. Originally from a small town about 90 miles outside Colorado Springs, he referred to himself as a refined mountain man. He could track and hunt anything, had actually taken out a grizzly when he was 17, or so he claimed, and could swim like a fish. His parents had died when he was a kid and his uncle had raised him, so no one complained when he joined the Navy on his eighteenth birthday. Jake never looked back. During basic training, he demonstrated his shooting skills and was immediately tagged for special ops training. He qualified as an Expert in record time. At six feet one inch, he was the opposite of Sam in coloring, physique, and disposition. Built like a linebacker, he carried 230 pounds of solid muscle. His long hair was pulled back into a braided ponytail, and he wouldn't be caught dead in anything other than jeans and cowboy boots.

Sam decided the door could wait. He sat down on the couch, pairing his scuffed boots with Jake's on the coffee table, and shared his vision for the house.

Chapter 5

Carlos took Kate to the theater, the symphony, and expensive dinners. The restaurant owners and staff treated them like royalty. Sometimes Carlos would drive and other times, they would use the consulate car, and Hector, an elderly gentleman, would chauffeur them. Each time they were out, Carlos made it a point to send flowers or sneak a note into Kate's handbag or pocket. She'd find it after he left. 'So you'll think of me until our next meeting' or 'I will dream sweet thoughts of you'; always something romantic. He was planning a siege, and Kate's heart was the citadel he planned to conquer. It wasn't enough to just make her heart race or her head spin. He intended to draw her into his charm and let him take more and more control of her and her time. He talked of his mother's hope for his happiness and grandchildren.

Tonight, Carlos was taking Kate to the symphony. He arrived at Kate's house right on time in the consulate town car with two men dressed in black suits rather than the usual chauffeur.

"Where is Hector?" she asked.

"His granddaughter is celebrating her fourth birthday today. The family is having a big celebration, and I didn't want him to miss it. Juan is driving tonight. And, I have some pressing business that unfortunately may require my attention this evening. Miguel is here to field any calls and will only intrude if absolutely necessary so I can give my undivided attention to you." Miguel opened the car door and they settled into the back seat.

The performance was Rodrigo's Concierto de Aranjuez for guitar and orchestra. He had specifically chosen it because it was Spanish and an extremely sensuous composition. When the lights dimmed and the orchestra began, he watched Kate lean forward; her left hand caressing her throat and collarbone. The simplicity of the solo guitar mesmerized her during the Adagio. It evoked images of old romantic Mexico. Breathing out a sigh, Kate closed her eyes and leaned back in her chair. Carlos watched her respond to the ebb and flow of the music. Saw her float as the sensuous waves washed over her. Carlos played with Kate's hand, tracing lazy patterns across her palm and letting his fingers skim over the silky skin on the inside of her wrist. She relaxed against him and as he gazed at her face, he could see the passion building in her expression. Having watched her response to the music, he planned on leaving at intermission. This would be the music he'd play tonight as he made love to her.

When the room erupted into thunderous applause, the spell was partially broken. It startled Kate from her dreamlike state. She turned to Carlos. Her face was flushed, her lips soft and parted. There was a fire being kindled in her eyes. She is ready, he thought.

"Kate, come, let's go. Let's go home." He reached out his hand. Kate moved like she'd been drugged. The music had hypnotized her and Carlos was in control. He helped her with her shawl, letting his hands linger along her shoulders, brushing them lightly across the sensitive skin on her tender nape. Kate drew in a breath and sighed it out slowly. His hands were warm. She trembled under his touch and a small shiver ran over her. Carlos was very pleased–it was the last step–it was time. He made a barely perceptible sign to his guard, who called for the driver to bring around the car.

"Senor Ramirez will be leaving now."

Carlos took Kate's hand, tucking it securely in the crook of his arm. He'd discreetly pressed his arm against her breast and felt her nipple harden in response. As he guided her toward the exit, the heat of her body shimmered through the silk of her dress. The car was already waiting at the curb. He imagined her lying back once they'd settled in the car's backseat with his hand sliding up her thigh. Carlos knew she would be moist and waiting for his touch. When they stepped out onto the sidewalk, Robert Cortino approached him. The black slacks and polo shirt he wore were in sharp contrast with his pale complexion. His jacket was leather, too heavy for the weather. He wore his dark hair loose tonight, slicked back from his face. Carlos saw the bulge and knew Cortino was carrying a gun in a shoulder holster. Cocking his head in curiosity, Carlos saw the menacing look on Cortino's face and the confrontational stance taken squarely in front of him.

"We need to talk. Now!"

Disgust curled Carlos' lips. Robert Cortino, a small dealer of drugs who purchased from the Ramirez Cartel had been warned once. But Cortino was boorish and stupid and tonight had made a big mistake. Carlos nodded. He turned, placing himself protectively between the man and Kate. He helped Kate into the back seat of the car and took her hand, kissing it lightly.

"Please forgive this minor intrusion. Give me a moment."

Closing the door, Carlos stepped away to speak with Cortino, nodding to Miguel, who positioned himself between the car and the two men. Miguel blocked Kate's view. Carlos stood calmly as Cortino's aggression amped up. Carlos waited patiently for Cortino to spew the anger and frustration radiating from him. Miguel stood near, but did not interfere. He was balanced on the balls of his feet, body tense, ready to spring. Miguel had his hand inside his jacket, anticipating and ready for action.

Cortino reverted to kind and poked Carlos in the chest. With his anger barely contained, he whispered, "The shipment is overdue. Your brother said it would be here yesterday. We do a lot of business with you and I expect to be kept informed when there are delays or problems. You're not dealing with some second rate distribution ring here. We know the ropes and have solid connections. Don't fuck with me, Ramirez!"

Carlos sneered and bowed his back. With murder filling his eyes, he placed his hand on Cortino's chest, shoving him away. "Back off, Cortino. You are interfering with my evening. If you ever approach me in public again, you will be dead. Do you understand?" Carlos cocked his head toward his guard. Miguel moved in and stood next to Cortino as Carlos turned on his heel and walked back to the car, climbing in next to Kate. Miguel stayed behind with Cortino.

He looked at her wide and questioning eyes. He could tell the spell had been broken. What would have been the perfect accompaniment to their lovemaking would now remind her of the encounter with that boorish imbecile. He was seething inside, but his expression was controlled and calm.

Carlos took Kate's hand and brought it to his lips. Thankfully, he thought, Kate could hear none of the conversation. "I apologize for that rude interruption. Apparently, the man had some business dealings in Mexico go badly and wants to blame me. He obviously did not want to wait to see me in my office to discuss it civilly. I hope he did not frighten you. You are always safe with me, Kate. I would let no one ever hurt you."

"Thank you, Carlos. This has been upsetting. Would you take me home, please?"

"Of course, *Carino*." Carlos' eyes darkened momentarily in anger. He was frustrated. The romance of the evening was beyond rescue. He knew Kate was an intelligent and observant woman. She would know something didn't ring true with the entire episode. Kate had enough experience in the world to have seen the bulge of the guns. She would have witnessed the body language and anger on their faces as he and Cortino talked. He sensed her pulling away and wondered if she was more frightened of Cortino or him. Kate was a cautious and guarded woman. She didn't give her trust easily. While he felt triumphant earlier thinking he had found a weak spot in her defenses, that moment had passed. He placed a protective arm around her and settled them back in the seat. "Juan, please drive us to Ms. Hunter's home."

After dropping Kate off at her home, Carlos texted Miguel. He would meet the offensive gentleman, Cortino, and Miguel in an hour at the garage in the river bottoms to 'finish' the conversation Cortino had started.

Carlos changed into black jeans and a dark t-shirt.

He pulled a black windbreaker on to hide his shoulder holster and grabbed the keys to the SUV. Cortino had made the mistake of coming between Carlos and his goal for the evening—having Kate. He was pissed. No one got in his way without regretting it.

Cortino was sitting on a folding chair in the three-bay garage next to an old wooden work table covered in discarded spark plugs and carburetors being rebuilt. Several years accumulation of cobwebs and dirt covered the concrete walls. Grease stains layered the concrete floor. He was leaning back in a folding chair, waiting for Carlos to arrive. Cortino had had time to think and was feeling nervous about the direction this meeting was going. It had been a couple hours since his last speedball, and while Cortino pretended to be calm and in control, there was a sheen of sweat on his upper lip and around his hairline. He was drawing blood, chewing his cuticles, clearly worried. Cortino looked up when Carlos walked in, trying to maintain a façade of bravado. Cortino leaned back on the two rear legs of his chair. The cocky attitude he displayed was all it took to push Carlos over the edge. In three quick strides, Carlos was on him. Kicking out the legs of the chair from under Cortino, Carlos knocked him to the concrete floor. Before Cortino could scramble to his feet, Carlos had him by the lapels and was dragging him to his feet.

"You stupid, two-bit thug." Carlos spat in his face. "You have gone too far. Do you think your measly one-hundred thousand dollars a week is enough to give you the right to approach me whenever you wish? You are a worthless piece of shit. I had plans tonight and your untimely interruption prevented them from happening."

Cortino swallowed hard, trying to regain some of

the arrogance he'd shown earlier. "So what? Did I get in the way of you getting some? Oh, I've seen how you look at her and escort her to all the fancy restaurants and stuff. She is a nice package and I wouldn't mind a go at her myself, after you weary of her, that is. She has a nice mouth and I can imagine it around my cock."

Carlos looked at him incredulously. He wasn't sure what made Cortino keep talking, trying to push his buttons. It was working, though. Carlos released his hold on Cortino's lapels and smoothed out the material, patting him lightly on the chest. Then, with the speed of a coiled cobra, Carlos grabbed Cortino by his hair and slammed his face down on the tabletop, breaking his nose and busting his lips. "You are a fucking idiot. You are lucky I don't kill you right now. As it is, I will leave you with a reminder to never, *never*, approach me again. Do you understand?"

Cortino slid down from the table, curled up in a fetal position on the floor, holding his nose and cringing, waiting for another blow. Carlos obliged him by sending a vicious kick to his kidneys. Cortino looked from Carlos to Miguel, who all this while had stood silently off to the side, watching. He smirked at Cortino's stupidity. Miguel knew his boss. Ramirez wasn't someone to cross.

Miguel came forward and uprighted the chair. He grabbed Cortino by the collar and threw him into it. Two other men moved in from the darkness and came to stand behind Cortino. Carlos crossed his arms and slowly nodded. The two held Cortino as one of them took his left hand. Cortino's eyes grew wide with fear. He yelled and struggled to pull himself free from their grip.

Miguel smiled and, with a nod from Carlos, pulled a set of bolt cutters from his back pocket. Slowly removing his jacket, Miguel draped it over the back of a chair. Cortino's eyes darted back and forth between Carlos and Miquel, finally settling on the cutters. Forcing Cortino to splay his fingers, Miguel neatly snipped off the pinky finger of his right hand with the skill of a surgeon. Cortino screamed, and when the men released him, pulled his bloodied hand to his chest, cradling it and crying like a baby.

"Never get in my way again." Carlos turned and, followed by his men, walked out. He was sure Cortino would continue to do business with the Cartel, but he'd be more circumspect in the future.

Chapter 6

Sam thought he recognized Kate's bouncing ponytail and tight bottom from a hundred feet back. Not knowing she ran, he couldn't believe the serendipity of running into her like this. Sam knew his sister and Kate were friends. They lunched together and, as Emily said, the invitation to join them was always open but their paths hadn't crossed. Sam hadn't been able to get her out of his mind and considered how he could use this accidental meeting to his advantage.

Kate automatically moved to the right so the faster runner could pass her. Sam came up next to her and slowed. The steady dual slap of their soles on the pavement caught Kate's attention. When she looked to her left, she saw Sam matching her pace. "Sam? What a surprise. I haven't seen you since the gallery preview. Do you run this route often? I've never noticed before."

Sam gave her a lazy smile. How lucky can a guy get? "I take the river run about three days a week, but if this is your regular route, I'll be sure to take it more often. Do you run every day?"

Kate adjusted her cap and wiped the sweat from her upper lip. Lips, Sam wanted to kiss. "I try, but sometimes work, and lately, life gets in the way. You?"

"Yep, military habit. Hard to break. I try to do three to five miles at least five days a week."

They continued for another quarter mile when Kate

slowed to a stop and bent over, resting her hands on her knees, panting. "Well, I have reached the end of my route and my stamina. I usually cool down from here and walk home. I hope we run into each other again."

Not wanting to let this opportunity pass him by, Sam pointed out his Gladiator. "Hey, my jeep is right over there. I have some water in a cooler in the back. We could sit and talk while we cool down and then I'd be happy to drive you home."

"I guess that sounds okay". Kate smiled with a shrug.

Sam grabbed a couple of cold bottles of water from the back of the jeep and they headed over to a shady spot along the river. He was struggling to come up with a conversation. "I understand you and my sister are hanging out a lot. I appreciate it."

Kate turned a perplexed look to Sam. "You sound like she's a charity case and I've taken her on."

"No, no, not at all. It's just that you guys hanging out means she doesn't spend so much time nagging me about construction debris and stuff." To Emily, stuff would be his not calling Kate for a date.

"Oh, that's right. Emily said you were rehabbing an older home in the Fairmont neighborhood. From what she tells me, it sounds like it's going to be fabulous. She keeps talking about your garden and the shower. I'd like to see it sometime."

The wheels were turning when Sam nodded. "I guess you gals could drop by one day when you go to lunch. Give us a warning, though, so Jake and I can clean up the construction site."

They sat silently on the top of a picnic table, enjoying the peace of the park. A light breeze carried the scent of the water. It was a pleasant, musky smell. They watched a couple of kayaks racing down the river, their competitive calls to each other carrying over the water. Kate leaned back on her hands and turned her face to the sky, breathing it all in. A couple of squirrels chased each other around the trunk of a tree. One of them ran up to Sam, looking for a treat. Sam pulled a pecan out of his pocket and, crushing it with the heel of his hand on the tabletop, cracked it open. He tossed the nutmeats to the squirrel that cautiously grabbed the bits and scampered off.

Kate let out a surprised gasp and a little laugh. "Do you always carry pecans in your pocket?"

Sam shrugged, confessing, "I've been doing it for a while now. That squirrel is one hungry little devil. It's like he has a built-in clock—he is always waiting for me at about this same time—just as I finish my run. He gets a treat. I get the fun of watching him get closer each time. I hope I can make him feel safe enough to feed him by hand one day."

Kate shook her head, laughing. "What a sweet thing to do. Emily says you're a tough, mean old guy and here you are a big ol' softie".

Sam and Kate chatted companionably for the next thirty minutes. They laughed at the antics of the squirrel and shared their mutual love of nature and all God's creatures. A trip to the zoo would be fun, they decided, and agreed to find a free Saturday to do it. Meanwhile, the squirrel ate all the pecans Sam had brought, perching within three feet of where they sat. Good progress toward the hand feeding. Agreeing to meet up again in the morning to run, Sam drove Kate home. It wasn't a date, but it was fun. Sam hoped Kate was looking forward as happily as he, to tomorrow morning's run and the future excursion to the zoo.

After he dropped Kate off, Sam returned to the park and ran another two miles to clear his head. Their meeting had been completely accidental, but in Sam's opinion, it couldn't have turned out better. During their cooldown that morning, Kate called the squirrel Rocky and promised to meet Sam regularly if he promised to bring more pecans. It elated him to think of starting his day off with her. She was hot, no doubt about it. She was confident and capable, but Sam's instincts picked up on a vulnerability she kept well hidden under all her bravado. It appeared she was being given the full-court press by Ramirez. Sam could only hope she wasn't interested in the smooth and criminal Carlos. Time would tell.

Chapter 7

Even after the messy encounter with Cortino, Carlos was determined to continue his siege of Kate's emotions. He wanted to spend every available moment with her, but she limited him to four days a week. She told him her house needed cleaning. The laundry was piling up, not to mention her work, and after all, someone had to pay the bills. It had been a couple of days since he'd seen her, so he planned a romantic evening to set the stage for his expected conquest.

With Kate's penchant for punctuality always in mind, Carlos arrived right on schedule Tuesday evening and rang the front bell. He had a bouquet of stargazer lilies that gave off such a heady aroma, it made him nauseous on the drive over. He had found it difficult to concentrate on his work earlier, thinking of Kate; how beautiful she was, her perfect face and body, and how much he would enjoy making love to her. When she answered the door, he saw the wait had only heightened his anticipation. Kate chose a sea green silk halter dress with a cinched waist. Her strappy dress sandals enhanced her trim ankles and the delicate arch of her neck gave her a regal look. Tonight, she had pulled her hair back in an updo. Carlos looked forward to taking it down later that evening. He imagined running his hands through her silken tresses and delighting in the feel of them sweeping across his naked chest.

Tonight, Carlos had selected Chez Robert for dinner. The quiet French restaurant held only twelve tables and prided itself on the finest food, attentive service, an extensive wine list, and privacy for their exclusive patrons. When they arrived, Chef and owner, Robert greeted them, and personally escorted them to a table in a corner, tastefully shielded from the view of other diners. The waiter anticipated their every need without hovering. It was almost as if they were his only table. They started the meal with cocktails. Carlos ordered Chateaubriand for their entrée and a Napa Valley Cabernet with the meal. When the first bottle was finished, a second one immediately appeared without Carlos having to ask. The meal was exquisite, and Carlos was the quintessential gentleman. Following their leisurely dinner, the waiter asked about dessert. Carlos was thrilled when Kate suggested they take it to-go so they could enjoy it with coffee at her place. He was more than happy to agree. He ordered two cherry tarts and asked for the check.

Back at Kate's house, Carlos switched the stereo on to some soft music while she made coffee and transferred the dessert to real plates. This was the first time he had been in her house beyond the foyer. He wandered around and looked at her books and artwork. Carlos noticed her small desk area, where she apparently did her writing. It was neat and organized, much like Kate herself. A hallway led to the back of the house where he imagined her bedroom to be. He wondered what soft feminine style she chose for her private sanctuary. Picturing soft hues and exotic patterns, he imagined himself touching and possessing her there.

Turning back to the living area, there was a couch and a simple side chair, which offered cozy comfort and invited conversation. Her TV was tucked away in a subtle entertainment center. There was a dry bar next to it, holding several bottles of exceptional liquor. She had good taste, but none were open. It seemed they were there for her guests. Seeing a bottle of decent cognac, he took it upon himself to pour two snifters. Warming them with his cupped hands, Carlos walked into the kitchen. "I hope you don't mind my making myself at home. I always enjoy cognac with cherries," he said, handing the glass to Kate. His eyes shone suggestively at his cleverly hidden meaning.

"I'm glad you feel comfortable." Kate smiled, accepting the proffered cognac. She had already had too much alcohol and really didn't need another drink, so after a small courtesy sip, exchanged it for her coffee. They sat at the island enjoying their tarts and coffee. When they had finished, Carlos took their snifters in one hand and Kate's hand in the other. He led her to the sofa, clearly telegraphing his intentions. Before sitting down, Carlos put down the snifters and, cupping Kate's face, lowered his mouth to her lips in a gentle kiss. It quickly built into a deeper, more urgent one. The embrace tightened and one hand slipped down her back. Molding her hips with his hands, he pressed them into his own. Kate could feel him growing hard and found her arousal at this intimate touch startling. She yearned for him to do more than just kiss her and was getting lost in all the sensations Carlos aroused. Kate stiffened and pulled back.

Carlos sensed her sudden reluctance. Easing back, he gazed into blue eyes darkened with passion and clouded with fear. Cupping her face once again, he laid soft lips to her cheek, whispering in her ear, "Perhaps it's best if I go."

Kate, with closed eyes, could only nod dumbly, impossible to speak at that moment.

He took her hand and when they reached the door, drew her to him once more for another embrace. Carlos drew in the scent of her. The ginger had faded. All he could smell was woman and desire. She was succumbing to his will. Carlos was confident he could have her, but would it be the conquest he envisioned? No. He wanted her to come willingly, to beg him to take her, to master her. Using gently curled fingers, Carlos raised her face to his. Her eyes were closed and her soft lips parted, waiting for his touch. Kissing her once more, Carlos could sense her surrender. He let his lips linger, feeling her soft sigh against his mouth. "I want you, Kate, but I'll wait—for now."

Kate closed the door, leaning against it. She drew in a shaky breath, willing her heart rate to slow back to normal. Carlos was handsome, intellectually stimulating, and let's not even mention the promise of great sex. God, he wanted her. Truth be told, at that moment, she wanted him too. She spent a sleepless night going over again and again, the evening and the kiss with Carlos.

Waking in a sour and confused mood, she made coffee and contemplated the dirty dishes from the night before. *I don't understand why I reacted like I did. He is handsome, rich, everything I've always wanted. Even the tall and dark part. What am I afraid of? He'd be so easy to get lost in.* Kate stared into troubled eyes at her reflection in the mirror. *Ah, that's the rub, isn't it?*

Maybe too easy. She tied her hair into a ponytail and pulled it through the hole at the back of her ball cap. She needed some fresh air and was meeting Sam for their run. Maybe it would put some perspective on everything.

****

Later that day, Kate sat at her desk shifting through her reaction to Carlos' romantic advances. She still didn't understand her feelings, but thought she might be overreacting. She contemplated what to do. Pouring a cup of tea, she picked up the phone and dialed Carlos.

"Hi, Carlos, it's Kate. I hope I didn't catch you at a bad time. Thank you for a lovely dinner. I'm sorry I was so abrupt at our parting. It had been a long day and I guess all your attention overwhelmed me."

"Not at all. It's a pleasure to hear from you and I am very happy you enjoyed yourself. I must apologize if I became too amorous after taking you home. You must have realized I am growing extremely fond of you."

"That's kind of you to say, Carlos. Things are rocketing along at warp speed and I'm not a fast mover. I hope you understand. I'm just not used to having a man sweep me off my feet. I think I lost my balance. How about I make it up to you by buying you dinner Friday night?"

"I would enjoy that very much. Lady's choice. Where did you have in mind?"

"Oh, excellent." Kate almost clapped her hands. "Do you like Lebanese? There is this little restaurant called Em Sherif. It's very authentic and one of my favorites."

"That sounds quite different and interesting. I am

looking forward to sharing something you consider a favorite. Is seven a good time to pick you up?"

"Perfect, see you then." Kate rang off.

Chapter 8

Sam and Kate had been meeting up to run almost every morning. Last night's rain had blown past, and the sun was peeking through the clouds when Kate arrived. Sam was already there and sweaty, as if he had run before meeting her. She'd see him doing push-ups and stretching before their run. She remembered one time she pretended she was on the phone just so she could sit in her car and watch him doing warm-up exercises. Kate enjoyed the way his thigh muscles bunched and pulled while stretching; his slim hips and obvious bulge. She wondered if the adage about hand size was really true. Kate studied him now as she pulled her hair up into a casual top knot and thought, *Oh yeah, most likely*. When he glanced in her direction and smiled, obviously aware of her scrutiny, she flushed guiltily and fumbled with her sunglasses. Kate gasped, hand to mouth, when Sam, grinning mischievously, deliberately turned and executed a forward bend, hamstring stretch, showing off a well-muscled buttocks. She could feel the heat of embarrassment flood her face. *Oops! Caught me red-handed, didn't you?* She laughed.

Kate was growing increasingly confused. Here she was, being wined and dined by Carlos almost every evening while looking forward to and enjoying her morning runs with Sam. She found both men attractive for very different reasons. Carlos was suave and sophisticated. He made her feel beautiful and desired. It had been a long time since she'd been in any kind of relationship. Kate was dry tinder, and when he touched her, she all but burst into flames, yearning for his kisses to quench the fire.

Sam was different. He made her feel precious, in a gentle and protective way. Almost brotherly. There was thought and purpose in his every action. He had a sincerity and quiet strength that drew her. She felt safe with him, secure. Goose bumps rose whenever they accidentally brushed up against each other. She'd sometimes catch him staring at her when he thought she wasn't looking. It made her heart jump from a slow simmer to a rapid boil. She didn't know what she wanted from Sam, but it sure wasn't to be treated like his sister. Kate was open to Sam, making a move. It all made her less confident in her feelings for Carlos. She decided that until something changed, until she was more confident of her feelings, an exclusive relationship with Carlos wasn't right for either of them.

They were feeding Rocky the pecans Sam had brought and his prediction of the squirrel eating out of his hand was progressing. Right now, the squirrel would run up to Sam, take the proffered pecan and scamper off a foot or so to consume it. Kate loved watching and even tried to feed him herself. Their cool downs became a special time for her. Sam had traveled and knew so many interesting things. He could match Kate on any subject. They discussed current events, favorite foods, books, and movies. Sam loved antiques and architecture.

With the sun glinting off the river and the squirrels

full of all the pecans they'd consumed, Kate decided to get the story firsthand. "Sam, Emily talks non-stop about your house and what you are doing to it. She mentioned something about an old fireplace and some pillars and all the demolition you've done. What are you doing to the place? It sounds like a complete gut job."

"Yeah, that's pretty much what it was to start. I picked it up from one of those we-buy-ugly-houses guys. It was in sad shape, so I gutted most of it. There are some amazing bones to the old place, but a lot, like the updated kitchen..." Sam made air quote signs... "is not worth the glue and nails holding it together. The first project was the guest bedroom. I needed somewhere to sleep beside the couch in the middle of a construction zone. When I started taking everything down to the studs, I reworked the entire floor plan. My buddy, Jake, flips houses for a living and he came in from Colorado to give me a hand. Things have been going much faster since then. We began work on the main suite upstairs. It's going to overlook the garden. The side yard has a pergola. I planted Wisteria and, given time, you'll be able to reach out the windows and pluck a bloom." Sam's excitement was contagious. Kate found herself able to envision every square foot of the house. She hoped for an invitation to see it in person.

"Everything connects in one big loop, you see? You enter through the front door into a cozy foyer with a set of stairs on the right, leading up to the second floor. The master suite is up there, along with a couple of small bedrooms. To the left will be my study, with a door in the back corner leading to the laundry room.

There is a door to the side yard and the butler's pantry there, too. Continuing around the loop, is the kitchen at the rear of the house. This opens up across the way to a family room. I found the original fireplace while doing the demo and was able to rescue it. I've sourced an old mantle. It will hold a lot of Christmas stockings. Moving through the family room is a guest bath tucked under the stairs. I told you about that being the first room I completed. The living room used to be right off the entry with a large cased opening, but I closed it off, adding double doors at the front. It will be the guest suite with an on-suite bathroom. It will open to the family room and the front foyer. So, everything connects back to the front entry. Then, as you stand in the foyer, there is a straight shot from the front door to the back and when you walk down that hall, there is a formal dining room on the left, opposite the stairs."

Sam stopped, noticing Kate holding back laughter. "You're laughing at me, aren't you?"

Kate quickly assured him, "I'm not laughing at you. I'm thinking you are just like me when I get a new story to investigate and write. It's so exciting and all-consuming. I get it, really, I do." She giggled. "Sam, it's just your enthusiasm is so cute. You're like a little boy with a new toy on Christmas morning." Kate may have thought Sam was cute, but she heard loud and clear his desire to have a home, a family. God, she missed her folks. They had been so in love. It was a love that had filled their home. Her brothers didn't get it. They didn't have the depth of emotion to understand and appreciate how unique and special their folks and their love for each other had been. Family meant nothing to them, as evidenced by the lack of communication since their folks had died. Kate suddenly felt alone and very lonely.

"Well, I guess it *is* like a new toy. I know I sound crazy when I talk about the house. It has such potential and I think it will make a wonderful home for a family one day." He looked at Kate and noticed her expression soften. There was yearning and an understanding in her eyes. He also saw her mouth soften, too. God, he wanted to kiss her.

Sam wanted to tell Kate about taking down the walls and the old framework and pocket doors. About his vision for the dining room that would one day host holiday dinners. Sam wanted to talk about the kitchen and the attempt by the former owner to modernize it with contractor-grade cabinets and green Formica counter tops. It was circa 1965 and ugly as sin. It needed to be ripped out and redesigned, but how do you tell the woman you think you were falling in love with, that you wanted her to help design the kitchen so she'd be at home there too? Too much, too soon, too frightening, he thought.

Extending their cool down over coffee and Kate's guilty pleasure, cream-filled donuts, Sam told Kate about wanting to find some vintage materials for the house. "There is a terrific architectural salvage warehouse over in the Fairmount neighborhood. I've been meaning to check it out. Would you like to join me?"

"That sounds like it would be fun and an adventure. If you give me about an hour, I can get cleaned up and join you," Kate said.

Sam couldn't hide the excitement of sharing the fun with Kate. She laughed out loud when he pestered her about the timing. "Sam, I promise an hour will be plenty of time to get ready. Drop me off and go get cleaned up yourself and come right back. Maybe we can grab lunch after?"

Sam rushed home, and within fifty-five minutes, was at Kate's house. He practically skipped to her door, whistling a merry tune.

Sam turned down a neighborhood street and parked around the corner under a spreading Oak. He jumped out and ran around to grab her hand, pulling her toward the doors to one of four unique buildings set on each corner. Walking into the main warehouse was a genuine adventure—like a historical tour. Ten-foot-tall Victorian doors opened into a labyrinth of winding aisles holding doors, windows, shutters, room dividers, and mantels. There were bins filled to overflowing with door hinges and knobs. They festooned the ceiling with hanging light fixtures–chandeliers, crystal and brass, old and mid-century modern. Someone had repurposed several items. They stopped to admire a craftily constructed bench made from an iron headboard and an antique piano turned into a desk. They moved across the street to the opposite corner. This yard housed exterior building materials, bricks, and old wrought iron. There were chimney pots and statuary covered in a perfect patina. A third corner used to be an old gas station, which they now used to display the kitschy art work created from the detritus of old buildings. There was signage and old tools, even a well-worn galvanized chicken laying box. Everything had just the right amount of rust to make it farmhouse chic. They devoted the final corner building to plumbing. Countless claw-foot tubs lined the side walls, pedestal sinks formed the aisles.

"Oh, Sam, look at all the claw-foot tubs." Kate clasped her hands. "They evoke such romantic images; candles and scented bath oils, peignoirs and champagne." Sam made a mental note to add one to the master bath design.

The back wall was stacked with faucets and fixtures. Sam had always been interested in architecture and history. He confessed his head was filled with useless factoids about old mantles, light fixtures and cabinet hardware, being able to tell if it was authentic or a reproduction, the period manufactured, and how it had originally been crafted. When Sam saw Kate was on sensory overload, they returned to the first building. Sam selected some original craftsman-style door and drawer pulls for the kitchen remodel and took her up on the idea of grabbing lunch. Pete's Greek Garden was in an old home near the hospital that had been turned into a small café. It boasted some pretty good gyros and cold drinks. There were postage stamp tables inside and a half dozen picnic tables outside in the backyard. They ordered sandwiches and root beer from the counter and scored a table near the blooming Carolina Jasmine.

"What are you writing about now, Kate? Emily says you're researching some charity events. She mentioned something about the children's wing at the hospital."

"Oh, yes, that. They invited me to a fundraiser. I invited Emily to be my 'plus one'. It was a lovely lunch but very predictable and, honestly, boooring," she said in a sing-songy tone.

"I guess when everyone knows why they are there, they don't expect much beyond rubber chicken and talking heads. But it got me thinking. There must be more inventive ways to motivate people to donate to a cause. There are several fun things to do that can engage your donors. One I found, is a wine tasting and silent auction being hosted by a church that offers a weekly free lunch to the homeless and working poor. It's a good cause and actually sounds like fun. Why don't you go with me?" she asked. "It's not until the fall, so we have plenty of time to plan."

"Sounds like fun. I'd like that. Emily would enjoy it, too, but I don't suggest we include her. You've never seen my sister at a silent auction. She tends to spend way too much. In fact, there was one time she actually bid herself up on an item. Since this is church-based, I'm sure the organizers will see a patsy and have a shill that bids up the weak and gullible. I'd enjoy watching that." Sam laughed but perked up. If Kate was thinking ahead to fall and still hanging out together, there might be hope. Of course, he'd have to get up the courage to make a move.

"Oh, Sam. Emily has a good eye for a bargain. If she is bidding too high for something, I'm sure she wants it and knows the money goes to a good cause. She has your heart, although you don't show yours as often. But I hope to engender interest in their cause and build participation and donations through my article. There is another event the wife of the Mexican Consulate holds to raise awareness and money for saving the monarch butterflies. I'd give my eyeteeth to attend that, but it's a closed event–very exclusive guest list."

"Maybe the attaché can wangle you an invitation. I've seen your picture in the paper when he escorts you to functions." Sam barely disguised his bitterness. He tried to make light of it, but inside, his stomach was roiling. "Excuse me for a sec–our food should be up. I'll go check. Want another root beer?"

Sam made a hasty getaway to the pickup window. His carefree smile was replaced with a grim, tight-lipped look. Kate could see the impatient drumming of his fingers on the counter. Was he jealous? Kate thought back on conversations she and Sam had where she talked about a show or symphony she'd attended. Surely Sam knew she was seeing Carlos. Everyone else in town did. Kate just didn't want to spoil what they were enjoying together. She liked Sam more than just a friend. She wished he'd make a move…

****

On Friday, Carlos knocked on Kate's door at 7 p.m. on the dot. He had checked out the website for the restaurant she'd selected and learned it was just a hole in the wall–they had actually converted from an old drive-in restaurant. Not really his style. Em Sherif was a BYOB that allowed patrons to bring their own wine. Upon learning that the only glasses provided were plastic, Carlos picked a pinot noir and packed up two Riedell wine glasses as a surprise. He was used to the best and thought Kate deserved nothing less. Since the restaurant didn't have the linen tablecloths and napkins he was accustomed to, he'd do what he could.

In keeping with the casual atmosphere of the restaurant, Carlos had selected black slacks and a sage green shirt. He had left the top two buttons undone. A thin gold chain with a crucifix graced his neck. Kate wore white cotton capris, clunky sandals, and a tailored blue oxford shirt worn untucked. The color set off the blue of her eyes and Carlos felt desire rise in his chest.

On the drive to the restaurant, Kate teased Carlos about his interrogation techniques into her personal life and stated that turnabout was fair play. Although he'd shared some things about himself with her, she wanted to know everything about him. As Carlos was helping Kate from the car, she saw Emily walking toward the door to the restaurant. "Emily, how nice to see you! You remember Carlos Ramirez, don't you? He was at the Gallery Preview evening."

Em offered a half-smile, glancing toward Carlos. "Yes, I do. How nice to see you again, Mr. Ramirez."

Carlos shook Emily's hand, looking at her with guarded eyes. He knew how close she and Kate were growing. The last thing he needed was some interfering 'friend' influencing Kate's thinking. That was his job. "It's good to see you, too. How is the gallery doing?"

Kate took Emily's hand and turned excited eyes to Carlos. "I can answer that. Emily is knocking it out of the park. I loved attending the preview and writing the article for the Guide. It was easy to promote such a wonderful variety of art. The presentation was slick and professional without being stuffy." Turning back to Emily, Kate remembered. "Emily, I've been thinking about the small bluebonnet landscape with the old windmill. Is it still available? I have the perfect wall for it."

Carlos noticed the sparkle in Kate's eyes when she mentioned the painting. He made a note to himself to check on the landscape and purchase it for Kate as a surprise; so much better than flowers. Perhaps both–she was worth spoiling and he could afford it.

"I'll have to check. If it is, Kate, I'll be happy to set

it aside for you when I get to the gallery tomorrow."

Remembering her manners, Kate inquired, "Are you here alone, Emily? You could join Carlos and me."

"Oh, no, no. Thanks for the invite. I'm meeting my brother and his friend. They're waiting for me inside. I'm late as usual. I'll see you later, Kate. Nice to meet you again, Mr. Ramirez."

"The pleasure was all mine, Ms. Slater."

Emily rushed in.

With a curt nod, Carlos placed his hand on the small of Kate's back. "Shall we?"

****

Jake looked around the cramped dining room, taking in the scarred wood tables and mismatched chairs. "I can't believe you want to eat this stuff after... how many months in Afghanistan? But I agree with you. I experience withdrawal symptoms if I don't have it at least twice a month. Unfortunately, there aren't many authentic middle-eastern restaurants in Durango, and I've yet to find a woman that wants to cook it for me. And before you say it, Slater, yeah, put up with me too!" Jake said as he slapped Sam on the shoulder.

"Jake, the problem is that you have too many women willing to put up with you. I am stunned by your attraction to the opposite sex. It's got to be the Harley."

Jake shrugged indifferently. "It's a lover's machine. You know, they tune the engine to the same frequency as a vibrator. Seems to have worked in the past. You should buy one."

Sam scoffed and rolled his eyes, scouting for an open table. The two were unlikely best friends–the yin and yang. Jake was more relaxed than Sam, prone to laugh at himself and others more easily, whereas Sam expected more from himself than anyone else. Jake wasn't a pleaser, and didn't carry the burden of having to protect and save everyone like Sam did. But there was no one else Sam would rather have at his back. They'd bled together over bullets and broken hearts.

Jake was the only other person besides Emily that knew about Sam's dream. Jake also knew the details and understood far more than Emily did. Lakia haunted Sam; her young life was cut short because Sam let his emotions take over. He'd been suckered by the kid that shot the cat. Sam hadn't seen it coming. Jake had been there, and had missed it too. Jake had watched the darkness of Lakia's senseless death seep into Sam's soul. Jake knew it was a case of wrong place, wrong time, a tragic accident. No one could have anticipated it. Jake had made peace with it, but he wasn't Sam; didn't have the same baggage Sam's dad had dumped on him. Shit, how can anyone protect everyone? Save everyone?

Back when Sam had led their 4-man fire team and occasionally worked special assignments only with Jake as Sniper/Reconnaissance, Jake had his back. He had it now, too. When Sam asked him to come to Fort Worth to help with the remodel, Jake figured he'd spend a few weeks working on Sam's place and then take his bike on a trip to the hill country. Everyone said it was a great ride. What he hadn't counted on was meeting Sam's sister, Emily. That was an unexpected bonus. Sam never talked about family while they were in Afghanistan. He had mistakenly thought she was Sam's girlfriend–although Jake couldn't see any woman putting up with Sam for long. Jake soon discovered

Emily was amazing and totally different from Sam. Petite, with brown hair and flashing green eyes; she was the antithesis of Sam. While Sam was serious and all business, Emily was funny, and saw the bright side of everything. She had an uncanny ability to get under Sam's skin and tease the bejesus out of him. Jake loved to watch her in action.

The guys had just arrived at Em Sherif and scored a table in the back corner–neither Jake nor Sam sat with their backs to a room–old habits die hard. Sam took a nice Spanish red from his backpack and pulled the cork. They used the restaurant's plastic glasses.

"Nothing but the finest for my best friend," Sam quipped as his phone tinged. "Yup, text from Em–she's running a little late. Surprise, surprise."

Jake took a sip of the red saying "Or… maybe she is late because she's getting gussied up for me! Or at least I hope she thinks I'm worth getting gussied up for. Man, why didn't you tell me you had a sister?"

"Because I know you, Edwards. You left too many broken hearts behind you everywhere they stationed us. I didn't want to have to kill you to protect my sister's honor."

"Screw you, recon man! No, seriously, is she seeing anyone? I mean, I don't want to tread on anyone's toes."

"Seriously? No. She lost her fiancé, Greg, three years back. He hit an IED while on patrol and didn't make it–a blessing all around. Lost his legs and lower right arm. He wouldn't have been a whole man, and Emily would have given up her life for him. She falls hard and loves completely. She also can take an accurate measure of a man, making sound decisions about who they are and if they are worth her time. So far, she hasn't found anyone to measure up to Greg. If you are serious, let me give you a friendly warning. If you hurt her, I'll hurt you." Sam had a steely look in his eyes, but one of brotherly affection quickly replaced it. Sam knew Jake was solid and honorable, no matter how much he liked to tease him about the broken hearts.

"Wow–warning heard and taken, buddy. Hey, there she is now–not too late and much gussied up." Jake stood to motion her over.

Emily threaded through the crowded restaurant to the table. "Well, if it isn't the two most handsome, eligible men in the room. I feel so honored to be included in your awesome presence. Sitting with your back to the wall as usual, Sam? And Jake–you too? Are all you SEALs so careful?" Em accepted a glass of wine from Jake. "Oh, I see. Sam brought out the good crystal. Hey, you'll never guess who I ran into right outside the restaurant. Kate and that Mexican attaché, Carlos Ramirez. She is interested in the bluebonnet landscape. You remember? The one with the old windmill? You know, I think he's really attracted to her and they only met a few weeks ago when she interviewed him for Texas Quarterly. I don't know, though. Something just doesn't feel right about him. Oh, he's smooth and very good-looking and, from all appearances, has lots of money, but my radar is pinging something awful with him."

The waiter approached, and they ordered the most amazing shawarma, hummus, lamb, and Mashwi beef with vermicelli rice. They enjoyed another glass of wine and light conversation. Jake and Emily did most of the talking. There was chemistry between them. Jake noticed how Emily relaxed as the evening progressed, enjoying the company. Sam would make one heck of a brother-in-law if it went that far. But he wouldn't forget Sam's warning about hurting him if he hurt Emily.

****

Over dinner, Kate made good on her promise to grill Carlos about his life.

"Yes, yes, yes." Carlos raised his hands in surrender. "I give up. I'll tell you everything." He laughed at her curiosity. "So, I grew up in a somewhat modest house in Guadalajara. A typical three-bedroom, two-bath. I am the middle son of three boys. Ric is the eldest and Eduardo is my younger brother. I am blessed and pleased to say that both my parents are happy and healthy. My father is in distribution, and as his company grew more prosperous, we moved into a larger home. Ric, as the first-born son, is apprenticing with my father. He'll take over when Father retires. My mother is a saint. She's a stay-at-home mom, very traditional. She had high hopes for her boys and wanted to give a son to the church. I guess all good Catholics feel that way." Carlos confided, "But I disappointed her and chose politics and the diplomatic corps instead. As you know, I was fortunate to attend university in Salamanca, Spain. My master's degree I earned from UCLA. Even as an average undergraduate student, I realized the importance of a good education. As I matured, that understanding grew when working on my masters. My little brother, Eduardo is a banker–he handles the company's finances and investments. Mother would love you, Kate. She wants her boys to be happy and, as you can see, I am very happy," Carlos concluded. He squeezed her hand and leaned forward to place a kiss on her cheek.

Blushing, Kate smiled, looked down, and moved her hand to her wineglass. Her thoughts were a whirlwind of emotions. Everything was still so fast, she thought. Although he was extremely Hollywood romantic lead handsome, Kate barely knew the man. It reminded her of the plot of a trashy romance.

*****

Thinking about hurting people, Sam had watched Carlos escort Kate to their table with a possessive arm around her waist. Too familiar from where Sam was sitting, but Kate wasn't exactly pulling away. They sat across the room, and Carlos was careful to seat Kate next to him in such a way as to keep her all to himself. Regardless, Sam had a clear line of sight. Damn the man, he was so smooth and sophisticated. He pulled out a bottle of wine, followed by two crystal wine glasses. This might be a modest restaurant without a liquor license, but they weren't slumming tonight. Sam wondered if Ramirez would pull a candelabra out of his ass. Carlos was attentive to Kate's every need and would often lean in and touch her hand to make some point in the conversation.

Kate ordered for them, which took Sam by surprise. Maybe this wasn't Carlos' choice of restaurant–maybe Kate had suggested it. This made Sam feel both better and worse. Better that Kate might enjoy middle-eastern food as much as he did and worse that she'd want to share that enjoyment with Ramirez. Sam could see her smiling at Ramirez and hear her laughter across the room. All of which didn't help his appetite.

Sam brooded watching Carlos make moves on

Kate. His jaw clenched in anger and frustration. The three finished their meal, and were leaving as Sam's cell phone pinged. Leaving Jake to escort Emily to her car, he answered. Twenty minutes later, Sam finished the call. Jake had sent Emily safely on her way home and was leaning on the back of Sam's jeep, arms crossed, waiting. Sam read the question in Jake's eyes.

"Jake, I'm sorry. Things are heating up. There are some fresh developments at work and although I had hoped to take a couple of weeks off to concentrate on the construction work with you, well, hell, that's not in the cards… I need to hit the office tomorrow and then fly to Miami on Monday. Look, man, you are welcome to stay, but I feel guilty about asking you to work on the house if I'm not here."

"Sam, it doesn't take a rocket scientist to see something's up. I know you work for Homeland Security." Jake held up his hands. "Nothing specific, but I suspect from everything I've seen in the short time I've been here, this has something to do with Ramirez, which complicates your interest in Kate even more."

Sam eyed his brother-in-arms. He should have known nothing got past Jake. Sam scratched his head and let out a long breath–silently admitting to Jake's evaluation.

"Sam, look, I'm between flips and have time on my hands. I'll stick around and putter in your place. I can read blueprints, you know. The least I can do is finish up the framing and hang the drywall. It will keep me off the streets and give me an excuse to stick around and spend more time with your sister. Hey, maybe I'll even texture and paint. You hate that part and besides, you suck at it," Jake pointed out. "Don't worry about a thing. I'll rough everything in and you can do the finishing touches." Sam thought he'd be back by late Wednesday. Jake agreed with the plan. When they got back to the house, Jake bid Sam goodnight.

Sam went out to the garden. He'd poured himself a glass of scotch, neat. His thoughts were on the case, but they kept straying to Kate. What was she doing with Ramirez? Was she just one of his latest conquests, or was she involved? Either way, he wasn't happy about her being mixed up in anything with him. Ramirez was a slimeball and a killer. All the evidence they had amassed so far pointed to him being a key player in the weapons smuggling. It sickened Sam to think of that creep touching her. He had to find out if she was mixed up in any of this.

****

Sam and Jake rounded the corner, finishing up a 5-mile run along the river. Jake's stream-of-consciousness conversation distracted Sam from another awful night. This time, the dream took a different tack. He couldn't find something precious. He searched and searched and then the rain came and obscured the tracks. Sam was calling to God for help, but there was only silence in response. The feeling of helplessness set his heart racing, and he woke with a jolt.

Sam was up and ready to run when Jake walked into the kitchen. Jake recognized the signs and knew what to do. He set a fast pace for the two of them. Sam would have thanked God for his friendship with Jake, but God hadn't listened in his dream or back in Afghanistan, so why would he bother now? Jake got it.

They walked in to find Emily waiting in the

kitchen with cold water and coffee. "Last night was fun. Thanks for including me. It was fun to see Kate, too, but wish she could have joined us." Emily jumped when Sam slammed the door to the cabinet. "Hmm, cranky this morning, isn't he?" Sam gave her a perturbed look over his shoulder. "At any rate. I'm going to set that Windmill painting aside for her." Adding to Sam's frustration and fuming, Emily continued talking to Jake as if Sam wasn't standing right there in the room. "I'm going to call her when I get to the gallery and invite her for brunch tomorrow. I like her. I think Sam does too. But you know Sam," she said pointedly to Jake, "he won't admit it."

Sam waved a hand in front of Emily's face. "Hello, I'm right here. No need to talk about me like I'm invisible."

Sam stood with his arms crossed. He'd listened long enough. "Funny, real funny. I have a meeting at the office. I'll leave the two of you to continue planning my love life." Flipping them off, he stomped out.

Chapter 9

"Thanks, John. This is good work." Sam was meeting with his team at Homeland Security, reviewing the intel gathered so far. They sat around a conference room table, but there was nothing formal about the meeting. There were paper coffee cups scattered on the table, several empty boxes of donuts, and a couple of empty gallon jugs of orange juice. This team moved on their stomach and Sam kept it filled. He pulled up pictures and graphics on the screen and continued. "The Ramirez family has been smuggling marijuana for years and when the US legalized it, conveniently switched over to drugs like cocaine, heroin, and fentanyl. They've had a successful operation for years, with the Mexican government turning a blind eye. Now they are graduating to weapons. We know the consulate is a convenient front for Ramirez. Everything points to him and his family being smack dab in the middle of this operation. So, we believe the consulate residence will be where we get our best intel."

Tag teaming with Sam, John picked up the stream of the briefing. "We confirmed the location of the warehouses they used in the past for the exchange, but they changed locations for each shipment, and we don't expect that routine to be any different for the next one. There is a good lead on the new handoff location. Confirmation of the warehouse and the date and time of the exchange is the next pivotal step to achieving our goal." They reviewed all the details, assignments, and answered questions.

Sam shut down the screen and flipped on the lights. "I don't just want to bust the smuggling ring. Hell, the Ramirez family will simply absorb the loss and plan another delivery. No, I want to get them during the exchange, so we get both the buyer and seller. Challenge is, we don't know what kind of firepower they will have on-site or what key players or numbers will be there. I don't want to tip our hand yet so stay back–give them room to hang themselves. Keep up surveillance on the suspects. Use the landscape company van to monitor the consulate residence. By the way, we've had a lucky break. They have contracted Aalem to cater a charity function for the consulate's wife."

Sam and John reiterated each team member's role in the surveillance. "We'll place the usual team as parking valets. That will give us access to license plate numbers and maybe part of the complex. We might also pick up some conversations. Aalem said he'll try to get us a guest list. Anything we pick up could be helpful."

Sam scanned the table, focusing on each team member. "I seriously doubt the Consulate's wife has anything to do with our case, but there might be some other intel we can ferret out. Just being inside will allow us to get a lay of the land. I'll be heading to Miami on Monday. There are some fresh developments there." Sam concluded the briefing, closing his laptop. He wondered if there was anything they overlooked when he got a 911 text from Emily. "Sorry, guys, I need to take this. I think we know what we need to do.

Everything for Operation Crossbow is progressing well."

Dismissing the team, Sam called Emily's cell.

"Emily, what's going on? Is everything okay?"

"Oh, Sam," Emily cried. "Larry sold the bluebonnet landscape before I could set it aside for Kate. He said it was an anonymous buyer that paid cash. I can't even track it to see if they'll sell it back. Sam, I promised Kate I'd save it for her. I'm so upset about this. What am I going to do?"

"Okay, okay." Sam took a breath and rubbed his fingers over his brow and forehead. He shook his head. "Not really a crisis, Emily. These things happen. I'm sure she will understand. Did you already invite her for Sunday brunch? You can break it to her then. Maybe offer to ask the artist to paint another one she'll like even more. Don't sweat the small stuff, sis. Now, I need to get back to work. Hey, why don't you take Jake some of that barbeque you brought me before? He'd appreciate the good food and company."

"Okay." Emily sniffed in agreement and hung up. Crisis averted, Sam thought.

****

Early Sunday morning, Jake and Sam went for a quick three-mile run. When Sam wasn't running with Kate, Jake and he fell into their usual routine from their time in the SEALs. Jake set a grueling pace for the two of them. Recalling Friday night at Em Sherif and Sam's full-on-alert and narrowed eyes watching Kate with Ramirez, Jake had to laugh. Yeah, Sam liked Kate. Jake knew Sam joined her for morning runs several times a week. He could tell how calm Sam was, how happy after the runs. Sam would whistle while he worked. It

89

was obvious as tits on a bull, Sam was happy spending time with Kate. In fact, Jake had noticed that on the days Sam saw her, he slept better, too. Now if Sam would just admit to himself that he was interested and make a move before Ramirez snatched her up from under his nose. Jake threw a look over at Sam and kicked into a quicker pace, thinking, with women, sometimes Sam moved as fast as a freakin' sloth.

Sam left Jake to his own devices while he cleaned up to go to work to sort through additional information on the weapons smuggling. Returning home shortly after four, Sam saw Kate's red Honda roadster parked in front of the house. Hearing laughter emanating from the garden upon opening the door, he headed in that direction. Jake, seated in the big Adirondack chair, was regaling the two women with stories from his and Sam's time in Afghanistan. Emily, her eyes dancing with laughter, perched on the arm of the chair, leaning over him to refill his glass. They were drinking margaritas. Sam could tell Jake was on a roll. He had a wicked sense of humor and could make the most ridiculous and sometimes mundane things enormously funny.

"So, then Sam thinks he hears something from his locker. He pulls his sidearm and snatches the cupboard door open. Inside is this cat curled up on his boot. It had pissed all over his clean khakis. Oh, it had dried by that time, but... well, you know cat pee—it sure smells. Poor Sam had to go see the colonel about the next day's mission and didn't have time to wash it out. He stunk to high heaven. Now, I got to tell you, Sam is one fussy dude."

Both girls gasped, hand to mouth, saying

simultaneously, "No!" then giggled, clinking glasses.

"I kid you not, ladies. Where Sam would have every crease ironed and his boots spit polished, I'd have a loose thread or button that would earn me the pleasure of dropping and giving the commanding officer 'twenty', so you can imagine Sam's chagrin."

By this time, Jake had the girls in tears, their hands covering their giggles. He continued, "I didn't think that cat would live to see another day, but the next thing I knew, ol' soft-hearted Sam was sharing his rations with the little runt. He called him 'Pissy'. After about a week, we discovered 'he' was actually a 'she'. Of course, it didn't take a rocket scientist to figure that one out. She ended up having a litter of kittens on his bunk. Well, what the heck do you do with a litter of kittens? You know, Pissy actually turned out to be the company mascot. We fashioned ourselves the Hell-Cats—never mind that every other crew referred to us as Pissy cats. Those little fur balls were good mousers–or actually good 'roachers' and let me tell you, the roaches in Afghanistan are the size of mice. Heck, the colonel even commandeered one for his office and, if memory serves, took it back for his little girl when his tour was up."

Sam cleared his throat, and with raised eyebrows, said, "I don't suppose Jake told you he took the runt of the litter to bed with him every night. He'd sing it to sleep with, 'Let me call you Sweetheart'."

Jake immediately jumped in crooning "I'm in love with you…." while looking at Emily. Sam realized Jake had probably never said truer words. Tossing his suit coat aside, Sam took off his tie and grabbed the pitcher. Seeing it was near the bottom, he offered to make another batch.

Emily jumped up. "I'll get more snacks while you do that."

The blender whirled and Em scooped more guacamole into a bowl surrounding it with chips. They could hear Jake through the screen door telling more lies, or stories, as he would later claim. He and Kate teamed up to sing a verse of "Let me call you Sweetheart" and burst out laughing. It was music to Sam's ears.

"I hope you don't mind that I invited Kate to come over. We were talking about the house and she was interested in seeing it. She says you have been talking her ear off about it and even took her to that architectural salvage place where you bought some kitchen knobs. She said she loves craftsman style architecture and restoring old houses and antiques just like you do. I showed her a little, but she really needs you to explain your vision."

Three pitchers of margaritas later, Kate reluctantly stood. "Well, I think I have imposed long enough on your hospitality and need to head home. Let me help clean up the dirty dishes before I go." Sam rose to gather empty plates and spent glasses, following Kate into the kitchen. Jake and Emily stayed behind in the garden. They were oblivious, giggling and canoodling.

Sam put the dirty dishes in the sink. "Before you go, did you want to take a real tour of the house? It won't take long. It's not that big a house."

"I'd love to. As long as you promise that these green laminate countertops are not part of the finished product." Kate smiled in answer. "Lead on Macduff."

"Haven't heard that one in a while–shows you're a

Yankee, you know."

Sticking her tongue out at him, Kate retorted, "Or, well-read, Mr. Shakespeare." Taking her by the hand, Sam walked through to the front of the house.

"So, you've seen the kitchen and dining room. The study is still in shambles, but I have my blueprints in there and perhaps it would be easier to show you those rather than chance stepping on a nail while walking through the half-finished rooms." They went into the shell of a study. "The original built-in bookcases were in pretty rough shape, about six layers of paint. I pulled them out to strip and refinish. When they are done, they'll go here and my desk will be over by the large front window so I can have a view when I work. I do a lot of work from home and need a quiet and secure place to spread out my paperwork and think."

A sheet of plywood on two saw horses held the plans. Unrolling them, he invited Kate to look. She leaned forward, running her hand across each page to get a clear idea of the details. Sam stood looking over her right shoulder. He pointed out the different elevations, explaining the finish details he envisioned doing. Orange ginger, he thought, breathing in her scent. When she traced a particular detail, her hand brushed against his. Sam felt like he'd received an electric shock at her touch.

Kate noticed the ombre tile design notated for the master bath and turned quickly toward Sam. He was standing so close that she hit her head on his chin. "Oh, I'm sorry," Kate said.

They froze, gazing into each other's eyes—silent. Sam reached up and ran his knuckle along Kate's jawline. Bringing it under her chin, he tilted her face up. She stood statue still, looking at him with those fathomless blue eyes. He read the desire coupled with wariness, quickly followed by trust. Swaying toward him, Kate closed her eyes, inviting him to plunder at will. Sam looked at her parted lips, so soft, so kissable. He stood there feeling the blood rush in his veins, feeling the throb of his heartbeat blend, then echo Kate's. She was intoxicating. Finally, Sam placed his hands on each side of Kate's face, feeling the racing of her pulse under his thumbs. Her breaths came in small pants of desire. Sam sighed. Kate was waiting, he read her anticipation. With eyes closed, he leaned in and knew fear. Sam kissed her on the forehead.

"I'm sorry. I may have overstepped my bounds. Please forgive me," Sam said as he disengaged himself from Kate.

Kate pushed her hair behind her ears, looking confused and frustrated. Taking a deep breath, she struggled to collect herself. "Perhaps I should go. I-I need to think."

Sam said nothing. His thoughts were so jumbled he couldn't speak. All he could think about was sweeping the plans off the makeshift desk and taking Kate right then and there. He could feel her trembling and drew in a deep breath through his nose, holding it for a second to regain control. He took her hand and walked her outside to her car. As Sam gazed into her eyes, all he wanted to do was kiss her.

"Call me when you get safely home." Sam took her by her shoulders and once again kissed her on the forehead, letting his lips linger for just a moment. "Good night, Kate."

****

Kate started her car. She watched Sam in her rear-view mirror until she turned the corner, slowly driving out of sight. Kate angrily brushed tears from her cheeks. "Damn you, Sam Slater! You look at me like that and then let me leave. And a goodnight kiss on the forehead?! Jeez Louise. Is there something wrong with me, Sam? Don't you want me? Cause I think I might want you."

Arriving home a little after 9:15, she found a note on her door from her neighbor. Mrs. Weekes had accepted a package delivered for her earlier and would be up until 10 if she wanted to retrieve it. Knocking on the door, Kate was greeted by a mature divorcee smoking a cigarette, dressed in straight-legged spandex pants and a midriff workout top. She was sipping a martini. The term cougar came to mind. She practically gushed about the tall, dark, handsome stranger that had dropped off the mysterious package and bouquet of roses.

"He didn't leave a name, but given the opportunity," she purred, "you'd have stiff competition for his attention."

Kate thanked her, but waited to open the card once back home, although she strongly suspected who the stranger was. She couldn't imagine what he had sent. Carlos had explained after their evening at Em Sherif that he had to go out of town and would miss spending time with her. Carlos promised to see her upon his return for the consulate dinner and then he'd help her with a little 'task'. She wondered if the task comment had anything to do with the package. Carlos did mention wanting to share something very important with her.

She opened the card, reading silently.

I look forward to seeing you soon and to hang this small gift on your perfect wall.

With deep affection,

Carlos.

P.S. Have you translated the Spanish phrase I taught you?

Kate opened the package. It was the bluebonnet painting. So that was what he had hinted at with the 'task' comment. Kate had to admit it was pretty sneaky, the way he picked up on her interest in the painting. Apparently, he was the anonymous buyer Emily said had purchased it before she could set it aside for Kate.

Oh, jeez. This is crazy. I'm so confused. I'm attracted to two totally different men. What am I going to do?

She put the painting on a chair by the wall and went to bed. Sleep eluded her.

Chapter 10

Emily and Kate had clicked from the start, so it was no surprise that while Carlos was out of town and not monopolizing her time, she and Em spent their free time together. They shopped, enjoyed mani/pedi days, and went to museums and art shows. Emily impressed Kate with all the knowledge she carried around in her head about art and history. Like brother, like sister, Kate thought. Their trip to the Kimball Museum was so much more interesting because Emily could give her additional insight into the works of art that Kate wouldn't know otherwise. Sam and Jake would join them occasionally or come over for dinner and a movie at Emily's house. It was an easy and fun foursome. But how fast Carlos was falling for her preoccupied Kate at times. *Surely, he couldn't be getting serious this fast.*

The nail tech led the girls toward their pedicure stations. Lately, Emily's conversations all centered on Jake. "Oh, Kate, you need to come see the progress Jake and Sam are making on the house. He put up the drywall and there is a real guest room and master suite. Did I tell you about our pizza night binge-watching Yellowstone? He is such an interesting man. And if you've never ridden a Harley—well, let me tell you. Ooh la la!!!" Kate felt herself drift off, relaxing into the massage chair while the technician worked on her feet. She moved on autopilot whenever she felt the light tap on her calf to switch legs. Jake had certainly caught Emily's attention.

"I know he's a bit rough around the edges. Not someone I ever thought I'd find attractive, but he is so funny and kind and knows so much about fixing stuff. I love to watch him work. He moves so confidently, sawing and nailing things. Sam is lucky to have him helping. Jake is really whipping that house into shape. And I'm kind of embarrassed to say it, but after he sands a piece of wood, he rubs his hand along it and I envision him rubbing me the same way. It's kind of sexy." Emily giggled.

Kate gave her a surprised, raised eyebrow look and laughed. "Why, Emily Slater! If I didn't know better, I'd say you are in serious lust with that man!"

"Oh, come on, Kate. You're one to talk. Carlos hasn't stopped calling or following you around for weeks. He has a serious case of lust too, if you ask me. Is it reciprocal? Every woman in town thinks he's hot and romantic. They practically trip over their tongues when they see him, but he only has eyes for you. I bet he'll propose."

"Oh, no. Bite your tongue. I—heck, I don't know. Everything is so weird with Carlos. I mean, I really enjoy his company but… I don't know. Maybe I'm just being paranoid. Lately, I feel like someone is watching me and I keep seeing this same car that might be following me. There was this one night we were leaving the symphony and a mean-looking guy approached Carlos. He looked like a real thug. Carlos put me in the car and then stepped away to talk with him. It looked like they were arguing. And, Emily, Hector, who usually drives us, was off and there were two other men in his place. Everyone was wearing a gun that night, including the stranger that approached Carlos. There is a lot more to Carlos than he lets on."

"Wow. That sounds scary. Have you mentioned this to Sam? He's pretty knowledgeable about this kind of stuff. Maybe he and Jake can watch out and at least see if you are really being followed or you're just imagining it." Emily tried to sound reassuring, but she didn't trust Carlos. Sam and Jake should know. If Kate wouldn't say anything, she decided she'd bring it up the next time the four of them got together.

****

Kate was enjoying the breathing room with Carlos out of town and out of the picture. He sent flowers and called several times. Most of their conversations never touched on his business or family, so most of their calls were short, chatting about her work, the weather, or current news events. Early on, Carlos reminded her about their dinner date when he returned. Kate found herself begging off, stating her schedule as a freelance journalist was very unpredictable. She had to make her own rain, as they say. Part of the process was to scour newspapers for stories that would benefit from an in-depth follow-up. She was always chasing key people to interview. When she landed a ghost-writing contract for a wealthy philanthropist who wanted to self-publish his memoirs, she took a breather. It was steady work and a lot easier than chasing the illusive follow-up features she usually wrote for publications. Kate wasn't sure it would be a best seller, but it was his money, and he was paying her well.

Kate wasn't one to let the grass grow under her feet, though. There were plenty of proposals she'd submitted to monthly publications in the pipeline that required follow-up on her end to see who was interested in what. Luckily, Kate had always enjoyed doing research and was often buried at the courthouse or library for several hours a day. She hadn't been able to shake the nagging feeling that someone was watching her but chalked that up to her imagination.

****

Emily worked ten-hour days at the gallery four days a week, and the artwork was flying off the walls. Few people truly understood the entire scope of her job. They thought it was all preview parties and writing up sales invoices. Emily was involved in the artist's success. She was organizing work on a specially commissioned mosaic for a client. It would be a one-of-a-kind tile insert in the foyer of their new home. Between coordinating with the installer and the contractor, Emily was also working with three other artists to produce numbered prints of their more popular works.

Almost daily, Emily took lunch to Jake, and they spent several evenings together just hanging out. She worried Sam was spending too many nights alone, and she picked up his not-too-subtle hints that she and Jake were moving too fast. Emily reassured him he wouldn't have to break Jake's arm.

Even with her busy schedule, Emily was the self-appointed social secretary for Jake, herself, and Kate. Sam was busy with his work, traveling back and forth to Miami, so the three of them got together for dinner or sometimes a movie as often as their schedules allowed. On a Sunday, the two girls dragged Jake along and went to the Nasher Museum in Dallas.

"Seriously, you will enjoy the different mediums used in the artwork," Emily said, enthused as they walked in the door. "The museum showcases modern sculpture and…" Emily watched Jake roll his eyes and make gagging motions. "You're not a big fan, are you, Jake?"

"Babe, I'm willing to try anything you like, seriously…" he choked out. Being a trooper, Jake trudged behind the girls. When Emily cried out in delight over several pieces of art, he turned his head in shock, eyes wide in total incomprehension. Although Jake was very respectful and curbed his disbelief that any of it was defined as art, he couldn't pass up the opportunity to comment. Pointing out the sign to Kate, he read quietly, "'Do not touch the art'—Hell, when I see a piece of art, I promise I won't touch it."

Kate snorted out loud, drawing scolding glances from Emily and the docents. Jake redeemed himself by offering to buy adult beverages for everyone following their tour. They snagged a table at one of the small bistros in Klyde Warren Park. The park was an urban oasis in the middle of Dallas, with fountains and grassy areas promoting a family-friendly atmosphere. The girls watched the performers entertaining the children in the crowd. It was fun to witness the wonder on the faces of the audience, child and parent alike. Jake went in search of adult beverages and returned shortly with three glasses of wine. The children played in the fountains or chased the water spouts. Some would just sit on the spout, waiting for the stream of water to erupt. It enchanted Emily, and she looked at Jake out of the corner of her eye; seeing him in a new light. She turned and took his hand. Holding her thumb and index finger a little apart and peeking through them, she bravely asked. "Did you enjoy it at least a little?"

Jake shrugged. "I have to admit, this has been an eye-opening experience."

"You read a lot of the descriptions of the sculptures."

"I did, and it all caused my eyes to glaze over multiple times. But I must admit that one made complete sense." Feigning a hoity-toity tone, he plagiarized a certain description he'd read, raising his glass of wine, regarding it critically. "I think of this glass material not as junk but as garbage. Cow pie, actually; it goes from being the waste material of one cow to the life-source of another." Emily tried to act aghast over his heathen ways, but watching Jake pretend serious intent and scholarship about his glass of wine, quoting such nonsense, couldn't help bursting out in laughter.

"You are such a philistine Jake Edwards!"

Jake could do that—always see the joy in life. Emily loved how remarkably balanced he was. That was what made him perfect for her and, as she knew, saved Sam so often from the darkness. As a cloud passed overhead, it also passed over her thoughts. She prayed Sam would find a way out of his darkness.

With an eager eye for fun ways to spend time together and do a little matchmaking, Emily planned a game night pitting the girls against the boys in Trivial Pursuit. It became a regular event when Sam wasn't busy or traveling for work. The four of them would get together for game night, trading off which team won. Sometimes they'd go to baseball games or on one occasion to an outdoor concert. The best time, though, was when they took Jake's suggestion and went bowling. It was a hoot. Everything was comfortable and casual. It gave everyone time to get to know each other better and, unbeknown to any of them, fall in love.

****

"Fishing?" Kate laughed at Emily. "I'm worse at that than bowling." It was Friday afternoon, and the girls were sitting at the salon getting a pedicure while Emily was planning their next big adventure.

"Oh, come on, Kate, you can't be that bad." She laughed—actually, she guffawed. "The one and only time we decide to try something completely different and you complain. Come on. It was hysterical. Jake was obviously sandbagging because he was in his element that night. He confessed to me later that bowling was the one thing he and his uncle had in common. That was why he was so damn good. Sam's just good at most any sport. He's a natural."

"I know. You and I were hopeless. I loved the way Jake didn't have to buy any beer that night. His fifth frame scam was priceless. Who knew it was the beer frame? What was it, something about the person with the worse pin count in the fifth frame had to buy the beer? God, we'd have incurred the national debt before the third game if Jake hadn't messed with the rules, so Sam always lost. Do you remember?" The girls giggled, recalling Sam's discomfort that evening.

"No, no, no, Sam," Jake had explained during the first game, "in the fifth frame, guys have to bowl with a ladies' ball, a pink one." Then for the next, "Oh, I forgot Sam. In the fifth frame of the second game, the guys have to bowl with their shoes on the wrong feet."

"My shoes are on the wrong feet, Edwards," Sam

growled. "They're on *my* feet!" That sent everyone into fits of laughter.

Just remembering it made Kate's cheeks hurt from smiling so hard. "Remember how by the third game we were all so worn out from laughing we switched to root beer and Jake cut Sam some slack, letting him win the frame? It was so unexpected and so much fun."

"So, see? Doing something different can be fun. What do you say, Kate?" Emily's query brought Kate's attention back to the present conversation.

"Seriously? Fishing?" Kate sighed in resignation. She didn't think Emily would take no for an answer.

"We can take a picnic lunch, drive down to the lake and just chill for the afternoon. I'm so tired of all the rain we've had lately. I need some sunshine. The weatherman says Sunday is promising to be a gorgeous day and because of the recent rains, the wild flowers are supposed to be glorious and in full bloom. Please, let's do it. I'll invite the guys. They can fish while we catch some rays."

Kate found Emily's enthusiasm hard to resist. She had been working hard on her latest project and a break would be welcome. Shaking her head and wondering what trouble she'd get into next, she agreed. "Okay, on one condition. I don't have to fish."

"Of course not. Why would you do that?" Em agreed much too quickly, arousing Kate's suspicion. Emily loved a good joke and Jake had gleefully become her partner in crime. Kate suspected she would be fishing before the end of the first hour.

****

They all met at Sam's at eight a.m. Sunday morning as planned. The day promised to be as beautiful as Emily and the weatherman had predicted—bright, sunny, and with the temp starting at sixty-eight, warming to eighty-one by noon. Not having fishing clothes in her closet, Kate decided on her periwinkle blue sun dress under her summer-weight white cotton sweater. Jake and Sam were packing up rods and 'fishing stuff'. Kate did not know what any of it was for. She and Emily were in charge of the food and drink; ham sandwiches, chips, brownies that Kate had whipped up the day before, and lots of water and cold beer. When everything was loaded up, Jake disappeared. He returned roaring up on his Harley.

"Em and I will follow you guys down to the lake", he told Sam as Emily put on a helmet and hopped on the back of the bike.

Sam and Kate exchanged shrugs and got into the Jeep. "They'll wish they had a vehicle with air conditioning later today," Sam commented. The drive down to the lake was perfect. Sam had taken the top off and the rushing wind was exhilarating. Instead of taking the direct route along the freeway, the guys took a route along the old farm-to-market roads. It afforded a grand view of field after field of beautiful wildflowers. When Sam crested a hill, they looked down into the small valley. A sea of green grass dotted with blue bonnets, orange Indian paintbrush, and poppies bedazzled Kate. Here and there, white Queen Anne's lace fought their way to the top and the sunshine.

"Oh, Sam. It's beautiful." Kate sighed out a breath of pure delight.

Sam eased the jeep to the side of the road and they climbed out to take in the sight. An old neglected windmill was standing in the field valiantly trying to turn as a light breeze ruffled its battered blades and Kate's hair. Following the rutted farm trail, Kate walked further into the field. Leaning against the side of the jeep, Sam watched as it drew Kate along the path. Like a sunflower, Kate turned her face up to the sun. The heat shimmered on her face and the rays of the sun caused little black dots to dance on the insides of her eyelids. Taking her hat off and holding it by the brim, she walked through the grass, trailing her hand along the flower tops. The blue of her dress and little white sweater contrasted with the colorful backdrop nature provided. A wistful smile crept across her face when Kate turned to look over her shoulder at Sam. He snapped a perfect picture of the scene with his cell phone.

Jake and Emily came roaring up on the bike. "Hey, guys, what's the hold-up?"

"Just wanted to enjoy the view. It's beautiful." Sam answered, looking at Kate instead of the field of flowers. "We're coming…" They jumped back into the Jeep to continue the journey.

****

The minute Sam had topped the hill, Kate saw the field of wildflowers. It was amazing, the burst of color. But it was the windmill that drew her. Kate felt an affinity she couldn't explain. This poor dilapidated windmill was so fragile looking. Kate knew, though, that the simple wooden structure could harness immense power to deliver life-giving water. Somehow, it all saddened her. How could something that had once been the difference between life and death now be relegated to farmhouse chic décor? Kate was pensive during the rest of the drive. She considered the symbol of the windmill. How necessary it had been to survive in days gone by. How forgotten it was now. It reminded her of the men and women who served in the military and how, as a country, their service and sacrifice were often overlooked. Kate could sense a story brewing and wanted to write it. She pulled paper and pen from her purse and jotted down notes. Sam glanced over at her furrowed brow. She was deep in thought, so he kept quiet to give her a chance to document her feelings.

****

The lake was full, and the fish were biting, which made Jake's teasing motivating enough for Kate to try fishing. "Just be sure to hand off the rod surreptitiously to one of us guys if the game warden comes by. I'd hate to see you go to jail for fishing without a license," Jake solemnly advised.

"So let me get this straight. I have to touch a fish to put on as bait to catch a fish, I won't even get to eat, because we're doing catch-and-release. And, I could go to jail because I don't have a license. Oh, no you don't. I'm not falling for that one." Kate wagged her finger in Jake's face.

Sam smiled and showed her how to put the minnow on the hook. She scrunched up her nose, holding the minnow out a full arm's length. He looked at her with teasing eyes. "Come on. Don't be such a girl. Here, I'll cast, then you can take the rod. Come on, I'll show you." Sam expertly cast out and pulled Kate in front of him. He held her around the waist, guiding her hands to the rod and helping her hold it and reel in the line.

Kate was enjoying having Sam's arms around her, so she didn't care that she was a dismal failure at

107

fishing. In fact, she was worse at fishing than bowling.

As the four of them enjoyed the sunset over the water, Emily decided it was time to mention Kate's suspicions about being followed. Emily could tell Kate was doing the same thing Sam did—pushing it to the back of her mind—refusing to face up to the actual possibility that she might be in danger.

"So, guys, based on your experience in Afghanistan, were there times you felt you were being watched or maybe followed? What did it feel like?" Emily asked. It was a general and somewhat innocent question, but Kate threw her a look, letting Emily know she was on to her shenanigans. Kate shook her head slightly and sent a warning glance.

Jake exchanged looks with Sam, deciding who would field the question. Sam stared down at his clasped hands, pressing his lips together. Jake took the lead.

"Well, that's an interesting question, babe." Jake pursed his lips, drawing in a long breath and blowing it out. He tsked and puffed his lips, cracking knuckles and rolling his neck and shoulders around a couple of times. It was more to buy time than anything else. "So, when you're in the field long enough, you develop a sixth sense of sorts. The hairs on the back of your neck stand up and then your eye is caught by a sudden flash of light or color. All these little things paint a picture in your mind that your gut, in a flash, says danger. That's assuming emotions don't distract you." Jake shrugged his shoulders and raised his hands, palms up. "Having a cat shot at is a good example of the emotional distraction that might make you miss certain clues."

Emily looked at Kate, hoping she'd open up and

share her feelings about being watched and followed, but Kate remained stubbornly silent. Emily shook her head. So much for that plan, she thought.

Ending the day with Kate's brownies while sitting around the fire pit, they packed up and headed home. It was late and Sam had to fly out in the morning for Miami. Jake and Emily left Sam in the dust on the drive home, zooming off on the Harley. Sam and Kate took a more leisurely drive home, content to enjoy the silence. Sam finally built up the courage to ask Kate what she had been jotting down earlier.

"You were very thoughtful after we stopped at that field of wildflowers. And then you made all those notes." Checking his blind spot, he smoothly merged onto the highway. "May I ask what you were thinking about?"

Kate took a moment before answering. Sighing, she replied, "I think I finally figured out why I'm so drawn to windmills. They are an iconic symbol of the pioneer's life. They were integral to the survival of the early settlers. Without the windmill, there wouldn't have been life-giving water out here on the plains. And yet, when you look at them, the foundation appears fragile. I mean, the framework is just a series of crisscrossing wooden beams rising to a platform on which sit the blades that are fragile unto themselves most times. They're wood or tin slats or sometimes a simple wire frame with a canvas covering. It all turns by the power of the wind. In Texas, that can be incredibly strong. People have forgotten the hidden strength and power of the windmill. We have neglected it over the years so that now they are just standing there rusting away. No one cares anymore. No one appreciates how they really were life savers. I know it's an odd connection to make but, somehow it all reminds me of our veterans. Every one of you who has served— you are just human beings with all the fears and frailties of everyone else. Yet you willingly put yourself in danger and can withstand the ultimate challenge presented to man; Death. Then, after you meet this challenge head-on for the freedom and safety of some stranger on the street, when your work is done, we forget you. We neglect you, even as you rust away in front of our eyes." Sam heard the sadness in Kate's voice. It spoke louder than any of the words she had just uttered.

He reached out for Kate's hand. There was comfort in holding it, feeling she got it. He wasn't alone. He wasn't sure how to respond to her. She had just shared something deeply emotional for her. He wondered if maybe, just maybe, there might be a third person in the world who would understand and could help him vanquish his demons.

Sam pulled up in front of Kate's house a little after nine. They had traveled the last forty minutes in silence but that was okay. People could communicate more by just holding hands than either realized. Sam walked Kate to her door. "You shared some powerful emotions with me today, Kate. Is there something else you'd like to share?"

She turned wide eyes to him. Her pupils had grown bigger, and she was gripping her hands so tightly, her knuckles were white. "Yes, maybe, but when we have more time to discuss it. I believe nothing bad could ever happen when you're with me. I'm sure it is all nothing, just my imagination."

Sam had picked up on the subtle communication between Emily and Kate back at the lake and didn't believe her for a second. He let it rest for now. "Thank you for your trust. I will always keep you safe." *With my life*.

Kate turned eyes filled with trust, to him. "I know, Sam." She sighed. "I know."

That was when Sam felt himself go under. She was everything he'd ever wanted. Sam desperately wanted to kiss her, but kept his emotions in check. He was still afraid he'd fall in love with her and fail her like he had failed before. Sam waited until she had entered the house and heard the deadbolt turn before walking back to the jeep and heading home. He was more determined than ever to grill Emily and learn exactly what the hell was going on.

****

Too much of Sam's time was occupied with work. Having previously closed a case in Miami, he'd traveled back twice to testify at the trial. It was on the second trip that he saw Carlos. Ron Marsh, his counterpart, at the Miami office had picked up rumors of a deal being negotiated at one of the known rendezvous points for drug dealers. Ron suspected it might have something to do with Sam's case in Texas, so he suggested they do a little stake-out to see what popped up. Pulling the light blue compact into the parking lot across from the restaurant, he found a shady spot and parked eyes forward. The windows were tinted dark and the fender slightly dented. It looked like every other working-class car in the lot. Ron and Sam sat in the car while their coffee went cold and waited. It didn't take long.

Ramirez came out of the restaurant like he didn't have a care in the world. Dressed in light tan slacks and a floral print shirt, he looked very Floridian. Sam watched as Carlos got into a high-priced rental car and drove off. Shortly afterward, one of the many suspected drug dealers in Miami stepped out. Coincidence? Sam didn't think so, but what exactly did this have to do with the weapon smuggling Ramirez was suspected of heading up? Maybe this was just Ramirez Cartel business as usual and not related to the weapons at all.

Sam and Marsh returned to the Miami office to review the surveillance photos they took and to complete a facial recognition program to tie all the faces to names and potential crimes. That's what good investigative work was all about—taking all the loose ends and following each one as far as it went. Sometimes it worked out. Sometimes it was just a tangle of more questions than answers. But, if there was any connection that gave them grounds for an arrest, they could pick someone up and, with luck, sweat information out of them. Marsh and his team would take care of this part after Sam returned to Fort Worth and contact him if there were any hits.

Chapter 11

"Kate, my dear," Carlos said into the phone, "Senora Quintana has requested me to invite you to her Save the Monarchs luncheon on Sunday. I said yes on your behalf. I think you will enjoy yourself and I know you agree that the purpose of the fund-raising event is well worth it. Please say yes."

Kate did a fist bump in the air. This was the big charity event she wanted to write about. Getting her excitement under control, she answered calmly and professionally. "How can I turn down such a gracious invitation? It would be an honor to be included in such an exclusive group of guests." Carlos gave her the details and offered to send a car to her at one-fifteen.

The black town car pulled up in front of Kate's house. Hector, the driver, was the same elderly gentleman who usually drove her and Carlos. He stepped onto her front porch and knocked, bowing politely, when she opened the door.

"*Buenos dias*, Senorita Hunter. I am here to drive you to the consulate residence at Senor Ramirez's instructions." He motioned for her to precede him down the walk to the car, where his perfectly timed steps allowed him to reach around and open the car door without her having to pause or wait for him. Seeing her safely ensconced in the backseat, Hector closed the door and made his way around to the driver's seat. He buckled himself in and started the car. Before driving off, Hector turned, looking at her over his shoulder. "We are honored you have accepted the invitation to this afternoon's event, Senorita Hunter. Senor Ramirez is looking forward to seeing you again. I should not be so bold, but it does an old man's heart good to see love blossoming between two such handsome young people. The staff is hoping there will soon be a happy announcement."

Kate paused from settling in, a small crease forming between her eyebrows. She gave Hector a puzzled glance. If he was thinking what she thought he was, this line of conversation was a little uncomfortable. With a slight smile, hoping to discourage additional comments, she gazed out the window at the lovely residential neighborhood they were entering. Kate appreciated how beautiful and enchanting the neighborhood was. The houses were immense, and all backed up to the river. High walls surrounded each estate. All one could see at the front of the properties and along the driveways were grounds filled with picturesque landscaping. They turned in at a manned gate where they were waved through to a long drive winding through trees, manicured lawns, and colorful flower beds. She gazed out at a charming house, designed in the colonial Spanish style. It had ivory-colored stucco and terracotta roof tiles. The wrought-iron railings on the Juliet balconies were covered with trailing bougainvillea in shades of red, magenta and orange. The drive curved around to the front door where a granite car park allowed for the cars to drop off their passengers. Hector pulled in and ran around to open the door to assist Kate out of the car.

Carlos beat him to it.

Carlos regarded Kate with pride and desire in his eyes. She was stunning in a tea-length sky-blue A-line dress with cap sleeves. The heart-shaped neckline showed off her delicate collarbones and graceful neck. She carried a royal blue shawl that matched her eyes. On her feet, she wore matching two-inch Manolo pumps. Taking her hands in his, he brought them to his lips, kissing the knuckles on each one. He recalled her response to this intimate greeting before and enjoyed watching her quickened breath and charming blush at his touch. In his mind's eye, he saw Kate stretched out naked before him, caressing and kissing her body from head to toe.

"You are a vision", he said between the kisses, never breaking his gaze. He held her hand, pulling it through his arm to enter the house. This was her first visit to the residence. The family had opted to live in Fort Worth rather than Dallas. Even though it was not an official government compound, they felt this gave them an effective presence in both cities. Carlos escorted Kate through a set of wrought-iron gates along a gray stone walkway that led to an arched wooden door opening to reveal a large, beautifully landscaped courtyard. Tropical plants and flowers surrounded a center fountain. Each corner bed was overflowing with Mexican heather and lantana. Hibiscus blooms the size of a man's hand anchored other beds filled with aloe and Guava. Bougainvillea cascaded from the 2nd story balconies here as in the house's front.

"Carlos, this is breathtaking. It feels as if someone turned back the hands of time. I almost expect Zorro to swoop down and carry me off." Kate laughed gaily, enjoying the moment.

"Ah, perhaps I can be your Zorro, the man of mystery who captures the love of a beautiful woman."

"Hmmm, very romantic." She squeezed his arm, changing the subject. "Is that Aalem Siddiqi, the caterer from Emily's gallery preview? And are these Spanish tapas?" Accepting a small plate, Kate delicately bit into a tiny croquette, rolling her eyes as she enjoyed the subtle flavors flooding her mouth. "I can't imagine an Afghan catering business providing such delicious and authentic fare. Of course, considering the Moors conquered Spain, maybe the culinary influence isn't too unfamiliar to Aalem."

Carlos listened as Kate spoke into a small hand recorder she'd pulled from her handbag, short-handing her comments. 'Afghani immigrants—how transitioning. Tie in with the rush to get the remaining interpreters and their families out safely; nice counter-point to the Art from Darkness story, Emily and the McGill Gallery." She tucked her mini recorder away and turned back to Carlos, ready to enjoy the company, finger foods, and Cranberry Pear Prosecco cocktails. The body guard from the night of the symphony stepped up to Carlos and whispered in his ear. Carlos' lips formed a thin line. He quickly masked his anger, leaning in to brush soft lips against Kate's cheek.

"Kate, I regret but I have a small matter to attend to. Will you be all right on your own?"

"Of course. Please, do what you need to do. I'll be fine." Kate nodded, noticing the set of his shoulders and the anger pulsing out of him as he moved to the exit.

Kate was in her element. She circulated, stopping to visit with the other guests, instinctively searching out potential story lines for future projects. She learned the cocktails were refreshing but also very potent when she was halfway through her second one. Since she felt it sneaking up on her, she selected a sparkling water in its place. After a time, the guests were called to the white folding chairs placed in front of a small stage where they enjoyed a brief presentation on the migration of the monarchs. The climax of the program was the release of hundreds of monarch butterflies. All the guests let out laughs of wonder and immediately pulled out their checkbooks. Kate observed the lucky guests on whom one of the delicate creatures lit, exclaimed excitedly, and commented they were doubling their donation. Kate had to give it to the person who organized the afternoon. It was an impressively orchestrated and successful fund-raising event.

Kate searched for Carlos. Apparently, he was still 'attending' to his small matter. She went to make her farewells to the consulate's wife, thanking her for a lovely time just as Carlos returned. Senora Quintana motioned to him. Ever attentive to her needs, he excused himself from the man who'd spoken with him earlier, coming to stand at her side. The senora spoke rapidly in Spanish to Carlos, who nodded, smiled, and translated to Kate, "Senora Quintana wishes me to express her genuine pleasure at having you attend her…" He waved his hands in the air to encompass the room. "… soiree. She wishes to share how happy she is and that she can see how much you mean to me. She hopes to see you more often and can't imagine me without you by my side."

Kate smiled sweetly at Senora Quintana and said in her best Spanish, "*Gracias. Sera un placer.*" Mentally sighing, Kate felt cornered. Wow, first Hector, and now Senora Quintana. Carlos must really be getting serious. Was he thinking of proposing? She felt a moment of panic.

Carlos smiled approvingly and, taking her arm, escorted Kate toward the front door. Taking her hand, he pulled her off to the side through a short hallway, away from the crowd. "You are amazing, Kate Hunter. Everyone can see how special you are." Drawing her into his arms, he kissed her deeply and possessively. His tongue teased, and she opened her mouth to his further exploration. Carlos ran his hand down her front and gently squeezed her breast. She didn't pull away and Carlos smiled to himself. *Soon, Kate, very soon.*

He led her to his office while they waited for the car to be brought around to take her home. Shutting the door, he twirled her around, catching her in his arms. His lips possessed her neck, face, and ears, delighting in every one of her sensitive, tender, erogenous zones. Kate sighed in surrender to his seductive touch. Pressing his body to hers, he kissed her greedily, walking her back toward the couch, planning on taking her. Before things could progress, his cell phone vibrated. "Lousy timing." He grinned at her. "I'll only be a moment." He stepped out into the hall to take the call.

When he closed the door, Kate collected herself and gave thought to the direction her relationship with Carlos was taking. He was so adept at arousing her physically and while touching her, kissing and loving her, she wanted him to take her, to master her. If Carlos proposed and she accepted, she didn't think she'd lack physical satisfaction. Kate tried to set that thought aside and busied herself wandering about the room. It differed from the office he kept at the Dallas consulate building. Curious, she examined the artwork and books. Kate believed you could tell a lot about someone by what they read and if he was going to propose, she needed to know him much better. Most of Carlos' personal collection was business, political biographies, and military history sprinkled in with some chemistry. A rather eclectic and odd combination, she thought. Kate crossed to the bank of windows behind his desk, idly running her fingers over the polished and organized surface. There was an antique inkwell, and a blotter set made of brass that she stopped to admire. That was when she noticed a file folder tucked under the leather writing pad. The tab was visible, and it had her name on it.

Carlos returned, walking toward her with a proprietary glow in his eyes. He stopped and she noticed him staring at what was in her hands, his gaze darting from her to the desk. She held up the file, looking at him with quirked eyebrows and a set to her mouth showing her displeasure.

"Carlos, why is there a file folder with my name on it?"

Calmly, Carlos crossed to her and took the file from her hand, putting it into his desk drawer. "It's nothing Kate—just standard vetting information for all guests of the Consulate. Security nonsense really," he replied smoothly, reaching to take her in his arms once again.

Kate stepped back.

"Standard security nonsense? Vetting? I see," Kate stated skeptically. "Oh, look at the time. I think I should go. Please ask the driver to meet me at the front door." Kate turned a cool cheek to Carlos for a goodbye kiss. She held in her fury and maintained her composure, walking out of the room to the front entry where Hector was waiting by the car to drive her home. Her jaw was aching from clenching it so tightly.

Carlos was concerned. Kate wasn't stupid, but then, neither was he. He would have to convince her that the file she had found was just as he had explained; a security background check. Calling his assistant into his office, he handed him a prepared statement to be leaked to the local papers about an attempted break-in at the consulate and the subsequent need for tighter security. Once Kate read this, she would be more inclined to give him the benefit of the doubt.

Carlos sat back in the leather chair behind his desk and surveyed his office. It spoke to the power he planned to possess, just like he'd possess Kate Hunter. Her liaison with Slater, however, was disturbing. Add the fact that Carlos had discovered Sam worked for Homeland Security, investigating the Mexican drug cartel smuggling. There was a possibility Sam could be investigating him. Based on what Carlos was learning, it was becoming clear that he would have to eliminate the competition for Kate's affection and the potential threat to his operation.

Chapter 12

The evening of the consulate dinner was finally here. It was a black-tie event and Kate chose her gown carefully. Because Carlos had to take care of some state business before the guest's arrival, he planned for the consulate car to pick Kate up. She was happy to see Hector again when he arrived at six p.m. Juan had been surly and a little scary. She had grown fond of Hector over the last few weeks. He was always solicitous and helpful. "Good evening, Hector. I missed you. How was your granddaughter's birthday party?"

"Oh, it was a wonderful evening." He was practically beaming with pride, talking about his beloved family. "Her Abuela and I have a lot of grandchildren but this one, she is very special. She was born in the United States and is a US citizen. She could be president one day! Her mother baked a delicious tres leches cake, and we had a piñata for the children. Everyone enjoyed it so much. Senor Ramirez sent a special gift for my little Maria, a silver crucifix. He is her godfather, you know. He is very thoughtful and you are most kind for asking."

Kate found his pride and joy endearing and thought Carlos, being a godfather, was also charming. He was a many-faceted and mysterious man.

Carlos had suggested she come early so he could properly greet her and get her settled in before he had to fulfill his official duties. It was misting when Hector picked her up so he had an enormous umbrella and was very solicitous making sure not a drop of rain touched her on the way to the car. When they finally arrived at the consular residence, the skies had opened and rain poured down in buckets.

The man at the front gate gave Hector instructions to take Kate to the porte cochère by the kitchen so she could enter without getting drenched. As he escorted her through the kitchens, she noticed a room off to the side with the door half open. Inside, four men were lounging around a table smoking cigarettes and picking their teeth, their dirty dishes cluttering the table. One had taken off his leather jacket and hung it over the back of his chair. He wore a shoulder holster with a large handgun and a knife on his belt. They didn't resemble the consulate security detail with which Kate was familiar. Those men were always clean-cut and typically wore suits and ear pieces. There was a toughness about these four men. They looked like the sort that could kill without remorse. It made Kate shiver with apprehension.

Carlos came up at that moment and mistook her shiver for being chilled. He put his arms around her to offer some warmth. The men in the room acknowledged Carlos, to which he simply nodded. He apologized for the inconvenience of entering through the service area and they left the hustle and bustle of the kitchen behind to make their way down a long hallway to a guest bedroom. Kate was hesitant to enter, wondering at Carlos' motives.

"It is such bad weather, I thought you might like an opportunity to repair anything the rain has ruined before

I introduce you, although you look perfect to me." He motioned for her to proceed through the door. Once inside, Carlos greeted her appropriately. Before taking her into his embrace, he held Kate at arm's length and admired her exquisite beauty. His eyes told her he thought she was perfection when they roamed over her V-neck midnight blue sheath with three-quarter-length sleeves. Pausing at her alluring decolletage tastefully displaying the right amount of cleavage and molding to her firm breasts, his voice grew husky and his eyes smoldered with desire. The bodice was lace-covered silk and a shear overlay shot through with silver threads, flowed from the high waist floating down to the floor.

His gaze completed the circuit, ending with her delicate feet peeping out from under the hem of her gown. At her ears, she wore drop diamond earrings. A simple pear-shaped diamond solitaire on a silver chain hanging at her throat drew one's eyes downward to her breasts. Carlos drew her closer and tenderly kissed her lips, teasing her with his tongue until she opened her mouth to receive a deeper, more urgent probe. Kate submitted to his attention, but with some hesitation. Releasing her, Carlos looked into her eyes. A lock of hair had fallen from her expertly fashioned coif and he tucked it behind her ear.

"Ah, even if the weather has not mussed your hair, I'm afraid I have. I asked the staff to place some toiletries and other things in the adjoining bath. Please make yourself comfortable. I'll return after I ready the reception line for the consular and his wife; about six forty-five."

Kate didn't realize she was holding her breath until

Carlos softly closed the door behind him. Lately, she had been picking up odd vibes from Carlos. The strange men in the kitchen made her curious. Taking advantage of the time to not only repair her hair and make-up but also explore the rooms in this part of the house, she snuck back to the kitchen area for a closer look at the four men she had spied earlier. Easing closer to the door, she listened to them discussing the rain and how it might delay 'the shipment'. Kate was hoping for more information so she'd know what shipment they were referring to when a fifth man entered through the outer door and shook off the rain. It was Miguel. Kate quickly stepped back into the shadows of the hallway, barely avoiding his detection. As he was closing the door to the room with the other men, she heard him say something about Rahim getting antsy for the guns. Just then, a loud crash of thunder sounded. It rattled her. She swiftly returned to the guestroom and puzzled over the comment Miguel had made. *'Antsy for the guns?' What did he mean by that?*

True to his word, Carlos returned at six forty-five and escorted Kate through the reception line where Senora Quintana practically gushed over Kate and her dress. She complimented Kate on her style and, in her stilted English, asked if Kate would consent to help her update her wardrobe. Kate smiled and graciously agreed, knowing full well it would probably never happen. Kate recognized it as one of those empty comments used by rich people to make others feel important. It was usually an insincere remark.

Moving on, Carlos signaled the waiter carrying a tray with glasses of champagne. Taking two flutes, he handed one to Kate and then expertly maneuvered her around the room, introducing her to other guests. Carlos had chosen a single-breasted tuxedo and crisp twill shirt. The black pearl studs contrasted dramatically with the whiteness of his shirt and silk tie. With his regal good looks and Kate's stunning beauty, they made a striking couple.

Carlos worked the room like a chess master. He'd spend a few minutes with the inconsequential guests, making them feel important but focused his time and attention on the more influential ones. By his manner and possessive hand on the small of her back, he made sure everyone knew Kate belonged to him.

When the orchestra struck up a waltz, Carlos took Kate in his arms and they glided onto the dance floor. He was an expert dancer, and they drew admiring and envious looks from the crowd. Carlos didn't miss a thing and was elated at the impression they were making. When it was time for dinner, Carlos placed her on his left next to an elderly gentleman who spent the entire meal dominating the conversation, demanding her attention and openly staring at her breasts. A dark-skinned man took the seat on Carlos' right. He acknowledged Carlos with a slight head bow and continued an intense exchange with the guest seated across the table.

Kate watched as Carlos sat patiently, making idle conversation, waiting for the dark-skinned stranger to conclude his conversation with the other guest. Every move appeared to be choreographed, every action scripted. Carlos was simply waiting for his cue to enter. When the waiter had removed the salad plate, the dark-skinned man leaned his head toward Carlos and whispered. Without so much as tilting his head, Carlos responded. The two men maintained indifferent countenances. They could have been talking about the quality of the wine for all any observers could see. It was difficult for Kate to eavesdrop on Carlos and the other man's conversation. She picked up a word or two; one was '*cuerno de chive*'. When the meal wound down, the crowd naturally gravitated to the back terrace for coffee and after-dinner drinks. The rain had stopped earlier, cooling down the evening air.

Carlos invited her to stroll through the grounds leading her toward the back garden, which was laid out more formally. Flanked by Italian cypress trees softening and hiding the twelve-foot concrete walls, an expanse of green lawn ran down an easy slope to the riverbank where a deck cantilevered out over the water. On it were comfortable seating areas and tables the staff had dried from the recent rain. Several of the guests had wandered that way, as it offered a beautiful view of the downtown skyline. The wait staff circulated with after-dinner drinks and coffee. Kate took advantage of the relaxed atmosphere to begin a subtle interrogation of Carlos.

"That was a wonderful meal. I hope your dinner conversation was more stimulating than mine. The elderly gentleman seated to my left spent the entire meal bragging about his sexual conquests back in his younger days, while his dentures clicked from lack of adhesive." She laughed, trying to disarm Carlos. "Who was the gentleman seated to your right? You two seemed to have a serious conversation. Solving the problems of the world?"

Without missing a beat, Carlos replied, "It wasn't too serious. He has business interests and would like to expand into Mexico. He inquired about Mexican laws and tariffs, then he told me I was the luckiest man in the room. I agreed with him." Carlos guided Kate along a dimly lit walkway away from the crowds. They came to a lovely arbor covered in honeysuckle. Checking that the bench was dry, he invited her to sit down. Taking her hands in his, Carlos looked deeply into Kate's eyes. Uncharacteristically unsure of himself, he cleared his throat and hesitated.

"Kate Hunter, I have grown very fond of you." With increased confidence following the latest report showing Kate's relationship with Slater was more platonic, he felt emboldened to express his true feelings. Looking down, he began toying with the ring on her left hand. When he spoke, Kate had to lean in to hear him. "Have you translated the phrase I taught you? *Seria tan facil enamorarme de ti*. It will be a little while until I see you again. I have to make another trip back to Guadalajara to pick up something special from my mother, but when I return, I'd like to ask you a very important question." He then turned his gaze up to her.

Kate floundered for what to say. She dreaded his words could only mean one thing. She didn't think she loved him. In fact, she realized she just might love Sam. But apparently, Sam didn't love her. All their conversations were strictly platonic. He acted more like a big brother, treating her just like he did Emily. She'd reached an age when the biological clock started ticking louder and considered what children with Carlos would be like. What was she going to do? She was almost in tears, thinking about all this. Carlos placed his finger against her lips and said, "No, don't say anything yet. Just promise me you won't go anywhere until I get back. Come, I'll take you home."

****

Emily looked up, smiling, as Kate came in carrying two lattes. "Looks like I came at a good time. How about a break? I need to ask your opinion about something," Kate said, setting down the coffee and flopping down into the chair across the desk. Emily leaned back to stretch.

"Sure. I could use a break. This is wearing me out. I mean, I'm thrilled that the artists I suggested are enjoying incredible success, but keeping up with orders is overwhelming. And I have a special commission that, ah, I'm working on." Emily shared with a wink. She licked the cream froth off her latte and took a sip. "What's up?"

"Okay, not sure what your wink means, but I'm sure you'll tell me in time." Kate smiled hesitantly, playing with the cardboard sleeve on her latte. "Em, you and I have become best friends, and I've grown to trust your grounded approach to life and your level-headedness. So, here's my dilemma. I need an impartial observer, someone who knows all the parties involved to help me sort something out. I'm sure you know that Carlos Ramirez has been putting on a full-court press."

"Only too well," Emily cautiously replied and leaned forward. She didn't like where this was going. "So why is this suddenly concerning? You know he has the hots for you—heck, you've known that since your first date with him. Do you have feelings for him? We talked about this before. I mean, he is pretty hot. Is he a good kisser?"

"Well, he is gorgeous and, yes, he is a good kisser." Kate half-smiled, sipping her latte.

Emily could see the gears turning. She could just kick Sam. It didn't take a rocket scientist to see there was chemistry between him and Kate. Emily knew Kate and had watched how she interacted with Sam. She wouldn't be surprised if Kate thought Sam might be a good kisser, too. Unfortunately, Sam, the idiot, was too afraid to make a move and risk falling in love. Emily chanced it. She lifted her shoulders and flipped her palms out in a casual shrug. "There might be others that kiss just as well, or even better."

"I'm sure there is, but I may never find out." Kate blew her hair out of her face, frustration sounding on every note. "That's just it, Emily. I don't know what to think. And the more I get to know Carlos, the more I am puzzled by him. Did you know he is the godfather to Hector, the chauffeur's granddaughter? I would never have expected that. And then, there is his protective nature. It's like he is always on the lookout for any kind of threat and has my safety at the top of his awareness. I think he is going to propose. I should be happy, right? He is handsome, rich, and treats me like a queen. And it's not like anyone else is breaking down my door. Life with Carlos would certainly be exciting. I doubt I'd ever want for anything, and we'd travel and lead an exciting life. Carlos is rising fast in the Mexican government and has political ambitions. He says I'd be an important part of that. He respects my career and hopes I'd continue working until I had children. And there it is. Family. He is close to his and wants to have children. I'd like to start a family before my biological clock times out."

Kate huffed out a heavy breath. "Emily, I want a love like my folks had, and I'm not sure I'd have that with him. Worst of all, I'm afraid that maybe the love my folks shared is a fairy tale. What if I say no? I could end up all alone."

"Ah, Kate, I may not be the best person to ask. I had what I thought was the love of my life with Greg, and then he died. I never hoped to find someone else I could love as much. Now I've met a man that makes me laugh and gives me such joy. I know there is someone that loves you with the same depth of devotion you remember your folks sharing. Please don't give up. Don't settle."

Chapter 13

Finishing her latte, Kate left Emily and drove down to the park where she sat on her and Sam's cool-down table. Rocky ran up, looking for a treat. "Sorry, little guy. I didn't bring anything with me today except my worries. You wouldn't like those as much as pecans." It was late. Most folks enjoying the park had called it a day and gone home. The sun was shining on the river and a light breeze blew Kate's hair back from her face as she sat in the shade and thought about her relationship with Carlos and Sam. A black Toyota 4Runner pulled into the parking space next to her car. A man in black jeans and a leather jacket got out and strolled over to her. "Lovely evening, isn't it? I have noticed you sitting at this table before. It's safe enough during the morning and with a friend. Now that it's growing later in the day and is less busy, you may not be safe."

Startled, Kate looked up into the eyes of the man that had approached Carlos at the symphony. He had a bandage on his hand and dark circles under his eyes, but they were no less menacing. Jumping up, Kate stumbled, running to her car. He followed her flight, laughing. Kate felt his evil burning a hole into her back as she ran.

Kate drove home, rushed into the house, and locked her doors. She turned on every light and called

Emily, getting her voice mail.

"Emily, it's Kate. That scary guy that argued with Carlos, he came up to me at the park. I don't think I'm imagining all the watching and following stuff anymore. I think it's real. Please call me. I'm scared." Kate hung up, holding her phone in trembling hands. She sat, eyes fixed on the front door. Twenty minutes later, someone was beating on her door like they'd break it down. Kate carefully looked out the peephole. It was Sam, and standing behind him were Emily and Jake. Kate flung open the door with a cry of relief. Sam burst in and, taking her shoulders, gave her a close inspection from head to toe.

"Are you hurt? What did he say? Did you notice what kind of car he was driving? Can you give us a description?" His panicked voice and quick action dazed Kate. Her mouth was working, but no sound was coming out. Finally, Sam took a breath and Kate could organize her thoughts to respond.

While Emily made coffee, Kate explained everything about the encounter with Carlos that long-ago evening and her feelings of being watched ever since. She told them about the black 4Runner that she thought had been following her. Then she described the man, his physical features, the bandaged hand, and his cold eyes. His words weren't threatening, but she felt he wanted to hurt her.

"I should probably tell Carlos, don't you think? After all, the man seemed to know him or have some connection." She looked at Sam for his agreement.

Sam bit his tongue. That bastard was the reason Kate was even in this danger. "I'm not sure Carlos is in any position to keep you safe. It appears he is the reason you are in this situation. But if you decide to tell him, that is your call."

Shocked that Sam would even think of letting Kate turn to Carlos, Emily shot him a withering look and put her arm around Kate's shoulder. "Kate, you're shaking. Why don't you spend the night at my place? Jake can come back here in the morning and add some additional security."

Kate took Emily up on her offer and followed her home. They watched some TV and went to bed. Neither slept well.

****

Sam was pissed. Driving home, the same thoughts kept floating around. His fist slammed down on the steering wheel. Jesus Christ! Ramirez is the reason Kate's in this bind and she thinks he can protect her? Damn Ramirez! And damn himself for not letting Kate know how he feels about her.

Slamming the door to his office, Sam plopped down onto his chair and stared at the phone. He rubbed at the pounding in his temples threatening to explode out of his head like an armor-piercing missile. The last thing he wanted to do was involve Kate in an operation that might put her in danger, but if he did nothing? Hell, it would be the same either way. He called his second. John picked up on the first ring.

Without preamble, Sam launched into the reason for his call. "Looks like we have another avenue to get to Ramirez. We need to put surveillance on Kate Hunter." Sam quickly outlined what Kate had relayed.

John listened, running the information through his computer. "Okay, from what I know, the guy that is stalking her has to be Cortino. Not only is he one of the cartel's business associates, but word on the street is that something went down between him and Carlos. No one else has the balls to confront Ramirez like this. Of course, maybe he's just plain stupid. Ramirez would kill him if he touched a hair on Ms. Hunter's head."

"You're right there. He is stupid, but when has a drug dealer, no matter how high on the food chain, ever been smart? Well, it may be our lucky break since it appears there is some bad blood and Kate Hunter is being used as a pawn for revenge. I'll be in first thing tomorrow—we'll confirm Cortino as our perp and lay out the next steps."

Sam hung up. He clenched his fists and imagined them around Ramirez's throat, squeezing the life out of him if anything happened to Kate.

****

Emily drove Kate to her house the next morning at ten to meet Jake. He would install new deadbolts on her doors and extra security on her windows. She watched Jake work, breathing a little easier when Jake explained everything to Kate.

"These deadbolts and window locks will give you some additional security. I'm putting a motion detector on your porch lights, front and back. I've also installed timers on your interior lights to turn on at dusk so you don't come home to a dark house." Jake gave Kate a reassuring pat on the back. "You'll be fine. Anyone messes with you, they'll have to answer to Slater and me."

Jake swept up his sawdust and packed up his tools. Emily sighed, taking a long look at his strong shoulders and deft hands. Raising her eyebrows to Kate, she blushed a little, remembering her fantasy confession.

Making sure all was in order; Emily kissed Jake and hugged Kate, noting the worried look lingering in her eyes. "I need to get to the gallery. Call if you need anything." Emily got in her car and drove straight to Sam's, ready to read him the riot act.

Bursting in the door, she found him at his desk, working. "Sam, we need to talk about what is going on with Kate. I watched you two last night. She called us because she trusts us to be there for her and you told her to tell Carlos. Don't you realize you are pushing her into his arms? Don't you care about her safety—don't you care about her?"

Sam slammed his hand down on his desk. Lashing out, he raked a hand through his hair. "Why the hell didn't you tell me any of this sooner? Christ, Emily, I care. I…care about her safety. I am not leaving Kate unprotected. Do you really think I'm that stupid? I set up a detail to watch her beginning last night. They will watch over her whenever I can't. And believe me; my team is much better at surveillance than Cortino. She won't see ours. Oh, yes…" He nodded at Emily's surprised face. "I already know who the bastard is that talked to her. But Ramirez got her into this mess and he is the best one to clean it up. I intend on letting him know, even if Kate doesn't. You have to trust me on this. Now, if you will excuse me, I have an errand to run." Sam stalked out the door, leaving Emily staring after him, open-mouthed.

****

Carlos was sitting at an outside table enjoying his coffee and reading the paper, idling away the time until his business meeting when a young kid rolled up on a skateboard.

"Hey, man, are you Mr. Ramirez?" The kid scooped up his board.

Carlos slowly folded his paper, laying it beside the cup of coffee, and looked at the young man. "Who's asking?"

"Look, dude, some guy just gave me twenty bucks to deliver this note. Are you him or not?"

"I am." Carlos reached out for the note. "There is another twenty in it if you can point out the man that gave you the note."

The kid looked over his shoulder across the street. "He's standing over... Oh, wait, he's not there anymore. I don't see him."

"The twenty is still in play. What did he look like?" Carlos asked, scanning the street.

"I don't know, man—tall dude, jeans, dark blue t-shirt, dark glasses, and a baseball cap. Looked like he could kick your ass, if you ask me. Can I have the twenty now?"

"Yes. And here is my card. If you see him again, get a better description and call me. Maybe the car he is driving. It will be worth fifty dollars."

"Shit! Deal." The kid stuffed the money in his pocket. "You two guys are nuts." He jumped back on his skateboard and rolled away, looking around, hoping to collect that fifty.

Carlos used his pocket knife to slit open the envelope and pulled out a generic white card. Printed in black ink was a concise message.

Your associate from the symphony paid a visit to Ms. Hunter. You started this, and it's gotten messy. You need to clean it up.

There was no signature. Carlos slowly returned the

card to the envelope and placed it in his breast pocket, looking around for the author.

He canceled his business meeting and called Miguel. Cortino had made a huge mistake. Carlos would personally clean it up.

Chapter 14

Things quickly settled back into the usual routine. They still met whenever he was in town for their morning runs and time with Rocky, the squirrel. A cadre of other squirrels had joined him, so Sam brought extra pecans and they enjoyed the antics of all their furry friends. It was nice to have someone to just hang out with. It wasn't like a date, so she didn't feel the pressure she did with Carlos, although Kate still hoped Sam took the next step. She had never felt comfortable taking the lead in a relationship. Her mom had told her that if a man was interested, he'd make the first move. Carlos certainly had. Good thing the squirrels were a safe distraction, getting more comfortable with them. Rocky was eating out of Sam's hand now. Just like the squirrel, Kate grew to trust Sam, and she valued his opinions. She was dropping more and more of her guard, sharing things with him that she had told no one else.

Kate was quiet and preoccupied following their run. It was the anniversary of her folk's accident and she was feeling nostalgic and melancholy. Picking a leaf off the tabletop, Kate broke it into tiny pieces and tossed them one by one into the air, watching as the breeze caught and carried them away, just like the pieces of her heart when her folks had died.

"You're quiet this morning. Something troubling

you?" Sam's tone held concern.

"I was just thinking about my folks. This is the anniversary of their deaths. They were so loving and supportive. Sometimes I really miss talking with them. You know how it is, something happens and you hear their voice in your head giving you sage advice. Their hearts were full of love for me and it reminded me how deeply they loved each other." Kate let go with a longing sigh. "I don't know if that kind of love even exists. They were both independent and strong-minded, but they still gained strength by relying on each other. Ever since they died, and I had to be the one in charge, I've had trouble letting anyone get that close. I think I've constructed some pretty high and thick walls around my heart. Someday, I'd like to get married and have children, but I don't want to lose who I am. I'm afraid I'll never find that kind of love." Kate absently played with a loose thread on her shirt as her voice trailed off and a small tear slid down her cheek.

Sam listened carefully, didn't judge, and when her burden became too emotional for her to continue, he held her hand, eventually putting his arm around her shoulders, hugging her to his side. "I know you miss your folks, Kate. But you still have them with you–in your heart and in your mind. How else do you hear their sage advice? My folks are still living, but I never recall seeing the kind of love you talk about. It was always duty for Dad. I think he felt guilty. He got mom pregnant before they got married. Mom was an artist. That's where Emily gets it from, I guess. She gave up everything to marry him and then she lost the baby. I'm not sure they would have gotten married at all otherwise. But like I said, Dad is all about duty. He drilled that into me ad nauseam." A twig snapped in Sam's fist. "It's my job to protect everyone–keep them safe. It's become ingrained in me–second nature. Then one night, when he and Mom were fighting, my dad raised his hand to her. I went berserk and beat the shit out of him. That night, I walked out of the house and never returned. I kept in touch with Mom, Emily, and Paul. Over the years, Mom would secretly send 'care packages', new underwear, and homemade cookies. She never left Dad, never pursued her art. I managed; worked my way through college and law school. Then Paul was killed, and I joined the Navy. You know some about Jake and me and our time in the SEALs. I didn't have the example of true love you had, but I'd like to believe it exists and that I'll know when I find it."

Sam feared Carlos was winning her over and if anything happened, Sam would fail her. Driving home after dropping her off, Sam listened to an old Scorpions CD absently singing along with 'Send me an Angel'. Maybe Kate was his.

****

The next day, after racing each other to the jeep for their water and pecans for Rocky and his buddies, they made their way to their favorite cool-down spot. Kate was telling Sam about the ghost-writing project she was working on. He was walking by her side, enjoying her animated gestures and expressions, when he stopped and touched her arm. He motioned Kate to be silent and listen. Triangulating on the sound, Sam walked toward a trash can with his head cocked to one side, Kate right behind him.

"Sure enough, that's a kitten mewling, and it sounds like it's coming from the trash can." Sam pulled off the lid and saw a black plastic bag inside tied off with a twist tie. Sam tore it open and out spilled four kittens, three of them already dead, but the fourth was a fighter and she was making a racket.

"What kind of a SOB decides he doesn't want kittens, and leaves them to die in a garbage bag? What is wrong with people?" Sam handed the kitten to Kate. He then gently checked the other three. When he confirmed they were dead, he re-wrapped them in the plastic bag and returned it to the trash can.

"Oh, Sam, look how small and helpless it is. Do something. You have to save her." Sam swallowed, mentally pushing down the panic rising in his throat.

Kate cradled the little kitten to her chest, dripping water from her bottle off her fingers into its mouth. "It can't be more than about five weeks old." Kate didn't know if it was a girl or boy, but all cats were 'she', weren't they? Bonding with Kate, the kitten sucked on her finger. "I think she's hungry. We should take her to the shelter or a vet. Do you think she's old enough to handle soft food?" Rocky and his friends were all but forgotten.

"Let's run over to the grocery store and pick up some supplies and you can take her home." Sam gave the kitten an ear rub.

Kate nuzzled the kitten, who was purring like a finely tuned race car engine. "No, wait. I can't take her until I check with my landlord. Remember? I live in a rental. You'll have to keep her until I find out if I can bring her home. Poor little girl." Kate was so focused on the kitten that she missed the sweat breaking out on Sam's brow. All he was seeing was dead cats and bloody Barbies.

Sam stuttered. "Kate, I can't–I'm not–it's not..." He knew he'd lost as soon as Kate raised trusting eyes to him.

Sam ran over to the squirrels and tossed them the pecans he'd brought, apologizing for having to leave so suddenly, and then he and Kate went to get the supplies needed to adopt a cat and head to his place. She was so small, black and white, with a little black patch on her chin. It made her look like she was saying 'Oh', so they called her Ophelia. She was very vocal and took to the kitten food right away. Then, like all cats, she walked around the house with her little tail in the air, inspecting every room. She must have approved because she found Sam's bed and made herself at home.

"Oh, no you don't, you little stinker." Sam scooped her up and placed her in the new cat bed in the laundry room. With a pointed look at Kate, Sam informed the cat she'd be moving on. "Don't get too comfortable. You'll be going home with Mommy soon. And if not home with Mommy, then outside to the garden."

Kate leaned against the doorjamb, watching him. The kitten fit in the palm of Sam's hand and he was so gentle with her. "Are you sure, Sam? I think she has your number." When he turned thunderous eyes on her, she quickly back-pedaled. "Okay, I promise, I'll talk to my landlord and get permission to keep her at my place. She is a cutie, isn't she? Yes, you are Ohh-phelia. So cuddly." Kate had pronounced the cat's name in that mommy sing-songy voice. It was a perfect name for the little fur ball.

Sam tamped down his dread. Maybe this was his test. If he could save a kitten...

****

"She looks just like you, Sam!" Emily teased when she and Kate arrived later that day with chips and guacamole for their evening game. She picked up Ophelia and cuddled her to her cheek, making cooing noises, and kissing her on the nose. "You really found her in a trash can at the park? Jeez, some people! I'm so glad you saved her."

Jake held the door open for Kate as she carried in brownies for her favorite people and catnip for the new baby. They'd fallen into the habit of gathering as often as their schedules allowed to play Trivial Pursuit or some other game. It was casual and relaxed. Tonight, Jake suggested Twister. He'd discovered the dusty old game in Emily's closet and when he brought it out, he winked at Emily. The two were engaged in a conspiracy to bring Sam and Kate together and get Sam off dead center.

Pulling out the game, Emily reminded everyone of the rules and suggested they continue to play as teams like they did with Trivial Pursuit. Discussing how to pair up to play, the guys pointed at each other and said immediately and simultaneously, "No way am I pairing with him!"

"Although it might be fun to watch the girls paired up", Jake remarked, looking lascivious, with his arched eyebrows and a wicked grin.

Jake and Emily called 'Dibs' for each other, conveniently leaving Sam to pair with Kate. Nothing obvious about this at all, Sam thought, but agreed that couple pairing was preferable. Kate simply laughed and blushed–a lot.

Typical of Sam and Jake, they made it a competition. "Okay, Edwards, the couple with the most moves before falling wins."

With Sam spinning and calling out the moves, Jake and Em went first, taking an impressive nine moves before they collapsed in a heap. "Well, hell, Em. You practice yoga. It's an unfair advantage."

Emily and Jake set the bar pretty high, but both Sam and Kate were up for the challenge. Sitting in the big chair with Emily in his lap spinning the pointer, Jake called out the instructions. "Right foot red", he said, the corners of his mouth curving up into a grin and devilish horns popping out of his forehead. Emily opened her mouth to correct him. He pinched her.

"Ow. Watch your hands, Edwards!" Then her eyes brightened as she figured out his strategy. Jake was intentionally calling moves to tangle Sam around Kate in such a way that when they fell, it was into a rather suggestive position. Jake and Emily giggled like pre-pubescent sex fiends.

Jake cheered when Sam and Kate fell after a measly six moves, high-fiving Emily. "Ha–you losers! Hey, since you hadn't a hope in hell of making nine like we did, Em and I will give you a rematch. You guys deserve a chance to win."

Knowing Jake and Emily like he did, Sam suspected a devious plot was afoot. He would also bet Jake was purposely orchestrating their moves. It was typical of his devious and devilish thinking. But since Sam wanted to get tangled up with Kate again, he accepted the challenge. "Bring it on, Edwards!!!" Two can play that game, Sam thought. When it was time for Sam to call the moves, he planned Jake and Emily's positions in such a way so that when they finally fell, Emily's bottom was in Jake's face and Jake's, well, let's just say there was a numerical component to their position.

The game quickly devolved from the number of moves a pair could accomplish before falling to which caller could create the most intimate Kama Sutra position. Jake took that championship hands down. When the evening ended, Jake left with Emily. He had tucked one or two of the suggestive poses away to try later with her, naked. They dropped off Kate on their way home. Sam took a cold shower.

****

The next morning, Emily took the bull by the horns. She cornered Sam after his morning run with Kate. Handing him his towel and water, she casually asked, "How was the run with Kate? Are you any closer to making your move? Jeez, it's so blinking obvious, you guys are in… I don't know–something, Sam. Look, I'm warning you, Ramirez might be planning to propose. He's out of town, not out of the picture. Kate hasn't officially broken up with him. I think she is waiting for you to say something. Anything."

Sam unscrewed the cap off his water bottle and swallowed half in three gulps. "I don't know how serious Kate is about Ramirez. I don't see her being in love with him."

"Really, Sam? Is that your keen investigative skills talking?" *How could he be so obtuse?* "Maybe you're just afraid to come right out and ask, fearing her answer. Well, let me clue you in. She's waiting for you to make a move. Every time you snuggle, she gets this hopeful expression in her eyes. If that girl isn't hoping it will lead to more, I'm a monkey's aunt. She is giving you every signal she knows how to give without

145

throwing herself at you. God, Sam, you are such a bonehead. Kate isn't a woman that throws herself at a man. She wants him to take the lead. You need to kiss her and confirm what she is feeling."

Sam looked at Emily like she'd slapped him.

Emily crossed her arms and smiled. She was sure she'd knocked some sense into her brother.

Chapter 15

Kate gasped and brought her hand to her mouth in horror. The television newsman professionally read his copy concerning a fiery single-car crash at I-30 and Hwy 287. It was backing up traffic and delaying the evening commute. Flashing a picture of the accident scene, the newscaster continued. "The crash appears to be the result of road rage, as the lone victim was shot twice in the head. Police are asking for anyone who may have witnessed the crime to contact them at..."

Kate recognized the vehicle. It had been following her earlier that afternoon as she ran errands, and she thought she'd seen it in the parking lot of the grocery store. Could this be a coincidence? She called Sam. Mere minutes after she hung up, he was knocking on her door.

"Sam, thanks for coming." Kate sighed in relief. "Where is your jeep? How did you get here so fast?"

Sam read the question in her eyes and realized he had to be honest. "I've been in the phone company van parked across from your neighbor. The man that has been following you is a known drug dealer named Robert Cortino. He is extremely dangerous. This isn't something to take lightly. So, I've been watching over you."

Kate stepped back. "Oh. Well, I guess if you're going to watch over, you might as well be comfortable while you do it. Did you eat? I was going to put together a light salad, but can make something more substantial if you're hungry."

Sam heard the tone in Kate's voice letting him know she wasn't entirely happy with his actions and was going to explain further when he received a text just as the doorbell rang. Sam walked to the door while reading his text. —Cortino dead–killed in a road rage incident. More details when available.—

Kate had come out of the kitchen just as Sam answered the door. He curled his lip in disgust. *Damn—flowers! Bet they're from Ramirez.* Tipping the delivery driver, he handed the bouquet to Kate. She read the card and was going to get a vase when her phone rang. It was Carlos.

"Hello, Carlos. Yes, I just received the bouquet. Thank you. They are lovely." Kate walked into the kitchen to get a little privacy while Sam clenched his jaw until he thought it might break. God, he wanted to rip the phone out of Kate's hand and give Carlos a piece of his mind. Instead, he went to the front window and watched the road, thinking about the text he'd just received from John. Road rage was certainly convenient.

Sam heard Kate say goodbye and walked into the kitchen to see her sitting at the island, holding her head in her hands, looking like she was trying to puzzle something out. He stood in the doorway, watching her. "I just received word that Cortino is no longer a threat."

Kate's eyes were glassy, her face pale. "He's dead, isn't he? That man?" There was an odd distance and flatness in her voice. "I called you because I saw on the news about the 4Runner and the road rage killing. Then

I got these flowers and Carlos called and told me he'd talked with the man from the evening at the symphony. He said he gave him a satisfactory solution to his problem. Carlos said he won't be bothering us anymore." Kate turned frightened eyes to Sam.

He took two steps and had Kate in his arms. She sagged against him, trembling as he held her and stroked her hair, calming her. Sam desperately wanted to kiss her. He tried to keep his emotions in check. After everything, he was still afraid he'd end up failing her. It was a losing battle; he surrendered. Sam tucked her hair behind her ear, letting his fingers trace along her jawline. He raised her face to him. They looked into each other's eyes and Sam gently lowered his mouth onto Kate's soft, moist lips. Tenderly kissing her, his arms tightened, drew her closer to him and the kiss deepened. When he pulled back, he searched her face for something, anything, that would tell him how she felt.

"Sam, I'm sorry. I'm confused by everything. I need some time to think. If it's true and Cortino is dead then, I'll be safe. I won't need watching over."

Sam wanted to argue that point—to tell her Carlos was more dangerous than Cortino ever hoped to be, but his job prevented him from doing that yet. Kate walked Sam to the door and quietly bade him goodbye.

Chapter 16

Sam's schedule had lightened up, so he suggested he and Kate finally make that promised trip to the zoo. Pulling up in front of Kate's house, he almost skipped to the door. He was looking forward to spending the day with her; had been all week. They had met almost every morning for a quick 2-mile run. The park's early morning beauty and their shared conversations brought a special peace to Sam and contentment for Kate. The two slipped back into their playful, relaxed relationship with only a little effort. Of course, neither talked about his sitting outside her house, protecting her, and certainly not the kiss. Talking about that would have been like touching the wires of an electrical outlet. In hindsight, he wondered if it was just frayed emotions. It all seemed like some weird made-for-TV drama. There had been no repeat of the kiss. He guessed they both needed time to figure it all out.

Sunday was promising to be a great day for the zoo, sunny and not too warm. The Fort Worth Zoo had recently installed its new Animals of the Savannah exhibit, and both Sam and Kate were looking forward to seeing it. When Kate opened the door, they saw each had dressed in "safari" themed outfits, crisp khaki shirts and shorts.

"Dr. Livingstone, I presume," Sam said in his best English accent, bursting out laughing. "The only thing missing is a pith helmet. I'm sure we can get them at a souvenir shop once we get there."

It was the perfect way to start the day, which only got better and better. They made their way past the entrance gate, dodging the Zoo Camp kids and enjoying the excitement of the little ones as they pulled their parents toward the gorilla exhibit. Exchanging smiles, Sam pointed out a pair of tow-headed twins in matching sun dresses. He liked kids, and Kate had mentioned she did, too. If they could have read each other's minds, they would have known that each was wondering what their kids would be like.

The two headed straight for the Savannah exhibit. Sam had traveled to South Africa during R&R from one of his tours in Afghanistan. He told Kate about his experiences. He watched her eyes glow with excitement as he told her about the first day out on safari.

"Five minutes out and we were passing a couple of giraffes. Then about mid-morning, we encountered a pride of eighteen lions walking out of the bush right in front of our vehicle. Keep in mind; this was an open-sided Land Rover. A lion could easily jump in and devour any of us. Our game spotter was seated on a chair mounted on the hood of the car. We all held our breath as he sat still as a statue and the lions passed one by one within inches of him. We followed them into the bush and they flushed out, chased down, killed, and ate a warthog right in front of us. Even our guide said she'd never seen anything like that."

"Do you have any photos? I'd love to see them." Kate took Sam by the arm and pressed herself to him with eagerness.

"Of course, but let's grab a sandwich. I'm starved."

They walked toward the Texas exhibit, where they could get some lunch, and passed the reptile house.

"Eww," Kate said, "let's not go in there."

"You are such a girl," Sam teased with a playful push.

The shady patio felt good after so much time in the sun. They enjoyed chopped brisket sandwiches and cold soda. Popping the last of his sandwich into his mouth, Sam jumped up, walked over to the sweet stand, and came back with a couple of ice cream cones. It was all Sam could do to control himself as he watched Kate lick her cone and almost lost it when the ice cream melted down her arm and she used her tongue to catch the drip. She was totally oblivious to what her actions were doing to him. Sam cleared his throat and shifted in his seat while Kate blushed and quickly popped the last bit of her cone into her mouth. Sam inwardly groaned. He had a clear vision of her mouth under his and on him.

"Well, I'm a mess," Kate said, laughing.

"Yes, you are." *And I love it.* They made their way toward the exit, passing once again through the primate exhibits, stopping to watch the Gibbon monkeys chase each other around the trees. Tired from the heat and laughing, they walked side-by-side back to the car. Sam's hand itched to reach out and hold Kate's, to bring it to his mouth and kiss it, then kiss her.

"What a wonderful day it's been, Sam. Thank you for suggesting it. Sometimes it's good to do something innocent and child-like. No pretensions, no having to be on your guard to make sure you do and say everything properly. I wish it wouldn't have to end."

Sam stopped and turned to Kate. "Wait, who says

it's ending? I promised to show you my photos from Africa. We'll order pizza, look at the album, and watch *Out of Africa*! But don't expect me to wash your hair…"

Kate looked at him quizzically, then laughed. "Oh, Sam, you are too funny. Let's go!" She almost danced instead of just walking to the car. On the drive back to Sam's house, they tried to outdo each other by singing all the songs they could think of about animals or the jungle ending with a terrible rendition of "The lion sleeps tonight".

Arriving at Sam's bungalow, Kate removed her safari jacket, revealing a gauzy little white blouse with antique hankies appliqued at each shoulder. She was so damn cute and delicate. Sam felt a tightening in his groin. She didn't know what she did to him. He longed to show her tonight.

Sitting down on the couch, Sam paged through his photo album with Kate. She was enchanted by how wonderfully he had put it together. Not only were they fantastic photos, but the journaling captured her imagination and let her see a deeper, more complex side to him. Kate read Sam's description of every shot, animal, geographic feature, and funny observations. Sometimes Sam would read one of his narratives and be reminded of something else, allowing him to expand on the stories with additional insights. Kate enjoyed his trip vicariously. There was yearning in his tone as he reminisced about the trip. He freely admitted he feared for the long-term survival of the magnificent animals he'd seen and hoped to return and share it with someone special someday. *Hopefully you, Kate.*

The pizza joint fulfilled its pledge for a thirty-minute delivery. Reluctantly setting aside the photo album, they got out plates and napkins and ate, sitting on stools at the green laminate counter. Sam was still waiting to finish the kitchen. He had selected and purchased the appliances but still pondered over the finish materials. He hoped someday he might not be the only one cooking in it and didn't want to select a finish or style on his own. As for the rest of the house, Jake had been making great headway on framing and drywall. The guest bedroom, bath, and master were finished. The office was almost done. The family room was actually–well, a room. It had more than just four walls and a ceiling fan. Sam had furnished it with a TV, sofa, two club chairs, and a coffee table. Everything was good quality leather, cushy and comfortable. It wasn't easy, but Sam tracked down *Out of Africa* on Netflix and had it cued up, ready to go. They cleaned up dinner and he grabbed the wine, leading Kate to the sofa to watch the movie. Kate confessed she had never seen it.

"Oh, you're in for a treat, then. It was the romantic movie of the eighties–Meryl Streep and Robert Redford. Oh wait. That explains why you looked at me so funny when I said I wouldn't wash your hair." He chuckled. "Well, it's been years since I saw it. My mom loved it and insisted I watch it with her one weekend when I was fifteen. She said I might learn something. I don't know if she was referring to big game hunting or romance or STDs." Kate raised her eyebrows in question. Quick to explain, Sam continued. "Oh, just another reference from the movie. You'll see. As for the takeaway my mom wanted me to make? Heck, I was a teenager. What did I know?"

Kate settled herself on the sofa, and Sam hit the play button. Ophelia jumped up and made herself comfortable too, but when Kate became too engrossed to pay attention to her, she flounced off in a huff out the pet door; confident she'd find better entertainment in the garden. While the opening commercials and previews played, Sam refilled their wineglasses and settled himself into the corner of the sofa, laying his arm comfortably across its back. When the music started, Kate turned bright eyes at him.

"Oh, I love this music. I guess I never realized what it was from whenever I heard it." She tucked her legs under her to the side and leaned back into the crook of Sam's arm. He could see her profile and watched as the beauty of the music and scenery in the movie drew her in. Kate's every emotion flit across her face and when the hair-washing scene came on, she sighed and unconsciously snuggled in a little more. Bringing his arm down around her shoulder, he drew her in closer.

By the time the final credits were playing, Kate turned tear-filled eyes toward him. "Oh, Sam, it's a true story, and it ends so sadly."

He ran his fingers along her jaw and caressed her cheek, whispering, "That's their story, not ours." Looking deeply into Kate's eyes, he kissed her. Sam used his tongue to tease her lips until she opened her mouth. The kiss deepened and their tongues met and mated. He felt his need for her building. Kate reached around his neck and pulled him in. Breaking the kiss, Sam began a slow exploration of her face with his lips. He kissed her temple, breathing in her scent. Moving to her ear, he nibbled at her lobe, then down her neck, stopping to kiss and nuzzle her pulse point. He could feel her heartbeat increase.

Sam pressed Kate down onto the sofa cushions, raining kisses across her collarbone. He unbuttoned her blouse and followed a burning path across her breasts. His tongue darted over their swell, arousing more heat. With a flick of his fingers, he unclasped her bra. Her breasts spilled out. He took them in his hands, kissing and grazing his teeth across each nipple. Kate moaned and arched her back in response, grabbing his hair and pressing his face tighter to her. Returning his mouth to hers, he regained control before his urgency and demand overwhelmed them both. Kate pulled away and, holding each side of his face, whispered, "Wash my hair, Sam."

At that moment, Sam knew exactly what his mom had wanted him to learn from the movie. He picked her up and carried her to the bedroom. Laying her down on the bed, Sam began slowly and sensuously to remove her clothes. First, the little cotton blouse made with antique handkerchief panels, then her bra. He stopped after removing each article of clothing, worshipping her with his mouth, touching and exploring every inch of skin he exposed.

Kate reached out to unbuckle his belt, but Sam stayed her hand. "Don't move," he whispered in her ear and, bringing her hands above her head, held them there. He continued to trail kisses down her stomach, stopping only long enough to remove her shorts and panties. Resuming his ministrations, Sam's mouth found her mound of Venus. He licked and kissed and sucked at her sex. While continuing to manipulate her with his tongue, he stroked her with his fingers. Sam watched Kate's face. Her eyes were closed and her tongue swept around and across her lips. She made little sounds of pleasure and panted ever so slightly. As he aroused her to greater heights, her breathing became faster, and her hips involuntarily arched to meet the thrust of his fingers, the heat of his mouth. He moved his mouth to her breasts, laving each taut nipple with his tongue. He released her wrists. She wrapped her arms around his neck, digging her nails into his back. Sam could feel the rippling of her as the waves of her orgasm built.

"Open your eyes, Kate–look at me. I want to see you. I want to watch you as you come," Sam whispered. She looked into his eyes as he made one last flourish with his thumb tip, bringing her over the top. She arched against his hand and cried out, never breaking their gaze. Sam kissed Kate, first softly, then more passionately as their tongues intertwined in a slow, sensuous dance.

Taking her cue from his earlier actions, she began slowly to undress him. She started with kisses along his neck and sent dancing fingertips and light feathered caresses across his back. She flicked her tongue around his lips, kissing and nibbling at him as he had with her. When he rolled her onto her back, she enjoyed the feel of Sam's broad shoulders and back. She ran her hands down to his firm ass, cupping each cheek and pulling him closer. But she wanted to look at him, to possess him as he had her. Gently pushing against his chest, she rolled him onto his back. Kate straddled Sam, leaning forward to feast. Starting with his neck, she ran her lips and tongue down to his shoulder and trailed kisses along his arm. She stopped momentarily at the inside of his elbow, sucking and nibbling. From there, it was a short jump to his pecs, where Kate focused on his nipples, kissing and brushing them with her fingertips. Her journey continued as she left a trail of kisses down to the flat of his stomach, stopping briefly to lick and blow on the sensitive skin just above his cock. Kate took Sam into her hand, marveling at his size while Sam, growing more and more aroused, reached for Kate.

Smiling wickedly at him, Kate said, "Don't move." Sam lay back with closed eyes and groaned when she took him in her mouth. All Sam could see was the ice cream cone from earlier in the day. He mentally reviewed disassembling, cleaning, and reassembling an AK47 to keep himself from losing all control. When he had completed his exercise and he'd reassembled the rifle in his mind, Sam could hold off no longer. He grabbed Kate, bringing her up to his chest. Then, with agonizing slowness, he lowered her and impaled her on his stiff cock. Kate rode Sam. He squeezed her breasts, rolling her nipples between his fingers, lightly pinching them. When he could feel Kate's muscles quiver and tighten, he knew her climax wasn't far off. He held on to her hips, tempering their mad gallop, and rose to take her breast in his mouth, sucking just hard enough to drive Kate to grip his shoulders with her nails, almost drawing blood. Grabbing her around the waist, he rolled her under him. She wrapped her legs around his waist and, with a final and forceful thrust, Sam exploded into her just as she cried out with her own climax. Sam collapsed and rolled to his side, bringing Kate's face to his. They kissed tenderly and lay contentedly holding each other until the turbulence of their lovemaking calmed and their breathing slowed. Sam kissed Kate's forehead, and this time, she didn't mind one bit. She ran her fingers through his chest hair and nuzzled his neck until he could no longer stand it. Reaching out, he mimicked her movements, playing with her breasts, tickling and teasing her nipples with his fingertips.

It wasn't long before Kate's little mews of pleasure and Sam's growing erection overcame them. Engorged with desire, he rolled on top of Kate, kissing her, possessing her mouth as completely as she possessed his heart while she guided him into her. She was wet and welcoming and so damn tight Sam thought he'd come right then. He paused long enough to regain control. They began their slow dance of love, crescendoing in mutual ecstasy and fulfillment. They lay forehead to forehead, sighing with satisfaction. Tucking her head under his chin, Sam held her close to him and they slept.

****

The Wednesday before Carlos was to return from his business trips, Emily called Kate to invite her to take a break from all her work and join her and "the boys" as she called them for dinner and a rematch of trivial pursuit, winner take all. Jake had actually suggested strip Trivial Pursuit, but reserved that for just him and Emily. He figured he'd lose to her, but then, it would end up a win/win!

"Count me in. Can I bring anything?" Kate asked.

"How about the salad? I'm making lasagna. Jake is bringing the wine and Sam is bringing the garlic bread. Be forewarned. Sam believes there is *never* too much garlic."

Kate let out a sexy laugh. "Perhaps he isn't worried

about garlic breath when he kisses someone Wednesday night." After an awkward pause, Kate cleared her throat and before she hung up, agreed to bring salad and see everyone at 6:30.

Emily smiled into her phone. *Well, well, well. Wait until I tell Jake.*

****

Everyone ate until they thought they'd burst. The lasagna was a recipe Emily had gotten when on a cruise. It had both meat and cream sauce and they devoured every bite. They had settled down in the living room and Emily went to get the game of Trivial Pursuit. Jake was opening a second bottle of wine, leaving Kate and Sam on their own. Kate settled herself on the couch and continued the dinner conversation about her work. She realized that after their night of passion, she had gotten to know Sam physically, and boy, that was amazing! But he never talked about his work. Everyone had heard long ago how Kate had parlayed her talents into a career as a freelance journalist. "You know, it's not as hard as you think if you don't mind going weeks without a paycheck." She'd laughed. But Sam never opened up about what he did, even during many of their one-on-one conversations following their runs.

Kate, using her best interview technique, set to find out. "Sam, can you tell me more about what's been keeping you so busy lately? You're doing a lot of traveling. Do you go to different places? All I really know about your work is that you are a lawyer, but you don't actually practice law. What exactly do you do?"

"I work for the government doing research and investigation. It's not really very exciting. Mostly reading documents and tracking down loose ends." Kate knew Sam did more than just research and investigation based on how he'd handled the Cortino situation but didn't push. Maybe his work was top secret? *My own James Bond.* She smiled.

"By the way—" Sam deftly changed subjects. "—I kept the butler's pantry, to connect the study and kitchen, and I finished refinishing the bookcases. I'm going to install them tomorrow." Kate smiled. She was enjoying Sam's excitement with the remodel. He was very passionate about what he was doing. It was like one of the birds in his garden, preparing a nest for someone special. After Sunday night, Kate suddenly thought it would be nice if she was that someone. Then she wondered if she was falling in love with him.

Emily returned with the game, and Jake plunked down on the sofa with the bottle of wine. He refilled everyone's glass. They began a *very* competitive game of Trivial Pursuit. Emily took the win by strategically working the dice and board to land on all the Arts & Literature squares. She was a killer with the dice and possessed a daunting skill for rolling the right numbers exactly when she needed to. For the next game, Jake suggested they revert to their pattern of playing as teams. Emily heartily agreed, but where Jake thought he and Em would team up as usual and kick some butt, Emily suggested girls against the guys with the loser having to do the dishes. Challenge accepted by all. It took almost two hours and a second bottle of wine before the men squeaked out a win and Jake spiked the dice while doing an end zone dance around the living room. Emily, crying tears of laughter, picked up a woven basket. Placing it on his head, she curtsied low and proclaimed, "We hereby crown you 'KING Goofball'!"

The gals dispatched the dirty dishes under the regal commands of King Goofball, using a wooden spoon like a scepter and calling the girls his wenches. It was late and time to leave. Their farewells said to Emily and Jake, Sam took Kate's hand as they walked to his jeep. They were still laughing over Jake's ridiculous victory dance.

"He's like that, hard as hell in combat but a big goofball. I can't think of anyone else I'd rather have at my side in a firefight. He was the one that pulled me from the SUV when the IED exploded. Took a couple of bullets in the shoulder and his back, dragging my wounded ass to cover."

Kate stopped and put her hand on Sam's chest. "This is the first time I've heard you open up like this, Sam. We always seem to do things with Emily and Jake, and they monopolize the conversation. You know, Sunday was very special for me. I want you to feel you can open up with me, Sam. I'd like to know more about what makes you tick and more than just what you're doing to the house. Promise? No more secrets?"

A moment of panic hit Sam. *No more secrets?* Swallowing hard, he inhaled and blew out a breath. *Like I love you and want to spend the rest of my life with you, secrets?* "Um, I'm free Friday night. How about dinner?"

"Hmmm, can't, previous engagement. How about Saturday? I'll cook."

"Even if something comes up, I will make it work. Is six a good time?"

"That will work. How does Paella sound? I'll mix

up some Sangria to go with it. We can have a quiet evening, just the two of us, and you can tell me more about Pissy," Kate laughed.

"Deal." Sam kissed Kate and helped her into the jeep. He wanted to take her back to his place for a repeat of Sunday's incredible evening. She was so passionate and loved with a fierceness he'd never encountered. He was deliriously happy and knew he was falling in love with Kate, but he needed time to think. Whistling under his breath, he walked around to the driver's side and climbed in to drive Kate home.

Chapter 17

Kate didn't know what to expect and was nervously setting out hors d'oeuvres. Carlos said he'd hang the picture he had purchased for her, but Kate wondered if he also planned to pull a ring out of his pocket. He arrived at seven as agreed, punctual as ever. It had been raining on and off all afternoon, and there was a threat of severe thunderstorms with a chance of tornados predicted for the evening. He suggested they order in instead of going out. Kate felt reluctant, remembering the last time she had invited him into her home and the Cortino situation, but agreed. It was pretty awful out. She ordered Chinese. Let the poor delivery guy brave the weather.

While Kate opened a bottle of wine, Carlos grabbed his tools to hang the painting. The wall Kate had selected was in the alcove where her desk was situated. It didn't have a window, so she hoped the painting would give her a sense of space and fresh air.

Carlos set to work but couldn't resist the opportunity to peek at some of Kate's work while she was busy in the kitchen. It surprised him to see his name on a file folder and looked at what was in it. 'CR, attaché Mexican Consulate', was the heading. Okay, he thought, it was about him. The file contained several notes, probably research for the interview she'd done with him. But then he saw other notes about restaurants frequented, business associates, and known acquaintances. He had just gotten to the notes about his family business, father and brothers when Kate came in with two glasses of wine, setting them on the coffee table. Carlos returned the file to the desktop and placed his toolbox on top of it. "Where exactly would you like it hung?"

Kate explained, and he got to work, hoping for an opportunity to revisit the file folder to see what else Kate was looking into. He was just finishing up when the food arrived. Carlos went to the door and paid the delivery boy. Handing off the bag to Kate, he went to pack up his tools before going to wash up. Carlos snuck the file into the bathroom with him. Using his cell phone, he snapped pictures of all the pages and returned it to Kate's desk before she'd finished setting out dinner.

"There's a soccer game on tonight, Cruz Azul vs Chivas. Aren't they the top-ranked teams this season? I thought you might like to eat in here and watch it," Kate suggested. It was a good game, and she knew Carlos was a fan of the sport. When the game was over, they sat on the couch and admired the painting.

"I think it suits you. I hope you think of me whenever you look at it." He put his arm across the back of the couch, toying with her hair. He leaned in for a kiss, but Kate avoided him, reaching forward to stack dishes to take them into the kitchen. At 10:30, she yawned, looked at her watch, and all but invited him to leave.

Walking him to the door, she thanked him for the gift. "It was so thoughtful of you, and thank you for coming to hang it for me. I promise I will think of you whenever I look at the painting."

"I hope you think of me more often than that," he said, holding her close to him, leaning forward for a kiss.

Kate gently pushed against his chest, separating herself. She leaned in, placing a chaste kiss on his cheek. Kate hooked her arm through his and turned to the door, where she bid him goodnight. Carlos took a step back and gave Kate a puzzled look. Then she noticed his eyes grow dark with anger.

Someone who had seemed gentlemanly and respectful in the beginning had suddenly become a dangerous predator. She watched him through the curtains as he walked to his car.

****

Shoving the key into the ignition, Carlos slammed the heel of his hand on the steering wheel. He dropped the car into first gear and sped away. Nothing but anger seethed through him after the way Kate had pushed him away and kissed his cheek. She'd kept a healthy distance between them all night and used the soccer game to avoid conversation. She'd actually rejected his advances. No woman had ever done that to him.

After driving down the highway at a reckless speed, he calmed down and reviewed the situation and his goals. Returning to his apartments at the consulate residence, he pulled up the photos he'd taken of her file and printed them off. Sitting down with a drink, he read through them once and then again. There wasn't a lot of substance, information readily available in various publications, but why was she looking into him? What was going on? There were newspaper clippings and photos of him at public and private functions. There was one of him with Ahsan, his Taliban go-between with Rahim. She'd written notes in the margin and had identified some of the other people in the photos and done background checks on them. Carlos didn't like the look of this. He'd have to be more careful. He wasn't sure what she would do if she discovered the plans for the weapons shipment. He considered the Homeland Security part of the equation. Was she working for Slater? Could she be a spy sent purposefully to romance him to get information?

Carlos instructed his men to keep Kate under closer surveillance while he flew to meet with his contact to discuss the next shipment. This was the final delivery of weapons to the Taliban dog, Rahim. They had all gone smoothly and the payment of five million dollars for each shipment had been received and transported back to Mexico via Carlos' little brother, Eduardo. He would meet with his contact at the end of the month to discuss the delivery of the goods his father was shipping over. Carlos was to coordinate this final shipment and exchange of goods for payment. He looked forward to surprising Rahim. These Taliban idiots thought they could buy weapons and attack America. No. America was the goose that laid beautiful golden eggs in the form of addicted adults, and no one was going to screw with that. The amount of money his family made smuggling drugs across the border was obscene. The Americans couldn't get enough of the cocaine, heroin, and opioids they provided. The millions they were making off this weapons scheme were a drop in the bucket. Carlos's plan was simple. The Taliban contact, Rahim was to bring the last payment to the warehouse with two semi-trucks which, upon payment would hook up to the semi-trailers filled with the weapons, most of which were secondhand, damaged and useless, and drive them away. Little did they know that once the money was paid and the semi-trucks drove off, the American authorities would receive an anonymous tip regarding the trucks and attempt to stop them. What happened after that was none of Carlos' concern because the five million would be safely on its way back to Mexico with his little brother, Eduardo. The cost of the weapons was a pittance compared to what they sold for, so the return on investment was well worth the operation. Carlos poured himself another drink.

Chapter 18

In Sam's opinion, Kate made excellent paella, and the Sangria was bright and fruity, a perfect pairing for the meal. They took their flan and coffee for dessert into the living room. Kate had been using her best interview techniques to draw Sam out and learn more about him, but he was a tough nut to crack.

"There's not much to tell." He spread his hands and lifted one shoulder. "You know most of this about me from Emily, I bet. We grew up in Arlington. I was first baseman on my high school baseball team and won a scholarship to TCU. That was when I moved to Fort Worth. Our Mom is the best. Dad was a general contractor and built homes, so I come by my skills honestly. His life's philosophy was that the man's role was to protect those he loved. He was always telling me as the big brother it was my job to protect my siblings, Paul and Emily. I guess that was where it all started, my drive to be in control and keep everyone safe.

"You know about my old man's temper. Mom, though, she is a gentle soul. She always gives everyone the benefit of the doubt and sees the silver lining of every cloud. She started working for the post office when I was eleven. Everyone loves Mom, and her smile can light up the entire room. They've retired to Florida now. Dad's mellowed, but, well, we don't see eye to eye. Emily tries to get out there a couple of times a year to visit them. Our brother, Paul, was killed in Afghanistan. I guess that's what made me join up. Even though I wasn't there when he was killed, and couldn't have done anything, I felt I had failed to protect him. I wanted to make them pay. I thought joining the SEALs was the best way to do that." Sam paused. Kate gave him an encouraging look over the rim of her coffee cup. Taking a breath to get his emotions under control, Sam continued.

"Jake and I met in basic and we instinctively knew we would always have each other's back. It was a match made in heaven or, if you think about all the killing we did, maybe hell. We pestered the commander until he agreed to let us serve and ship out together. It was a shit-storm most days, but sometimes you got to know the locals. Jake and I saw the beauty of the country and the people. The regular Afghanis didn't want the Taliban or the violence. They wanted to live and love and have families like anyone else.

"I remember our interpreter, Hadi. He was just eighteen and loved the Dallas Cowboys. Go figure. Even over there. Hadi had a little sister named Lakia. That means 'treasure found'. She was nine and so cute; reminded me of Em at that age. I asked Emily to send me a Barbie doll for Lakia. Emily chose the Christmas one that comes in the fancy red sparkly ball gown. Lakia was over the moon with that doll. She never went anywhere without it. But it was Pissy that really stole her heart. Lakia would visit the base every afternoon after school and love on that cat. All the guys came to love Lakia, but I was her favorite. 'Uncle Sammy,' she called me. She'd come running up to me with that Barbie tucked under one arm and Pissy hugged to her heart. She'd crawl up into my lap to tell me all about her day and what funny things Pissy had been doing. Lakia was sweet and untouched by all the horrors going on around her. The light in her made the darkness of my day fade. I promised her a kitten next time Pissy had a litter. "

He paused again, his throat working to get out the next part of the story. "We had just returned from taking out some Taliban kill squads when Pissy was shot by some stupid thug. Shit, actually just some stupid kid. He thought it was funny, taking potshots at a cat. I lost it and jumped into our hum-vee. Jake was right beside me. We took off after the kid's car and that was when I hit the IED. It was all a plan by the Taliban to draw us out, and it worked. It was an ambush, and we got sucked in. We were so stupid.

"Lakia and her classmates were walking by at the same time the IED exploded. I had just clipped it so it only flipped the hum-vee, throwing Jake clear and trapping me under. Jake hit the ground, almost running, and took cover. Quickly assessing the situation, he ran back to the wreckage and retrieved his rifle and me, dragging my ass to safety. We radioed for help and our guys came charging in to our rescue, like the freakin' cavalry. Jake had taken a couple of rounds to the back and shoulder; he was bleeding like a stuck pig. I had a twisted knee, broken collarbone, fractured leg, and shrapnel in my knee. I still carry that little souvenir. Both our injuries were enough to sideline us, and they shipped us home. That was the easy part. When the bomb exploded, most of the power of the detonation went opposite our vehicle and right toward the girls. Do you know what they put into those homemade bombs?

There were nails, bolts, BBs, bits and pieces of scrap metal and broken glass in the device. You can't imagine what that does to the human body. Oh my god, they were babies... Lakia was... She was clutching that damned Barbie doll. It was the only way I knew which body was her."

Sam hadn't realized he was crying and pounding his knee with a clenched fist. Kate reached over, taking his hand, and brought it to her lips, kissing his white knuckles until his fist relaxed and he stopped smelling the carnage, seeing the images, the blood, the gore and his failure. Sam turned to Kate and lost himself in her tear-filled eyes. Crushing her to his body, he feverishly kissed her mouth, face, ears, and neck. He held her head and returned to her mouth, crushing her lips with more kisses. Kate responded in kind and when he picked her up and walked to the bedroom, she didn't resist. She welcomed it.

Sam needed her, her light, her life. His hands were insistent, lifting her skirt and tearing away the delicate lace of her panties. He unzipped his pants and thrust into her. She was hot, ready for him, even though there had been no foreplay. She met him thrust for thrust, arching her hips and crossing her ankles behind his back. They gave themselves completely and fully in angst, in passion, until they were both spent. Sam fell on her and wept. Kate held him, shushing him like a mother comforts her child. They fell asleep in each other's arms.

Later, Sam woke, realizing what had happened, feeling guilty. He gently tried to move away when Kate reached out to him. Sam stuttered over an apology for his brutality. Kate placed her fingers on his lips.

Without a word, she pushed him down on the bed and pulled his shirt over his head. She gently kissed his lips, cheek, and brow. Moving her mouth along his jawline and down to his neck, she feathered her fingers and lips across his collarbone, shoulder, and chest. Her fingers traced the scars that were a daily reminder of pain and loss and a symbol of Sam's bravery and sacrifice. Letting her teeth lightly graze his nipples, she trailed kisses down his abdomen. She finished unbuckling his pants and pushed them down. Sometime earlier, Sam had kicked off his shoes and his socks came away as Kate removed his pants. He reached out, removing Kate's clothes. Reverently, he touched her face, chin, and finally cupping her breast, he drank in the beauty of her. He kissed her breasts, suckled, then moved his mouth to her neck and earlobes, letting his hands explore further the wonderful curves of her soft flesh and inviting warmth.

Sam watched her face as his fingers manipulated her secret place, and she moaned and rocked her hips in response. He moved lower and used his mouth to bring Kate to the brink repeatedly until she dug her nails into his back, crying out. When he moved on top of her, he touched her cheek. "Open your eyes, Kate. I want to look into your eyes and drink you in as we love each other."

She opened her eyes and gazed at Sam with such passion that he thought his heart would explode; so great was his love for this woman. He entered her tenderly this time and slowly moved, building his rhythm and pace. Kate rose with him until, arching her back, she pulled him in deeper. As she soared over the top, he spilled his seed. Sam trembled, holding his weight off her. His was an exhaustion borne of grief and love and he knew he'd never find anyone else that filled his soul like Kate. He pulled himself out of the warmest and safest haven he'd ever found and, gathering the rumpled bedclothes over them, Kate snuggled in and they fell asleep in each other's arms.

Sam lay propped up on his elbow. There was a satisfied grin on his face as he watched the sun rise and Kate slowly wake with a contented sigh. He kissed her on the nose and said, "You're adorable when you sleep. When you're awake, too. Come on, hurry and get dressed. I want to go tell Emily the good news." Sam was acting like a little boy on Christmas morning singing an old Scorpions song "When you came into my Life" to himself.

Kate laughed and confessed, "I don't do a lot in the morning 'fast', without first having a cup of coffee. Let me make us a pot." Kate put on her robe and padded to the kitchen, calling back over her shoulder, "What good news are you talking about?"

Sam was already in the shower and didn't hear the question, and Kate promptly forgot about it when she left the coffee to brew and joined him. She stepped in and put her arms around his waist, laying her cheek on his back. "I think I like you naked Slater".

Sam turned and, looking down at his growing erection, unashamedly admitted, "I know I like you naked!" That was all it took for them to forget about Emily or anything else. Sam ran his lathered hands slowly and sensuously over Kate's body, finding all her secret places and caressing them. Then, using the hand-held wand, he rinsed her body off, concentrating the spray of pulsating water where it was devilishly effective, exciting her more. Kate's legs trembled, growing weak as Sam used the water and his mouth to tease and tickle her breasts and body. Then, leaning against the shower wall, he lifted her as if she weighed nothing and lowered her until they joined in joy. As the water ran over them, Sam brought her to the brink time and time again, always stopping just before she came.

Finally, Sam carried her to the bed, where he took her up and over the mountain. Kate felt as if she were floating down to earth from having circled the sun. Sam's arms were around her and she mewed and stretched. An hour and a half later, Kate heard the ding of the coffee maker's auto turn-off. The pot she'd made earlier was beyond done.

Sam nuzzled her neck and nibbled her earlobe. "Isn't making love in the morning just as invigorating as a cup of coffee? And with me, you'll never have to set a timer to turn me on."

They finally crawled out of bed, got dressed, and went to the kitchen for a bite to eat. The paella and dirty dishes from last night were still on the counter, so while Kate cleaned up, Sam made an omelet for the two of them. They took their coffee into the living room and Sam finally noticed the painting of the bluebonnets.

"I thought some mysterious anonymous buyer purchased the painting," Sam recalled. "Wait, don't tell me. The buyer was Ramirez, wasn't it?" Sam shot her a jealous look. "What did you have to do to get it, Kate? Did you sleep with him too?" Kate just stared at Sam, speechless. She was shocked at his reaction and hurt by his lack of trust. "Are you playing me?" Sam stared at her, the volume of his voice rising. Slamming down his cup, Sam turned to grab his jacket, heading for the door.

Angry at his outburst and lack of trust, Kate said, "Are you serious? You must not know me very well to assume I'd jump into bed with you if I was interested in Carlos. Come on, Sam, that's not it at all. Why would you think that of me? I didn't ask for it…"

Sam cut her off mid-sentence. "Oh, I'm sure you played the innocent with him and he forced you, right? This is BS, Kate. I thought you were different. I thought you were special—worth it." Sam raked a hand through his hair, looking as lost as a little boy. "God, what a fool I've been." He turned and stalked out, slamming the door behind him.

"Please, Sam! It's not what you think… I love you." Kate called after him, but he was already gone. All the anger that had bubbled up in her when he'd first said those horrible, hurtful words cooled. It flowed out of her as she realized he'd walked out her door and maybe even her life. Kate sank onto the couch and cried.

Sam, in his anger, failed to notice the black SUV parked around the corner from Kate's house. The camera inside clicked furiously, taking multiple photos. *Looks like the competition just got kicked out. Senor Ramirez will be happy with this report.*

****

Sam walked through the front door to the house, slamming it behind him. He grabbed the bottle of scotch and a glass and went straight out the back door to the garden, slamming that door, too. He had totally ignored Jake and Emily, who were sitting at the kitchen counter planning their day. They exchanged concerned looks.

"Shit, something must have happened between him and Kate," Emily said.

Jake nodded. "Yeah. Looks like something pretty serious too. I haven't seen Sam grab the scotch at eleven a.m. since Kandahar. I'll wait until he's roaring drunk before I chance a conversation with him."

"And you are more than welcome to it. I'll probably have better luck talking with Kate. I'm glad you care enough for me not to be stupid, Jake Edwards." Emily kissed Jake on the nose and headed out the door.

Sam was halfway through the bottle when Jake decided it was safe to approach. He carried a huge mug of black coffee out to the garden, placing it on the arm of the Adirondack chair, and sat next to Sam, but still out of reach. You didn't poke an angry bear. Jake sipped his coffee and waited. There were tracks of tears running down Sam's cheeks. He had chipped away most of the loose paint on the arm of the chair, worrying at it while he tried to drown his sorrows. Jake sat silently watching Sam and waited. It reminded him of the time following the IED. Sam had blamed himself for the deaths of Lakia and the other little girls. He beat himself up then and Jake could see a similar struggle now; an agony greater than the human spirit can hold. *If I could only take away some of this pain.*

Sam laid his head against the back of the chair and closed his eyes. He let out a heavy, agonized sigh. "God, Jake, I saw it, saw that fucking painting hanging on her wall. I think she is fucking Ramirez. He bought her that damned bluebonnet painting. She probably sucked his dick when he gave the painting to her. The bitch. Christ, she is a tigress in bed, Jake–scratching and biting and crying out with pleasure. She gives as much as she takes–even more. I can just see Ramirez enjoying it. His hands on her, touching her in her most intimate places, putting his cock into her, into... Oh God, Jake, I love her and I want to kill Ramirez because he has her. He probably doesn't even appreciate how special she is." Sam turned tortured eyes to Jake, and breaking down, he sobbed. "I love her, damn it. Oh, God, I love her."

Jake put his hand on Sam's shoulder, feeling the sobs racking his body. He loved this man like a brother and he hated Ramirez as much as Sam did, but he didn't hate Kate because he had seen the way she looked at Sam. Kate wasn't involved with Ramirez. He'd bet his life on it. Kate loved Sam too. He only prayed that Emily had luck talking with Kate to find out her side. Maybe, between the two of them, they could figure out how to help their two best friends heal their wounds.

****

Kate stood nervously in the doorway to Emily's office the next day, waiting to be invited to sit down. "Hi, Emily. Can we talk?" She had dark circles under puffy eyes and looked like her entire world had fallen apart.

Emily shrugged. "Sure. This is a surprise." Emily hoped today's conversation would yield more information about what had happened with Sam. All Kate had done before was cry and insist on watching *Out of Africa* repeatedly. She'd ignored her best friend's offer to listen and understand.

"You didn't bring any movies with you, did you?" Seeing the hurt in Kate's eyes, Emily backpedaled. "I'm sorry. Seriously, what can I do for you?" Em had the tiniest bit of an edge in her tone. She liked Kate and knew Sam loved her even though he was angry with her right now, but Kate had hurt Sam in some way and that was unforgivable.

"No, I didn't bring any movies, and I'm sorry about that afternoon and anything else I've done to disappoint you." Kate apologized. "I was such an idiot. I thought earlier yesterday I had good news to share with you, but it turns out I was wrong." Kate paused. She took a breath and cleared her throat, pulling herself together.

"What is it you feel you've done, Kate?" Emily cautiously asked. She didn't like the direction the conversation was taking, but also believed this would answer the question of what had happened between Sam and Kate. "What suddenly concerns you?" As she watched Kate's emotions play across her face, she moved from fear to hope for the answer that would heal the two lovers.

"I'm sure you noticed that Sam and I have," Kate struggled to continue. "We'd grown closer. I thought we loved each other. Well, it doesn't matter what I thought now, does it? Yesterday morning, Sam saw the bluebonnet painting Carlos bought for me. He accused me of two-timing him and screwing Carlos for the painting. I was so angry at him, his lack of trust in me and our relationship. I didn't know what to say to his accusations. How does one respond to that? How can he not know how I feel? He walked out so mad and, well, Sam made it abundantly clear he doesn't want to see me anymore." Kate looked up at Emily and finally lost it. "Oh, but, Emily, I love him. I keep trying to call him, but he won't take my calls or return my messages. He

ignores my texts. I love him and he...he hates me."
Emily ran around her desk and put her arms around a
sobbing Kate.

"Oh, honey. You poor, silly woman. Sam loves
you more than life. He's just hurt and angry right now.
He is dealing with his emotions like a little boy that
fears someone took his favorite toy. All he wants to do
is run away and hide." Kate hiccupped and took the
tissue Emily offered to wipe her eyes. Never one to
watch those she loved hurt, Emily said in her no-
nonsense tone, "Kate, you are coming to my home this
evening. I'll get Jake to bring Sam. We are going to
hash this out. I want to have you as my sister-in-law,
and I'll be damned if I'll let Sam muck it up because of
his stupid pride," Emily said determinedly. She
confided Sam worked for Homeland Security and
besides being concerned about Ramirez as a romantic
rival, he also was looking into Carlos for another
reason. Emily wasn't sure of the details, but she knew
he had been investigating Carlos and was getting closer
to the truth. Emily and Kate made a plan. "Go home
now, Kate. Try to do something about your puffy eyes.
They aren't very attractive, and we want you at your
best."

****

When Jake's phone signaled, with the 'Let me call
you sweetheart' ringtone he'd specifically assigned to
Emily, he stepped outside to answer. "Hey, babe, how's
my favorite girl? What's up?"

"Jake, I know this is short notice, but you have to
get Sam out of that house and bring him to my place
tonight. No, babe, don't ask why. Just make sure he is
sober and, for God's sake, make him take a shower."

Emily hung up. She could only hope this evening would give Kate a chance to explain everything and tell Sam she loved him. Emily also hoped he would be honest with himself and admit he loved Kate, too. Men can be so stupid.

Sam and Jake were there at six on the dot. While Emily got out cheese and crackers, Jake was in the kitchen helping her with the lemonade. There would be no alcohol tonight until everything was settled, and Kate and Sam had made up.

"I'll just grab a scotch," Sam called from the living room.

Emily threw up her hands in exasperation. Jake picked up her silent message and picked up the pitcher of lemonade to go discourage Sam from the scotch.

Jake was walking into the living room when Kate knocked and stuck her head in the door, calling out, "Hi, Em, I'm here. Mind if I let myself in?" She had done her best to erase the ravages of crying her heart out. She had thought about the file she put together on Carlos and tucked it into her satchel. Maybe there would be something in it that would help Sam and his investigation. She didn't work for Homeland Security, but she was a damn good investigative reporter.

Sam put down his glass, casting a disgusted look over his shoulder at Jake. He walked out the back door with every intention of leaving to avoid coming face-to-face with Kate. Jake was right behind him and, before he got to the gate, grabbed his shoulder. Sam spun around and took a swing at Jake. Anticipating, Jake went low, rushing Sam, pinning him against the fence.

"You bastard," Sam spat. "You know how I feel and yet you and good old meddling Emily orchestrate this little meeting. Who the hell do you think you are? You stupid son of a bitch!" Shoving Jake off him, Sam gained enough space to reach for the gate, but Jake spun him around once more and, grabbing his shirt by the collar, pulled him up.

"I'm the stupid son of a bitch? No buddy–you are. It's obvious as hell you love her, Sam. And she loves you."

Sam wasn't hearing any of that and was about to land an uppercut to Jake's chin when he heard the words that stopped him dead in his tracks.

"He's right, Sam. I love you. No one else." Kate was speaking so quietly it was a miracle her voice cut through the noise and commotion. "I've never been with Carlos. I think I've always wanted you since the night of the gallery preview when you took my hand. All the time Carlos kept pushing toward me, it felt like you were pushing me away. But, Sam, I kept hoping and praying that would change and it did—we did. Please, Sam, look at me. Look into my heart and hear the truth."

Sam dropped his hold on Jake and stared at the ground, shaking, and slowly dropped to his knees. He looked at Kate, praying she was speaking the truth. He couldn't go on without her anymore. Kate ran to Sam, dropping to her knees, as well. She hugged him, burying her face in his chest. Jake and Emily went back inside, leaving the two alone. After a half hour, they heard Kate's car start up and drive away.

"I think our work here is done," Emily sighed, resting her head on Jake's shoulder.

****

Sam drove them to her place. Once inside, Kate led

him to the bedroom, where she showed him with her body the love she felt in her heart. They made slow and beautiful love.The peaks and valleys of their emotions and shared ecstasy brought them to dizzying heights of fulfillment. When they rushed headlong toward their shared climax, it plunged them into an ocean of carnal pleasure and sensuous release time and time again until exhausted. They lay wrapped in each other's arms, completely sated. That was when they finally talked.

Kate knew Sam would never be the first to bare his soul, so she started. "I've never believed I could find a love like my folks shared. Love at first sight was a fairy tale in my mind, but, Sam, I felt your soul when you took my hand at the gallery preview. I was dazed and confused, but knew in my heart we were meant to be. I kept waiting for you to give me some sign of your feelings, and then you kissed me on the forehead that first time. How romantic!" She punched him in the arm and chided him for taking his time before making a move. "I kept snuggling close to you when we'd play Trivial Pursuit. I thought you'd get the hint. Emily and Jake said something about 'slow like a sloth'. I didn't realize they were referring to you." Sam gave a rueful laugh. Returning to seriousness, Kate fanned her hand across his chest, feeling the slow, steady beat of his heart. "I learned to rely on your strength and presence, your calming influence in my often-chaotic world. Sometimes I was frightened, Sam, but I knew that no matter what, I'd always be safe with you."

Sam brushed his lips against the top of Kate's head. "I was afraid to love you, Kate. I was always the big brother, the responsible one. When Paul or Em got hurt playing, Dad would cuff me on the head and blame me for not watching out for them, not protecting them. I grew up with his expectation that I was duty-bound to protect those I love. Protect them even from my dad. But God, Kate, it can be a heavy burden sometimes. I have been haunted. I have demons, Kate. Loving you keeps them at bay, but it frightens me. I never want to fail you. That was why I took so long to let you know my feelings." Sam took a deep breath and ran his hand over his face. Holding her a little closer and tighter, he continued. "Kate, like you, I knew deep in my soul that this was supposed to happen the first time I ever saw you. I was afraid of failing you like I've failed everyone else I loved and that loved me."

Sam paused, conquering his demons. Opening up finally, he told her about all his doubts and fears. He talked of how he had lost faith when his brother died, and had questioned his role of protector, of big brother. Wondering if God had forsaken him when the IED killed Lakia and the other schoolgirls, he turned from hope and all faith. But he knew when he got lost in her eyes that it restored his faith. He knew God hadn't abandoned him or his hope for happiness. When silence fell, they held each other and marveled at their happiness. Sam rolled over and took his phone out of the pants he had left on the floor in their haste to love each other. He called Jake. Getting voice mail, he left a brief message. "Mission accomplished."

****

Jake returned Sam's call the next morning at 6:30 a.m. "You and Kate should come over here. It's about Crossbow."

Sam had been lazing in bed watching Kate sleep. He didn't think he'd ever grow tired of doing that, but when he got Jake's call and heard the HSI code word, he was on high alert. "Be there in an hour." He gently turned and rubbed her shoulder. "Kate, wake up, honey. We have to go to Emily's. Come on babe–I told them we'd be there in an hour. Let's go."

They made it to Emily's place in forty-eight minutes. Jake met them at the door. He took time to look around outside before closing and locking the door. He exchanged a significant look with Sam and led him and Kate to the kitchen, where Emily had prepared coffee and laid out some cinnamon rolls. Jake slid Kate's file on Carlos across the island to Sam. Sam spotted the name on the tab and looked at Kate.

"It started out as my interview file. I do basic research to develop my questions. As I got to know Carlos better, I saw and learned things that alarmed me. Then, one day, while visiting the consulate residence, I found a file he had on me. It had *everything* on me. It also had info on my associates, friends–you guys–and pictures of us together; Emily, you and I, shopping; our outing to the ballgame, and, Sam, you and I running. He tried to pass it off as 'security nonsense' but there was a smoothness that I just didn't buy. I decided what was good for the goose was good for the gander, so I dug a little deeper into his background. Starting at the library, I scoured every publication I could find to build a file of my own on Carlos. I ran into several dead ends, which in and of themselves were innocuous, but what I didn't find made me more suspicious. Some of what I learned seemed to tie the Ramirez family to dishonest politicians and cartels. There were rumors of potentially illegal and violent activities, but I couldn't find any proof. Carlos said he was close to his mother. I wondered how close he was to his father and brothers. Was he involved in any of the questionable activities? I resolved to ask him about what I had learned. Yes, Sam, I know. I shouldn't have, but I wanted to see if my suspicions were valid and if so, to… I don't know; tell the police?" Kate shrugged, watching Sam's reaction.

Sam bit back a retort. She could have put herself in danger. He took the file and his coffee to the living room. Em put a hand on Kate's arm to stop her from following.

Sam was astounded at the amount of information Kate had unearthed. It was almost as complete as what his team had uncovered after months of digging. There were newspaper clippings with photos of Carlos at social events with various people. When the caption identified the others in the photos, she did a mini-investigation into those people, eliminating the innocent. She got guest lists and did mini backgrounds on the guests. She had created a calendar of Ramirez's travel itinerary cross-referencing it to illegal activities. After thirty minutes, Sam returned to the kitchen and poured himself another cup of coffee. Turning, he laid the file on the island and looked at Kate. "This is incredibly thorough and I don't want you to pursue it any further."

Kate picked up the file and hugged it to her chest. "But why, Sam? Isn't it helpful? I think I can find out more, given the chance."

Sam took the file from her, handing it to Jake. He turned Kate to face him. "No. You must trust me on this, Kate. Ramirez is a killer. Just because he thinks he is in love with you doesn't mean he won't hurt you if he finds out you have this kind of information. I can't risk you getting hurt. Please promise me you will stay away from him and keep yourself safe." Sam crushed her to his chest and fiercely whispered into her hair. "I thought I'd lost you once. I won't let it happen again."

Sam stepped away to call his team, setting a meeting for later in the day. Jake would join them. It wasn't protocol, but Sam would talk with Commander Collins. He needed the best right now, and Jake had proven his abilities.

Chapter 19

Sam was focusing all his energies on the investigation, ignoring the house and remodeling. Kate was spending most of her time at Sam's. During the days, she tried to keep herself occupied with work but was having trouble concentrating. Visiting over coffee one morning with the dynamic duo, Emily and Jake, Kate looked around. "Jake, this house is taking so long to come together. You and Sam have been working so hard and even after you come home for the day, Sam stays and puts in extra hours. The kitchen and dining room are the last two spaces to complete. What can we do to help?"

Emily ran her finger along the countertop and it came back covered in dust. "I just don't know how you can live like this. No wonder you spend so much time at my place."

"Now, Em, don't be coy. You know why I spend so much time at your place." Jake grabbed her and gave her a big, smacking kiss.

Emily playfully slapped at him. "You stinker! Now everyone will know."

Kate looked on, enjoying their playfulness. She loved these two goofballs. "Okay, seriously. Enough, you horny toads. Look, I know Sam has not really settled on the ultimate design for the kitchen, but I have some wonderful ideas, backsplash choices, countertop, cabinets, paint color. Heck, even pendants for over the island. Sam is out of town for the next few days. Can we at least make a start?" Ophelia jumped up on the table, where Kate was placing some samples she had tucked in her satchel to show them. She plopped down in the middle of the action and groomed herself while Kate held her breath.

Jake shrugged. "Kate, the reason these two rooms haven't been finished yet is because Sam was waiting. He delayed designing the kitchen because he wanted it to be a room that made his bride happy."

Jake and Emily exchanged knowing looks. Sam hadn't proposed, but he certainly loved Kate and all the signs were pointing to the fact that he would. Jake nodded to Emily and spread his hands in surrender. "I think whatever you want to do will be okay with Sam."

With that, Kate was more determined than ever. She excitably scooted Ophelia off the green laminate counter and explained her ideas. "The layout will remain true to Sam's initial plan with some tweaking. This is what I'm thinking. As you enter from the butler's pantry, the refrigerator will be on the right inset into the wall–it will take up room in the pantry, but there is plenty of space there anyway, so that will be okay. Now, here on your left," —Kate gestured— "is a thirty-inch cabinet and then the stove. The six-burner gas model Sam picked out is perfect, as well as the other appliances he selected. The cabinets turn the corner and under the back bank of windows is the farmhouse sink. I like white. Do you guys agree?" Kate didn't wait for their answer. She saw Jake and Emily raise eyebrows and smile and then barreled on. Apparently, the question was rhetorical.

"The dishwasher will go to the right of the sink. I really prefer to load a dishwasher from that side, don't you? Now, I think shaker cabinets in a rich oak topped off by quartz that has the look of soapstone. The backsplash will be a creamy white crackle twelve-inch subway tile installed horizontally, so it resembles bead board. The island will be this shade of blue–it's called Yard Blue. Instead of the soapstone, we'll go with white quartz on the island that will echo the backsplash. We'll do the wine cooler on the end facing the family room–easy access for the bartender without interfering with the chef's workspace." Kate laughed. "The island will allow for two stools on each side here at the end, see? And there will be a drawer microwave in the corner across from the sink. I'm thinking Folly Green for the walls and there is a great Picture Gallery red that will really sing as an accent color in the dining room. We'll use dark pewter pulls, the cup style. Sam picked them out at the Architectural Salvage Shop and there will be a three-light pendant over the island in the same pewter finish with seeded glass globes."

Kate looked from Emily to Jake and then back to Emily again. She was flushed and breathless with excitement. "Do you think he will like it?" she asked, suddenly unsure of herself.

Emily gave Kate a big answering hug. "If you like it, I'm sure Sam will love it. It sounds wonderful. Question is, Jake; can we pull this off in the short time until Sam returns?"

Jake puffed his lips, blew a raspberry, and shook his head. "It's a big job. Good thing we don't have to worry about the floors or appliance lead time. There won't be plumbing or anything else to move. I found a guy that can get us good quality birch cabinets. I'll call him. Kate, can you and Emily source everything else?"

"Absolutely," both girls said simultaneously. They smiled at each other and thought about all the fun this would be. "Shopping!!"

Everyone set to work, calling and ordering. Jake connected with his cabinet guy and although they had to do a little juggling with delivery, the cabinets were a go in a miraculous three days. The bigger challenge was the island, but since that would go in last, it might just work. Kate gave Jake the name of the quartz guy. He called to place the order for those coordinating with the cabinetmaker.

While Jake was busy working his magic, Kate and Emily purchased the paint and tile and returned with everything they needed to get started. Setting up the ladders and drop cloths, Jake decided he could not paint walls without painting Emily's butt, too.

"Emily, can you cut in around the ceiling while Kate and I roll?" he innocently asked.

"What? Why me? I'm not wearing a dress for you to look under when I climb the ladder, Jake Edwards," she teased.

"Oh, I know, honey, but you are the best choice for painting a straight line, so I'm assigning jobs to the appropriately skilled workers." He grinned like the Cheshire cat. "Here, let me help you." With his hand covered in enough paint to leave a mark on her bottom, he gave Emily a boost up the ladder. Every time Emily would bend over that hand print would make Kate giggle, and Jake grin like a twelve-year-old.

Eventually, Emily figured something was up and when she discovered the handprint on her bottom, chased Jake around the room with a loaded paintbrush, finally cornering him and painting a smiley face across the front of his t-shirt. He retaliated with a dot on her nose. They called 'uncle' at the same time. Kate, in the meantime, took care of her own war paint while brushing her hair out of her face. There was a broad stripe across her cheek and a streak along her brow and chin. No one escaped unscathed.

By the time Jake called for a break, all three were exhausted and starving. It had been hard work, but with Jake around, nothing could be entirely serious. Ordering pizza, they popped three beers and sat back, admiring their work. Tomorrow, Emily and Kate planned on sourcing the light fixture, bar stools for the island, and the area rug for under the round table. Kate was thinking about an oriental pattern. Jake would work on the recessed cans and buy the under-cabinet lighting. The plan was coming together nicely. The three of them worked tirelessly. When they were in over their heads, Emily drafted the wounded warrior artists from the gallery to help. These men knew and understood love and loss. They were happy to pitch in.

When Sam returned from Florida, he walked into a house that smelled of fresh paint and apple pie. Hoping Kate was there, and she had baked the pie special for him, he dropped his bag by the front door and made his way toward the kitchen, only to stop short and stare in amazement. Kate, Jake, and Emily were standing off to the side, so Sam had an unobstructed view of the finished kitchen. The look on his face said it all. He stood there moving his mouth, but no words came out. Picking his jaw up off the floor, he turned toward the three of them, still speechless but with such a look of joy, they knew without a doubt he was pleased with their efforts.

With two strides, Sam was hugging all three, saying, "What the heck? Did you guys do this? How did you ever get the materials and do the work so fast? It's perfect–exactly how I imagined it would look."

"Jake did most of the work. Kate and I painted and mostly stayed out of the way," Emily said. "He has some amazing contractors that put in extra hours as a favor. Kate chose the finish materials and the layout. You shared so much of your vision when you guys talked. I think she knew what you had in mind."

"You know, you owe your sister a huge thanks," Jake said. "There are some very talented vet artists and they respect the heck out of Emily. When they learned about our project, well, they all came over to lend a hand. In fact, they are waiting in the garden to meet you and see your reaction before tearing into the smoked brisket and drink more of your beer."

Sam turned to Kate, who was silently waiting with her fingers crossed. God, what if he didn't like it? She pressed her lips together and held her breath, looking at him expectantly. Sam, smiling from ear to ear, grabbed Kate, swinging her in circles of delight. There was no doubt he approved. Jake went to the door and waved all the guests in to enjoy the surprise and congratulate Sam on his new kitchen and finally finished house. "Guys, meet Sam. Sam, meet the guys. Somebody, give the man a beer!"

Everyone cheered and slapped Sam on the back, sharing their own stories about the project. Throughout the evening, they told Sam about what they did on the project, how they liked the house, and how happy they were for him. With a lot of winks and nudges, everyone asked if he had a particular lady in mind that would make use of the kitchen. Sam happily accepted their teasing, looking at Kate as she helped set out the meal. *Yes, I do, I definitely do.*

Finally, after enough brisket, beer, and pie was consumed, the party wound down and the last guest departed amidst jokes and whispered questions about when they could expect the wedding invitation. Sam walked into the kitchen, reveling in the design's perfection. It was indeed everything he had envisioned and Kate had made it all come true, even down to standing at the sink doing dishes. Yes, this was his vision; a home with the woman he loved. Coming up behind her, he wrapped his arms around her waist and nuzzled her ear. "I love you, Kate Hunter. You make me incredibly happy."

Emily and Jake came in from the garden. "Sam, there is one more finishing touch that Jake and I want to contribute as a housewarming gift."

Jake went into the study and came back with a package. "Kate, this is probably as much for you as it is for Sam. Why don't you two open it together?"

Sam placed the package on the island and unwrapped a beautiful framed painting of a field of wildflowers with a young woman in a blue dress walking toward a windmill and looking wistfully over her shoulder. It was an oil painting of the photo Sam had captured of Kate when they went fishing. It was perfect.

"Oh, Sam, it's beautiful. Emily, Jake–it's a wonderful gift," Kate said, hugging them.

Sam was silent, his eyes moving from the painting

to Emily and Jake and then to Kate and back to the painting again. He didn't think he could adequately express how perfect it really was. A slow smile spread across his face, and he knew precisely what to say.

"I know exactly where to hang it. It will go on the wall facing my bed. I'll wake every morning for the rest of my life looking at this painting of the woman I love and the real thing in bed next to me, assuming she'll marry me." Sam turned to Kate and got down on one knee, taking her hand in his. "Will you, Kate? Will you marry me?"

"Oh yes, Sam! Oh, hell yes!!!" Kate exclaimed as Sam rose to his feet to give her a passionate, all-consuming kiss.

Jake finally had to clear his throat to break the spell. "Ummm…Hate to interrupt…"

Emily chimed in, "But I think this calls for champagne. I thought there might be a reason to celebrate!"

****

Sam spent every free moment he had with Kate, but work took him away more often than he wanted. It had been two weeks and the case in Florida was falling apart. They called him back several times to clarify and testify. Kate continued to do research into Carlos and had discovered additional information about him and his family. It was like unraveling a tapestry. She explained her research methods to Sam. "You just pull on one thread at a time and look where it leads you."

Emily and Kate kept each other company in the evenings when the guys were busy. She tried to keep her distance from Carlos, but that didn't stop him from calling. He sent Hector to the house once with flowers.

Kate didn't answer the door, pretending she wasn't home. The last thing she wanted to do was arouse his suspicion. She tried to give the impression that she just wanted to break it off, even returning the windmill picture with a note stating she no longer wanted to see him. She tried to let him down gently at first, but he was maddeningly persistent. He started sending flowers every other day. With her house looking like a funeral parlor, she called to acknowledge receipt of yet another bouquet, and make it very clear he should stop contacting her.

"Carlos, please stop sending flowers. I don't want to see you anymore. I wish you luck in finding a woman who will make you happy, but I am not that woman," Kate stated unequivocally. "How can I make this any more clear? I do not want to see you anymore."

It fell on deaf ears. He wouldn't take no for an answer. When he tracked her down to her nail salon and interrupted her pedicure by seating himself in the chair next to hers, she'd reached her limit. Kate raised her voice, not caring who might overhear.

"Carlos, I don't know how many times I have to say no for you to figure it out. Is there a language barrier?? I'm *not* interested. *Comprender*?"

Catching the tech off guard, Kate jumped up, threw a couple of twenties in her direction, and picked up her shoes. She stormed out, struggling to put on her flip-flops. She hurried to the parking garage and her car. Carlos caught up with her.

"What the hell do you mean *not* interested? You can't tell me that. I bought and paid for you; the dinners, theater, flowers, the fucking painting, you bitch, even though you returned it. I won't take no for an answer!" he railed at her.

"I don't think you get it, you idiot. I'm seeing someone else. I'm not interested in you AT ALL!"

"Seeing someone else? You mean that lawyer? You slut! I bet you're screwing him." Carlos sneered in her face.

"Oh, you bet I am, and enjoying every second. He's a man who takes what he wants and gives back equally. You're a narcissistic bastard who thinks his money and good looks will win him all the love and physical affection he craves. So, go! Go on! Find some bimbo that falls for your kind of shallow guy. Go buy it from someone else! You won't get it from me!"

Carlos grabbed Kate, digging his fingers into her shoulders. She paled as his eyes filled with hatred. She believed he wanted to kill her. His hand slid down to her arm, and he started dragging her toward his car. Kate resisted, but he was much stronger. When Carlos opened the car door to push her in, it gave Kate enough maneuvering room to haul back and slap him. Surprised, Carlos loosened his grip enough for her to break free. She shoved him back, sprinted to her car, and jumped in, locking the doors. Carlos was quick but didn't make it in time. Dropping it into gear, she sped away, driving straight to Sam's house.

Kate jerked the car into park, jumped out, and ran up to the door, hysterically banging on it. Sam was in the master bath, working on some finishing touches. The radio was blasting a R.E.M. hit, and he was thinking about Kate and their plans for the night. He didn't hear the banging right away. When he finally heard the commotion, he ran to the door and opened it, only to have Kate burst in and wrap her arms around his neck. She was crying and shaking, and her clothes were in disarray. Panic set in. "What is it? Jesus God, what happened?" She was a mess. It took some time to calm her down to find out what had upset her. Sam led her to the kitchen and seated her on a stool at the island. He grabbed a bottle of water from the refrigerator and opened it, handing it to her. "Here, drink this; take some deep breaths."

Kate took a sip and hiccupped. Wiping her runny nose against her t-shirt sleeve, she told Sam about Carlos and his persistence. She told Sam everything. The flowers, the calls, the feeling she was being watched or followed.

"Then he showed up at the nail salon. It was so humiliating. He caused such a scene, followed me to the parking garage, and we got into a real shouting match. I called him names and said horrible things to him. Oh, Sam, he grabbed me and hurt me. He tried to force me into his car. He looked at me with such hatred. I was so frightened. I slapped him and pushed him down. Then I ran to my car and drove straight here. Oh, Sam. I'm terrified. He is so angry. The darkness, the evil I saw when I looked at him. There was cruel violence in his eyes…" She buried her face in Sam's shoulder and shuddered.

Sam's fear presented itself as raw anger at Ramirez. He could barely control his fury. "Why didn't you tell me this before, Kate? How long has he been bothering you?" Kate was too upset to answer, so Sam just held her and finally carried her to the sofa, where she curled up in his arms and finally felt safe. Sam stroked her hair and eventually she quieted in the security of his arms. The emotional drain had taken it all out of her. Sam pushed back the hair from her tear-streaked face and gently kissed her forehead. He returned her head to his shoulder, and they just sat there until the sun went down and the house grew dark. All the while, Sam went over every detail Kate had shared. He fumed. *That bastard. I'll kill him. If he touches or comes near her again, I swear I'll kill him.*

Kate spent the night at Sam's and in the morning, he packed himself a bag and they returned to her house. It made little sense for Kate to move her stuff to his place when he was traveling so much, and he would not leave her alone and unprotected. He'd move into her house temporarily. When he wasn't around, Emily could spend the night if needed. Carlos' actions had upped the ante. Sam had to find the last piece of evidence he needed to close the noose around Ramirez's throat and quickly. With Kate being threatened, it was more important than ever to solve the case.

For the next three days, Sam stayed close to home and Kate. He delayed returning to Miami, telling the investigators that his case in Texas was heating up and he couldn't break away. It wasn't, but they didn't need to know that. When his Intel told him Carlos had left town, he finally felt it was safe to fly to Miami. Sam gave Jake all the details of what happened and asked him to keep an eye on Kate. Jake recruited Emily and between the two of them spent the next few evenings keeping Kate company. It was Thursday and Sam was due back from Miami.

Chapter 20

The threesome had just finished carrying in the groceries when Kate shooed the both of them to the door. "Really, you two. You have been babysitting me for the last few days. I'm fine, really, go on. Sam texted me. His plane lands at five twenty. He'll be here by six forty-five at the latest. I promise I won't go out anywhere. I will lock the door after you leave, but please, leave. All I want to do is cook dinner and have time alone with Sam tonight. You two go home and enjoy some alone time yourselves."

"Okay." Emily hugged her. "If you are comfortable with that, I guess you'll be safe. Jake, honey, what do you think? Do you agree?"

Jake nodded. "It's been quiet, and Ramirez is out of town. I haven't seen anything to cause me concern. I'm sure you'll be fine for a couple of hours. Just keep the door locked."

"Cross my heart. Now get out of here, you two. I need to clean up and get cooking." Kate locked the door behind them, being sure to turn the deadbolt. She did a quick sweep and mop in the kitchen, straightened the living room, and changed the sheets. After prepping the chicken parmigiana and double-checking the lock on the door, she went to take a shower. She selected the white handkerchief blouse and shorts that Sam liked so much. It set off her tan. She had worn it to the zoo, and he had first taken it off her that evening. That was a magical day, and Kate wanted Sam to return to an equally magical night. She left her hair loose, framing her face and falling on her shoulders; just like Sam liked it.

Kate went to the door and unlocked the deadbolt so Sam could get in with his key when he got home, and then she walked through the living room into the kitchen, turning on some soft music on the way. Putting on an apron, she sang along to the radio while chopping veggies. Kate heard the door open, thinking Sam must have gotten an early flight. "Hi, babe, I'm in the kitchen. Hey, you must have lucked out and gotten an earlier flight. Why didn't you text me?" Kate put down the knife, rinsed her hands, and was reaching for the towel when she heard his voice behind her.

"How domestic."

"Carlos!" Kate spun around. Glancing toward the door, she asked, "How did you get in here?"

"Oh, Kate, I've had a key from the first time we went out. Don't you think I would have made sure of that? A simple wax impression was made when I opened your door after our first date and there you have it, a duplicate." Carlos moved toward her. Kate grabbed for the knife on the counter, but this time Carlos expected her move, and was quicker. Taking hold of her wrist, he twisted until she cried out in pain and dropped the knife. Kate beat at him with her fists. Carlos, being stronger, held both her wrists in his right hand and, using his left, grasped a handful of hair and pulled her head back, exposing her neck to his mouth. Kissing and sucking hard enough to leave marks, he moved up her neck to her ears and finally brought his mouth down on hers in a bruising kiss, thrusting his tongue between her teeth. Releasing her hair, he ran his hand to her breast, squeezing and pinching her nipple until she cried out.

"Hmmm, do you like it rough, Kate?"

Kate twisted her body to bring her knee up into Carlos' groin. He had expected this and turned to the side. Her blow only contacted a muscular thigh and did no damage. Carlos back handed Kate so hard she was stunned, slumping to the floor. He picked her up, throwing her over his shoulder, and carried her toward the bedroom. Kicking open the door, Carlos threw Kate on the bed and, removing his tie, bound her wrists to the headboard. For good measure, he used his handkerchief to gag her. He then straddled her.

"How do you like it, Kate? How does Sam do it to you? Is he gentle or does he hurt you just a little? I will hurt you *un poco*, and you will beg me to love you to extinguish the fire I ignite between your legs."

Kate cried and begged Carlos to stop.

****

Bad weather was moving in and planes were being rerouted. Luckily, they landed just before the front moved in and the airport closed to traffic, twelve precious minutes early. Sam grabbed his bag off the carousel and practically sprinted to the parking garage to retrieve his jeep and drive home to Kate. He had missed her. By this time, the severe thunderstorm was raging with a vengeance and visibility was poor. Hail the size of quarters slowed traffic and reduced visibility to almost nothing. Sam didn't notice the Mercedes parked in front of the neighbor's house. He parked and ran up the steps with his key out when he heard her scream.

Unlocking the door never entered his mind. He simply threw his body at it and burst through, rolling across the floor and making a quick assessment of the situation. The scream had come from the bedroom. Sam jumped up and ran toward the door, only to have Carlos meet him with such brute force, it knocked him back against the couch. Ramirez was on top of him, swinging like a crazy man. Some of his punches were making solid contact, and it took Sam a moment to shift his weight and roll over, getting on top of Carlos. They held each other by the collars of their shirts and fought their way up to a standing position, continuing to swing. They were equally matched in strength, but Sam could only see red. He threw punch after punch at Carlos, who tried to cover his face and head but lost the battle. Sam delivered a right hook and heard the satisfying sound of crunching bone as he made contact with Carlos' aquiline nose. With one ultimate effort, Carlos shoved Sam and, stumbling back, got away, running out the door. Sam let him go.

Breathing heavily and bleeding from a cut above his eye, Sam rushed into the bedroom, fearing what he'd see. Kate was lying on the bed, wrists bound. Her eyes were tightly shut, closing out the pain and degradation Carlos had inflicted on her. Sam took in everything in an instant. Besides her blouse being ripped open, Kate had a cut to her lip and the start of a black eye. There were hickeys on her neck and nipples, and bruises on her breasts. The most important thing, though, was she was breathing. Sam felt such anguish and kneeled by the bed, gently touching her face. He untied her wrists and covered her nakedness. Cradling her in his arms, he held her, shushing her as she cried into his chest.

When Kate had fallen asleep, Sam called Jake at Emily's.

"Oh, God, Sam, I'm sorry. Everything was cool. Ramirez was out of town. There had been no action. There was no way I'd have left her alone if there was any possibility…"

"Look, Jake, I know man, I know. Everything looked good–even the team said it was clear." Sam gently eased his guilt. "There was no reason to suspect Kate would not be safe for the few hours until I got home. Don't beat yourself up."

They discussed and agreed on the next steps to be taken. Sam packed a bag for Kate and took her home to his house. Jake and Emily were waiting for them when he arrived with Kate. He sent her and Em upstairs. Moving into the study with Jake, they assembled an arsenal. Jake never traveled without his M9 sidearm. Sam had two Glock 19s. He handed one to Jake. "They hold more rounds," he explained. Each Glock used a 17-round magazine and Sam never carried less than two clips for reloading. Add to that his service revolver. They were well-equipped.

****

Sam and Jake had been working together since the discovery of Kate's file on Ramirez. They were currently chasing a new lead from the Rio Grande Valley surrounding the weapons smuggling, using the southern border to ship guns and explosives to terrorist cells. ICE and DEA were working with them to close the crossing point and capture the terrorists, but Sam had been pursuing the distribution angle. He had finally narrowed down the bad actors working with the Miami office and confirmed the Ramirez family was behind it all–Carlos being the key contact point here in the States. They knew how the weapons were crossing the border and had identified the location of the warehouse along the I-35 corridor south of the city where the contraband was to be stored awaiting last payment and hand-off. All that was missing was the specific date and time. Sam was in his office going over some miscellaneous information when his cell phone rang. His screen showed it was from an anonymous caller. Sam usually ignored these, but something told him to answer.

"Mr. Slater, we don't know each other, but we have moved in the same circles. In other circumstances, we might be adversaries. However, I have an offer to make you. My name is Joseph Cortino. Robert was my son. He was young and foolish and rash, but he didn't deserve to die as he did. I think we both know who was behind the accident. I wish to, shall we say, return the favor."

Sam sat up straighter in his chair and grabbed a pen. "And how would you propose to do that, Mr. Cortino?"

"Let's just say that the enemy of my enemy is my friend. The date and time you are seeking…"

Sam couldn't believe his luck. Cortina was ratting out Ramirez. The partnership between the two families went back to when old man Ramirez first started running drugs. Cortino controlled all the northeast distribution and purchased his goods from Ramirez. Sam had to wonder if Cortino was cutting off his nose to spite his face, but really didn't care at this point if it would give him Carlos.

"I will take care of the triggerman personally. I trust you will not interfere. It will be discreet, I assure you. I wish you success with your mission." The call ended. Sam just stared at his phone and the information he'd written down. A slow, satisfied smile spread across his face. Diplomatic protection wasn't going to help Carlos this time.

****

It had been three days since Carlos had attacked Kate. He had gone underground. The best Sam's team could tell, he'd left the country. It relieved some of the tension, but not all. Sam and Jake had insisted the girls hunker down at Sam's and they were going stir-crazy.

"Oh, come on, Sam, Jake. This is like being under house arrest, and Kate and I aren't even the criminals. Let's grab lunch at Angelinos. We can sit on the terrace, enjoy the sunshine, and put all this drama out of our minds for a while."

Kate held prayerful hands to her lips and gave Sam a hopeful look. Reluctantly, he agreed as long as it was after the usual lunch hour, so the crowds would be lighter. Whooping with delight, the girls ran up to the bedroom to change into pretty clothes.

The hostess seated the foursome at a table along the concrete wall separating the restaurant from the sidewalk. Sam and Jake sat across from each other so they each had a clear view in every direction. Their eyes were constantly scanning the crowds and traffic for any motion with lethal intent. Jake watched an elderly man take a seat two tables over. His wife gave him a pat on the shoulder telling her she needed to go powder her nose–no threat there. A table of four co-eds were celebrating someone's birthday, drinking too many pitchers of margaritas and flirting with the waiter, who didn't seem to mind a bit. Only threat there was to the waiter, or maybe the co-ed he'd get lucky with later. A young couple and a toddler were seated at the table next to Sam. Emily and Kate were chatting with the young mother, cooing to the baby and enjoying the normalcy of the afternoon.

Traffic was light; there were no slow walkers or visible watchers. Everything was quiet until a black SUV turned the corner, cruising by the restaurant, blasting its stereo. It could just be some young punk, but memories from Kandahar came flooding back and the hairs on the back of Sam's neck stood up. They used loud music as a distraction, drawing attention away from the real threat. Jake tracked the SUV with his gaze and now a second vehicle was moving rapidly down the street from the opposite direction, the windows rolling down.

Sam knew instinctively what was happening and yelled out, "Everybody, down–get down! Shooter, shooter, shooter!!"

Jake tackled Emily, throwing her under the table while Sam grabbed Kate and threw her behind the concrete wall, shielding her with his body just as bullets erupted from the second SUV. The barrage of bullets swept across the terrace. Everything moved in slow motion. The old man never knew what hit him when he was catapulted backward into the plate-glass window from a hail of bullets to his torso. The father of the toddler stood up in confusion, staring at the vehicle, not fully comprehending the situation. He took two shots to the head. Three bullets hit the elderly woman just returning from the powder room, throwing her back against a waiter carrying a tray of glasses. The toddler's mother sat frozen in horror, a sitting duck for the endless stream of bullets that made a diagonal path across her abdomen and up her neck. The force of the bullets threw her back into the high chair, causing it to fall. Screaming hysterically, the co-eds crawled under their table against the 12-foot-high plate-glass windows, which when hit by the flying bullets shattered, raining down sharp shards of glass, impaling and killing two, seriously wounding a third.

Amid the glass breaking and the screams of the innocent victims, Kate watched in horror as the crying toddler crawled out from under his mother's body. Sam and Jake were busy returning fire. Without thinking of her own safety, Kate jumped up. She snatched the child up, tucked him under her chin, and rolled behind the concrete planter. Curling herself protectively around him, she kept her cool. Kate took in the scene and handed the toddler to Emily. She belly-crawled over to where her cell phone had fallen, then stood to take pictures of the departing vehicle as it sped away. She jumped over the concrete wall of the restaurant terrace to chase down the shooters. Sam tackled her, rolling behind a parked car. Grabbing her arm, he pulled her up, turning her around, and shaking her.

"God damn it, Kate! What the hell do you think you're doing?"

"My job!" Kate shouted right back, impatiently shaking him off. "Damn it, Sam. I'm getting pictures for the police and the papers. What do you think?" Kate had the fire in her eyes that came with a reporter's instincts. Then she saw the blood on Sam's forehead and everything else faded into the background. "Oh, my God, Sam—you're bleeding!"

"What? Yeah, it's just a scratch. Head wounds bleed a lot." Kate's concern momentarily distracted Sam, but it didn't take long for the fear and anger to come flooding back. "But you—what the hell do you think you were doing? No scoop is worth getting killed over. Are you okay? Jesus. Any bullet wounds? How about your head? I threw you down pretty hard."

"I- I…" Kate fainted.

Jake and Emily had taken charge of the scene and were instructing survivors to call 911, getting napkins for bandages, and covering the faces of the dead. It didn't take long for Fort Worth's finest to respond, and soon police and ambulance were converging on the scene.

Sam scooped Kate up and carried her to a quiet area away from the first responders dealing with the dead and wounded. He grabbed a napkin, wetting it in a pitcher of ice water on the way. As he gently laid her down, Sam noticed she had fresh blood oozing from her upper arm. Forcing down his panic, he pushed up her sleeve to examine the wound. It wasn't too bad, a graze, probably from flying glass. A good cleaning and butterfly bandage would do. He'd seen and treated much worse in Afghanistan. Creating a cushion with his handkerchief, he used the napkin to wrap around her arm.

A paramedic saw them and came over to provide first aid. Kate was coming around. Sam told her to stay put and went to find the officer in charge. He exchanged contact information and returned to Kate.

The paramedic closed his triage case, stood, and

put a hand on Sam's arm. "She'll be fine. Flesh wound. Some aspirin to take away the sting, but really, it's nothing to worry about." He rushed off to see to others.

"I feel so stupid. I guess it was the adrenalin rush and the sudden come down that caused my fainting." Kate took deep, even breaths to clear her head. "Sorry for being such a sissy."

Sam didn't say a word. Anger wasn't an adequate word for what he was feeling right then. Damnation. She had put her life at risk. He looked at her, barely controlling his wrath–no, his fear for her. Pulling her to her feet, he walked her to the car and practically shoved her into the passenger seat. Slamming the door shut, he climbed behind the wheel and drove them home, forgetting about Jake and Emily left behind.

Sam's cell buzzed. It was Emily, in a fit of anger and panic. "Where the hell are you? Are you two okay?"

"Shit. Yeah, sorry I left you guys. I had to get Kate to safety. We're headed to the house. Meet us there," he said and clicked off. When Sam and Kate got home to his place, he took Kate to the kitchen, sat her on a stool, and unwrapped her arm to look at the field dressing the paramedic had put on.

"Look, I know it was stupid to jump up, but what a chance to get pictures of the shooters. This could be what helps the police make an arrest, not to mention the possibility of a front-page story and by-line. They were leaving by the time I stood up, anyway. I mean, I wasn't in the line of fire anymore, you would have done the same…" She let her sentence trail off as she noticed how tightly Sam was clenching his fists; the knot of anger in his jaw. The sky was clouding up, and fat drops of rain clinked against the window, a perfect match for his mood and the dream.

Sam went to the sink to wash the blood from the scene off his hands. He stood quietly, gazing out at the backyard. He then turned back to her with a glass of water and two aspirin.

"Here, take these. It will hurt for a bit, but you'll live." Sam walked out onto the front porch to wait for Emily and Jake, leaving a stunned Kate sitting where she was.

Jake and Sam stayed on the front porch to talk while Emily checked on Kate. After a little while, Sam drove off.

"Oh, Emily, Sam is so angry and I am so stupid. Part of me knows he is right. I should never have stood up to get those pictures. Everything was moving in slow motion. I knew I was okay and could get the pictures safely. This is how I'm wired. It's what I do. I can't change who I am and my career with the flip of a switch. If I can't be me, I won't be who Sam fell in love with. I emailed the best shots to the police and copied the editor on the paper. I'm sure they'll make the front page and help catch the criminals." Kate hugged herself, feeling chilled by the damp evening air.

"I understand what you're saying, Kate. Part of me agrees." Emily laid a calming hand over the ones Kate was twisting in her lap. "You can't easily change who you are, but Sam can't easily change who he is either. After living independently and taking care of ourselves, it is difficult to appreciate someone else might want to take care of us. Jake wasn't happy with me either, but I didn't really put my life in danger like you did. Sam has seen too much death and danger. You put yourself in harm's way on his watch. He doesn't take that lightly. And now that you'll probably be identified as the woman who took the pictures and helped identify the gang that did that drive-by shooting, well, you've put yourself in harm's way again. Did you ever consider that?"

Kate raised stricken eyes. Emily was right. There was nothing she could say.

Sam may never forgive her.

****

Sam went straight to the police station and spoke with the lead investigator on the shooting. Respecting the authority of the local law enforcement agency, he offered any help Homeland Security could give. He spent the next couple of hours working with the tech staff. They reviewed the different camera angles the police had lifted from business security cameras, bystander cell phone video and, yes, maddeningly, even Kate's photos. The vehicle used in the shooting had been stolen and was found submerged in the Trinity River on the north side of town. No prints. The first vehicle that had driven past blaring his radio was different. There was a clear shot of the license plate and they tracked it to a worthless gangbanger. When the Fort Worth PD picked him up, he claimed he knew nothing and clammed up, asking for his attorney. The authorities were sweeping all the city surveillance camera footage to see if they could backtrack the gangbanger's SUV to determine if or where it had met the other vehicle. With luck, they might tie him to the shooting directly and coerce him to give up the shooters. The best lead they had were the pictures Kate had taken. She got a reasonably clear shot of one perp before he pulled his head back into the vehicle. They were running facial recognition software.

When Sam had done as much as he could, he drove down to the river and sat on the table he and Kate used for their morning cool down. The park was silent, but the conversation in his head was deafening. He was so angry. The tense muscles in his jaw ached and the knots in his shoulders set like concrete. *What the hell did she think she was doing? How could she put herself in danger like that?* He wanted to shake some sense into her one minute, and hold her tight the next. Damn it! Hanging his head with a sigh, Sam worked to get control of his emotions. He accepted she was simply doing what any good reporter would have done, but seeing her risk her life like that was a punch to the gut. He respected her and her work. And, on closer examination, he wasn't so much angry as frightened. Frightened for Kate's safety. As well as for the possibility of his failing her. Which meant he was actually furious with himself? Hell, this kind of circular thinking was unproductive. After an hour, he gave up and headed home.

Sam pulled into his driveway a little after 11 p.m. Ophelia greeted him at the door, stretching and yawning and rolling over so Sam could give her a good belly rub. Then, after twining her long tail around his legs, ran back to the family room, where she jumped up next to Kate. She'd fallen asleep on the couch waiting for Sam to come home. He wondered what he'd done to deserve such an extraordinary woman.

Brushing her hair back behind her ear, he whispered, "Hey, sleepy head. It's time for bed. Come on, babe." Sam reached under her and picked her up.

213

Kate snuggled into his chest as he carried her into the bedroom. He laid her down and curled up next to her, spoon fashion. He kissed the top of her head and tucked it under his chin, sighing in contentment. Ophelia joined them, and the three of them were soon asleep.

****

Jake and Emily left Kate waiting alone at Sam's and went home. It had been an emotional day. Emily felt the tears slip down her cheeks. She was exhausted and emotionally spent. There had been so much blood and death. Emily couldn't fathom Jake's stoic attitude. She buried her face in his shoulder. She didn't see the turmoil he was feeling inside. They clung to each other, taking comfort that neither was harmed.

Standing in the tiny kitchen with his arms wrapped around her, Jake swayed side to side in a slow dance. He was softly humming under his breath, "Let me call you sweetheart" when Em stepped back from him. "Are you humming that cat song? How romantic." She laughed, playfully punching his shoulder.

Jake stopped and cocked his head to one side, as he often did when a new idea struck him. He nodded decisively, and taking Emily by the hand, led her to the sofa. Sitting her down, he took her hand in his and shared his most precious memory. "You know my folks died when I was eight, right? My uncle raised me but he wasn't a very loving guy—no hugs or bed tucks. Just get up and get to work. I don't remember a lot about my folks. But one thing I remember and the vision of it is as clear as a bell. I remember my folks dancing in the kitchen. Dad would hold Mom in his arms and she'd tuck her head under his chin, resting her ear against his chest, listening to it rumble while he sang "Let me call you Sweetheart" under his breath–for her ears only. For me, that song has always symbolized complete and perfect love. So, when you ask why I'm humming that cat song, I'll tell you honestly, I'm not. I'm singing a love song to the woman I want to spend the rest of my life with.

"Emily, I know I'm not the best catch. Certainly not the most handsome or smoothest guy you've ever met. I'm better with my hands than with books, know nothing about art, and probably will always be the philistine you think I am. I carry an extra thirty pounds around that in twenty-five years will probably turn to fat and I'll be old and crotchety, but I promise you one thing. I will love and honor you and work every day of my life to make you happy. I love you, Emily Slater, and if you'll have me, I'd like to marry you." Jake took Emily's face between his big mountain man's hands and kissed her gently as if she were made of the most delicate spun glass.

"Oh, Jake. I love you too. I may not be the prize you think I am, either. And since weight gain after three kids runs in my family, I suspect I won't be a size six in twenty-five years. We'll match. That's assuming you want three kids," Emily said.

"Make it an even half dozen and we'll teach every one of them to sing 'Let me call you Sweetheart.'" Jake picked her up and whirled her around in circles, laughing joyously.

Chapter 21

Carlos sat at his desk swirling the ice cubes in his scotch while he watched the action at the warehouse. Carlos had done all the coordination for the shipment, and now the exchange of money for guns would be handled by Ric and Eduardo. The entire transaction was live-streamed because Carlos had set up closed circuit cameras. It allowed Carlos to observe the culmination of their last deal with Rahim and his ultimate demise. Carlos would monitor everything from his office, giving him perfect oversight and an ironclad alibi. Eduardo would verify payment and Ric would hand over the keys. Once the deal was done, Ric and Eduardo would drive to Spinks Airfield, where they'd take the family jet back home. Rahim and his drivers would hook up the trailers and drive off. Carlos would use a burner phone and call the tip into the Homeland Security office. *Ya esta*, or *voila*, as the French would say. The deed would be done to everyone's satisfaction. So simple. So easy.

Ric watched Eduardo pace nervously. "Relax, Eduardo. We've only been waiting since three thirty. The men around the perimeter will text when the trucks and Rahim pull into the warehouse complex. Everything will be accomplished quickly and easily. We'll be on our way in no time, five million richer." Ric's cell pinged at 3:59, alerting him to Rahim's arrival. "See, you worry too much. They are right on time."

Punching the button, Ric watched the massive garage door roll up, allowing Rahim with his men to drive up the ramp into the warehouse, and the semi-trucks to position themselves to hook-up to the trailers. When they came to a stop, Ric walked toward the full-size sedan. Eduardo hung back, wiping the sweat from his face. Three very large and formidable looking Arabs with bulges under their jackets from their side arms got out, advancing on Ric to pat him down for weapons. Trusting bastards, Ric thought with a sneer. Upon a nod from the tallest of the group, Rahim exited the car and approached Ric, hand outstretched. Ric looked at Rahim and his extended hand with disdain. "Did you bring the money?"

Carlos watched the silent tableau unfold as Rahim motioned to the driver to bring the suitcase, and Ric motioned for Eduardo to step forward to receive the payment. Ric held the keys to the semi-truck trailers in his hand. With the funds verified, Eduardo gave a slight nod to Ric. Rahim caught the keys Ric tossed his way. Two of Rahim's men jumped out of the semi-trucks and took the keys. They unlocked the rolling door of each trailer and climbed inside to confirm the ordnances. Ric glanced up. He knew Carlos was watching. He gave a slow, smug smile to the camera.

****

Sam's team had taken up positions surrounding the warehouse earlier in the day. When the buyer entered the complex, they quickly neutralized the four Ramirez men outside the warehouse. They coordinated with the local authorities to establish a roadblock and awaited further instructions. Sam and Jake, reverting to their Seal training, approached the warehouse from the west and circled to the side entrance. Two armed guards were standing outside the rear entry door, smoking. Jake brought the MK12 SPR sniper rifle to his shoulder. He checked the silencer, and with two small piffts, took out the guards with kill shots to the head.

Sam and Jake ran to the door and verified the kill. They radioed the location of the door to the 12-man HSI team, and when they arrived, entered the building. Fanning out, the team spaced themselves in a horseshoe along the west side of the warehouse while four circled to the east side, covering the garage door exit, effectively surrounding Rahim and Ric and their respective men. Sam and Jake took a more direct route. Sam turned on his body camera and hunkered down to get recorded proof of the buy as it was going down. He signaled for Jake to go high, climbing to the catwalk, into sniper position. Sam silently crossed over to the conveyor belts and forklift, ensuring a clear camera shot of Ramirez and the exchange.

Ric saw Rahim's men confirm the contents of the trailers. "Well, it looks like our work here is done. You are welcome to hook up your big rigs and be on your way." Ric smiled. He walked toward his Escalade where the driver opened the rear door for him and Eduardo.

Sam double-checked his team's position and then stepped out from behind the forklift, weapon ready. Training his gun on Ric's head, he shouted, "Homeland Security! Everyone freeze! You're under arrest."

Taking their cue, the HSI team tossed two flashbang grenades into the center of the room, stunning several of the Arabs. Those left standing raised their weapons, shooting at any movement, and ran for cover behind a stack of pallets. Like all grand plans, it didn't go exactly as expected. It never does. The three men that had come with Ric ran around the semi-trailers toward the exit, skidding to a stop when they came face to face with four HSI officers. Wisely, they raised their hands.

"Drop to your knees, hands behind your head," John shouted. Wrists were zip-tied and leaving one officer to guard them, the other three made their way toward the shooting. There were ten armed Arabs, plus Rahim. Four were stunned by the flashbangs. Jake, from his shooter perch on the catwalk, watched the downed men to make sure they wouldn't be a threat anymore, but they made the mistake of raising their weapons. Jake finished them. He didn't believe in taking prisoners. Six had taken cover behind stacks of pallets, Rahim and his driver made it to the sedan and were putting down heavy fire, pinning the HSI team in their tracks. Jake took out another bad guy hunkered down behind the pallets, but they followed the trajectory of his shots and discovered his location. Two started concentrating their shots at him, effectively shutting down his ability to offer backup to the team on the floor. Shielding himself behind an A/C condenser, Jake thought, Okay, guys, you're on your own now. Two of the team put down cover fire while the other six fanned out to flank the pile of pallets.

There were three others that had subdued the Mexicans and they concentrated their fire on Rahim's sedan. Now Rahim was in trouble. He shoved his driver out from behind the vehicle, creating a diversion so he could jump behind the wheel. His driver found himself wide open and took two shots to the abdomen. Rahim thought he'd made a clean getaway, but as he passed the trailers, John, the team lead, stepped from behind the tractor-trailer and emptied his clip into the windshield, blowing Rahim's brains out the back window. The sedan careened off the loading dock and rolled twice before landing on its roof and bursting into flame. Rallying the team, they pushed around the pallets and finished the rest. One of John's men had taken a gunshot to the chest and was in serious condition. Two others had minor injuries. Otherwise, all was good.

Jake had been pinned down so sought a safe path across the warehouse. Stray bullets were flying all around as he ran. Carlos was watching his brothers on the camera. Everything was unfolding in agonizingly slow motion. Ric turned toward Sam when he first stepped out from behind the forklift. He eyed the Glock pointed at his head and raised his hands over his head, pretending to surrender.

"I see you have discovered our little business transaction. So, you get the big prize."

Ric's driver used the diversion of the flashbangs to pull his weapon and raised it slowly to take aim at Sam. Without breaking his gaze at Ric, Sam calmly and swiftly shifted his gun and pumped two shots into the center of the driver's forehead. Ric ran to the driver and, using his body as a shield, fired his weapon at Sam. Sam dove for cover and let go a hail of bullets. Ric returned fire and yelled at Eduardo to get in the car while he had Sam pinned down. Eduardo covered his head with the briefcase of money and ran for the car just as Jake made it across the catwalk. Jake fired a single shot, hitting Eduardo at the base of his spine. Eduardo stumbled and fell, crying out.

Carlos watched in horror as his little brother fell from the shot. Ric looked up and saw Jake on the metal walkway overhead. Roaring in anger, he sent several shots toward Jake. Ric ran to Eduardo and dragged him toward the car, leaving a trail of blood.

Sam had used the time they pinned him down to put in a fresh clip and, rolling out from behind the forklift, he came to his knee.

"Give it up, Ramirez. You're done."

In answer, Ric brought his gun around, sending bullets flying. Sam rolled behind cover and fired three successive shots into Ric. The velocity threw Ric back against the side of the silver Escalade, his arms thrown out in a macabre embrace of death. He slid down the door, leaving a streak of blood. Approaching the Ramirez brothers, Sam kicked their weapons away and checked for any sign of life. Ric had died almost instantly. Eduardo would most likely live, but probably never walk again. Jake climbed down from the catwalk and walked up to Sam, who had just closed Ric's eyes. They stood staring at the bodies. They weren't proud, but it was part of the job. Sam checked in with the team, asked about injuries, and issued orders. They called in medical for the wounded and the local authorities to help with the crime scene clean-up.

The paperwork and cleanup took the rest of the day. When Jake and Sam arrived home, they found Emily and Kate waiting anxiously. While they excused themselves to go clean up, the girls fixed sandwiches and soft drinks. The guys went into the back garden sitting quietly to decompress. It was like that after a kill day. Somehow, you had to fill the holes in your soul. Some did it with alcohol, others with prayer, some never succeeded. They were the ones who ate their guns. Sam and Jake did it in silence. They drank in the sweet scent of the flowers, took in the stars, and listened to the splashing of the water in the fountain. They let the world wash over them, cleansing the blood from their minds and souls. After a while, they stood and hugged. This was their shared brotherhood–blood and death—but waiting were the two women in the world that could make them whole. They went inside.

Sam took Kate's hand, and they were heading to bed when they heard Jake exclaim, "Oh hell no! That bastard, that lying bastard!"

Hurrying back to the family room, they saw what Jake was shouting about. Live and in living color, Carlos Ramirez and the weapons bust was the lead story of the 10 o'clock news. Carlos was standing on the front steps of the Consulate residence being interviewed. "I'm sure you can appreciate that this is all very upsetting for me and my family. I was here at the residence all afternoon working. When the police contacted me, I learned of this tragic event. Why my brothers would be there is a mystery to me. I cannot imagine them being involved in something illegal. Recently, I was informed my brothers were working with the Mexican authorities to set up a sting operation regarding illegal smuggling. I am reaching out to my family to learn more. It would be tragic if this was a case of miscommunication by the American agencies involved. I am sure the authorities will sort everything out and discover the truth. I have every confidence they will hold the responsible parties accountable."

Carlos had moved his pieces into position. Checkmate.

****

Carlos gave interviews to all the major news sources and planted his seeds. His brother Eduardo, after several hours in surgery, had medevacked to Mexico City. Carlos followed later in the day, making sure the media covered his departure to Mexico. Being a diplomat, the authorities couldn't make him stay in the country. He flew home on a commercial jet accompanying the body of his slain brother, garnering even more sympathy than before. Playing the lie out to the nth-degree, he landed in Guadalajara in the afternoon. The interview he'd given the media hinting about the sting operation set in motion an investigation into Sam and his team. Homeland Security looked guilty as hell. The Mexican Ambassador who owed his cushy position to the Ramirez family was happy to oblige in building a case against Sam, calling on the American government to explain what exactly had happened. The fact that the bodyguards Ric used were actually Mexican police officers on the cartel's payroll just added an extra layer of "truth" to the story.

Meeting with his father, Carlos planned the next steps he'd need to complete his revenge. It would ruin Slater professionally, and he might even go to jail. The Americans were turning against their law enforcement community all across the country. Why not Homeland Security too? Ah, but sweeter still, would be the killing of the people Sam loved most in the world, his sister and Kate. Sam would live, knowing it was his actions that led to his sister's death. If her boyfriend, Jake, died too, all the better. Kate, Carlos decided, he'd enjoy for a while and when he grew tired of her, perhaps get her hooked on heroin and put her into a brothel in Mexico City where she'd willingly satisfy the drunken lusts of every man that wanted her in order to get her next fix. Carlos would be sure to send pictures of Kate performing her duties to Sam. Or maybe he'd just kill her, too. Sam would live with the memories of his failure either way. Carlos smiled. It would be so satisfying.

Carlos took a private jet to a small airfield south of Whitney, TX, where he picked up an older model car left for his use and drove to the rendezvous point to meet his outfit. His men had armed themselves and tracked the movements of the targets. They knew where Slater and the others were staying and all the security measures. The pieces were in place. The plan was simple. Step one, ruin Sam. Step two, kill Emily and Jake. Step three, snatch Kate. And so it began.

****

The shit storm that ensued from the bald-faced lies Carlos told the media, insinuating a mistake by the American agencies resulting in the killing of innocent Mexican citizens, was explosive. Every media outlet was calling and knocking at the HSI office. They even camped out at Sam's house, asking for an interview. The local paper had the gall to reach out to Kate, asking her to write a piece on the weapons bust. "It will give you the chance to spin the story the way it should be," they'd told her.

"Commander Collins, you know this is all bullshit!" Sam exclaimed when he was called into a debriefing with his boss. "Ramirez is lying through his teeth, and the Mexican authorities are being paid off to lie for him. God, even that bought and paid for Ambassador is in on it. You know they have been in the Ramirez pocket for years. The old man set it up when he started dealing drugs forty years ago. His sons just continued the practice. Hell, the fact that he had police as his enforcers at the warehouse shows they are thick as thieves."

"Or, it means it was a legitimate sting operation, and we F'ed up. Sam, you need to get your ducks in a row because the Mexican Ambassador has reached out to the Secretary of State, and our esteemed senator is butting his nose in. He's up for re-election and this is the best free publicity and TV time he could ask for. There is blood in the water, the sharks are circling and I don't know if I can protect your ass. I'm in hot water myself for approving Jake Edwards to join the team. Those three guys your team took into custody work for the Mexican police. Yes, I know they could be on the Ramirez payroll, but it all lends credence to their story. And the fact that you two didn't leave any other live witnesses isn't working in your favor. Think about that. As of right now, I need your badge and gun. You're damn lucky you haven't been arrested for murder."

Sam slowly stood. He was screwed. Ramirez had woven a web of lies and Sam had to figure out how to prove the truth. He pulled out his badge, dropped the clip from his gun, and put it all on Commander Collins' desk.

His team stood waiting as he exited the office. John put his hand on Sam's shoulder. "This sucks, Sam. It was a righteous bust. We got the bad guys and we'll prove it. Lie low, man. Look, here are the keys to my cabin. It's in the Kildeer Hunting Reserve along the Sabine River, plenty remote. The media won't be able to track you down. Get out of town for a little while."

John was right. They needed to get out of town and out of the spotlight. Sam let Commander Collins know where they were going in case he needed to turn himself in. The team would work on the proof they needed while Sam and Jake, with Kate's help, reviewed all the info they had uncovered. Sam arranged for Ophelia's care and the four packed up their stuff and stole away like thieves in the night. Sam felt like shit about the whole thing, but they'd figure a way out.

****

"How the hell he explained the broken nose and black eye you gave him is what I'd like to know." Jake was leaning over the front seat, punching anger out with his voice.

Sam checked the GPS for the next turn off on their drive to John's cabin and passed a slow-moving pickup along the highway. He sent Jake a quick look in the rear-view mirror. "He told the media someone had rear-ended him in the rainstorm and his airbags deployed. They bought it. It actually added to his alibi. I mean, how could someone recently in a car wreck be involved in weapons smuggling? No offense, Kate, but some media are idiots."

"None taken, Sam. He is a very convincing liar. I think we can connect him to the weapons buyer from the newspaper articles and photos I uncovered, but it will all be circumstantial."

"We need to pin down Carlos' whereabouts during major drug deliveries. I sent a copy of your file to Ron at the Miami office and he's pulling together everything he has on Carlos, especially the last visit he made when we surveilled him exiting the restaurant. If Ron can come up with a connection, it would help the case."

They continued to puzzle over all the information until it wore them out with worry. Emily suggested a walk down to the river for lunch and a swim. Donning their suits and grabbing towels, they loaded up the barbeque they'd picked up on the drive down, along with some beer, and headed down to the river. The temperature was eighty-eight degrees, so the water felt cool and refreshing. Jake and Emily found the rope swing and had a go at trying to kill themselves with their high-flying antics. After an hour of foolishness, the girls set out lunch, and Jake popped open the beer. It felt good to relax and just forget about all the mess for a little while. Swimming always made Kate hungry. She made short order of her ribs. The food, beer, and company made her smile. Kate closed her eyes and stretched like a cat, enjoying the feel of the sun's rays. Dozing, they all enjoyed the downtime.

Sam was the first to rouse himself. Leaning over, he tugged at the strap of Kate's top to plant a kiss on her shoulder. "Hey, you are getting a little pink. Did you bring sunscreen?"

Kate pressed fingers to her skin, gauging her sunburn. "Yes, it's in my bag. Would you grab it and rub some on my shoulders, please? And I'll get your back too." Sam rubbed lotion on Kate's back, loving the silky smoothness of her skin. He moved aside the straps of her top, amazed at how tanned she was. He wouldn't expect someone so fair-skinned to be so brown, but Kate was perfection. When he had finished with her back, she rolled over, giving him a saucy look.

"Would you rub lotion on my front, too? Or we could head back."

The rising bulge in Sam's shorts showed he agreed with her suggestion. Adjusting himself, Sam rose and helped Kate up. Even with the peace and calm of the river, it was definitely time to return to the cabin.

"Hey, guys, we're heading back. Are you ready?" Sam tapped a napping Jake's foot with his.

Yawning, Jake stretched both arms over his head. "Why not? We're out of cold beer, anyway."

It was an easy walk from the river to the cabin. Jake had his arm around Emily and they were whispering to each other and laughing. Sam and Kate brought up the rear, carrying the picnic hamper. He held Kate's hand, rubbing his thumb across her fingers. Absently, he brought her hand up to his mouth and kissed it, tasting a little of the bar-b-que sauce from their lunch. With Ramirez out of the country and the media unaware of their location, the foursome felt a lightening of the pressure at least until they could discover how to bring in and neutralize Ramirez.

Everyone was thinking about a nap in the hammock when a shot rang out, hitting a tree just to the right of Sam. Diving for cover, he pushed Kate down and crawled over to Jake. "Shit, you guys okay? Jake, are you carrying?"

"No, didn't think I'd need it for a swim. It's back at the cabin. You?" Jake scanned the trees for the shooter.

"Yeah, just because I turned in my service pistol, doesn't mean I'm not carrying my personal weapon. Lately, I'm never without it. I think the shot came from that hill. You take the girls and move over to that ravine and circle back to the cabin. I'll hang back and cover our rear." Leaving their picnic paraphernalia, they crab-walked and crawled through the underbrush. They almost made it back to the cabin when another shot rang out, trapping them a mere ten feet from the back door. Sam signaled to Jake, who gathered the girls, making ready to sprint to the door of the cabin. Jake nodded and Sam rushed out to draw fire while Jake hustled the girls into the cabin.

Kate was off like a shot when the signal came, while Jake followed with Emily. When she stumbled, he used his body to shield her, taking a shot to the shoulder. Adrenalin blocks all pain and Jake never missed a beat, hustling Emily into the cabin. He shoved both girls into the corner behind the refrigerator, hoping it would provide some protection. Crawling over to his backpack, Jake grabbed his Glock and crawled to the window.

As agreed, Sam had taken cover behind the woodpile and when Jake knew the girls were in a safe spot, gave Sam a thumbs up. Firing off a couple of rounds, Sam leapt up and sprinted across the front yard. Launching himself over the shrubs, he rolled behind a birdbath just as Jake burst out the front door, throwing himself across the front porch, loosening a barrage of gunfire. Just then, an SUV pulled up and four more bad guys jumped out, taking cover behind their vehicle. The odds had just gotten worse. Now it was at least five to two. Jake scrambled into the house, turning to provide cover shots for Sam to somersault through the door inside. Jake slammed the door shut behind him.

Sam crawled over to the window to see what the new arrivals were doing. Right now, they were hunkered down behind their SUV, sending random rounds toward the cabin to keep the occupants pinned down.

"What do you think they're waiting for? How are you set for bullets?" Sam asked Jake.

"I spent about nine covering you, so eight in the magazine, plus a full clip of seventeen. How many did you burn?"

"Shit, I blew through over two-thirds of my clip, covering you and the girls. With my full clip, that gives me about twenty-two rounds, if I'm lucky. Did you bring your M9?"

"Never without it." Jake nodded. "That adds fifteen rounds. We can't waste any shots."

Sam studied the positioning of the men outside, assessing their position, strengths, and weaknesses. Turning back to Jake, he saw the ashen color of Jake's face and the sheen of sweat. Then he saw the blood soaking through his shirt.

"Damn, Edwards. You're hit."

"Yeah, took one in the shoulder getting the girls in. Don't let Emily know."

"Know what? Oh, God, Jake, you're bleeding," Emily cried out and crawled over to where he sat propped up against the couch. "Let me see." Kate was right behind her with three kitchen towels, a bottle of water, and the vodka they'd packed. Emily tore open Jake's shirt and cried out again. It looked bad and was bleeding like crazy. She turned to Sam with panic in her eyes.

"It will be okay, Emily. Here, take Jake's M9 and watch out the window. If you see movement, fire one shot at them, just one," Sam said calmly. "Kate, this is a good start. Go see if that first-aid kit in the kitchen has anything else we can use. If it doesn't, grab duct tape or anything we can use to bind the wound up."

Kate crawled off and quickly returned with the first-aid kit. It had been designed for minor cuts and bruises, but had a roll of gauze and tape.

"Good job, babe. Go keep an eye out with Emily." Turning to Jake, he warned, "I'm going to plug that hole to stop the bleeding. It will hurt like hell but I need you conscious, so stay with me." Sam used the first towel to wipe away the blood. The bullet hole looked clean, but was bleeding more than he'd hoped. He was afraid it might have hit Jake's lung. His breathing sounded wet. "Here, take a good hit and give it back."

Jake gulped three hefty swallows and, with a lopsided grin, handed the bottle back. "Do your worst, Slater. I'm ready." Using the vodka to disinfect the wound, Sam stuffed a wad of gauze into the hole. Jake jerked up. "Shit! Fuck! Damn, man! That stings like hell!"

Sam covered the wound with a gauze pad, and the second towel folded into quarters. "Buck up, you pussy." Tearing the third towel into strips, he bound it all in place. It wasn't pretty, but it would hold, for now.

Jake's face paled. "Here, take the water and drink it down." Sam left Jake and crawled over to Emily to take over the watch. Touching her forearm, he tipped his head in Jake's direction. "He'll be fine, but we need to get him to a doctor sooner rather than later. Go to him, Em."

Dusk would set in a couple of hours, and there were at least five guys out there with unlimited ammo. They were trapped in a two-bedroom cabin with too little ammo and cell service John had told them only worked at the top of the hill. Shit!

Jake had recovered enough to crawl over to Sam to review their situation and make a plan. The girls went to get water and some energy bars. Everyone needed hydration and sugar. Sam and Jake agreed they didn't have enough for a long siege. They concluded that sitting in the cabin playing the waiting game wasn't an option. After some discussion, the two came up with a plan. There was a trapdoor in the floor that Sam would use to exit and crawl under the house coming out by the Jeep. When he knocked three times on the floor, no joke intended, Jake would begin firing outside and Sam would run to the jeep. Using it as a weapon, he'd drive straight at the shooters, scattering them and hopefully exposing them to Jake's shots.

"When the shit hits the fan, Kate, you and Emily burst out the back door and go for help. Head to the river and follow it around to the north. You'll get to the road. Continue to follow that north and in about two miles you should come to the trading post where we bought our supplies earlier. Take your cell. If you get a signal when you reach the road, call for help. If not, the trading post has a landline. As plans go, it is pretty lame, but with limited ammo, we don't have better options."

"Wait, Sam." Emily grabbed his forearm. "I can't run like Kate. I do yoga, remember? But I can use a gun and I'm a good shot. I'll stay here and help cover you. With three of us making the attack, Kate's chances of getting away increase."

"I don't want to leave you guys, but Emily makes a good point," Kate added. "One runner will be less noticeable and I can make better time on my own. No offense, Emily."

"None taken."

Sam reluctantly agreed to the plan's revision. Sam held Kate in his arms, hating to put her in this danger. "I love you. When it's time, run like the wind."

Jake gave Emily a long kiss and handed her the extra clip for the M9. Sam tipped the table over and put it under the window against the wall. In front of that, he slid the couch, creating a shooter's blind with hopefully enough cushioning to stop the bullets the bad guys were shooting at them. "Don't get brave on me, you hear?" Jake told Emily as he leaned against the barrier, laying out the spare clips and weapons like a doctor prepping for surgery.

"That goes for you too, mister," Emily said as she grabbed his good arm and gave him one more kiss. "I love you, Jake Edwards. Don't die on me."

"Not in the cards, babe. I won't die and I won't lose you either!" Jake and Emily took up their position behind the barrier Sam had set up, readying for the three knocks.

Sam handed Jake his partial clip and jammed the full magazine into his Glock. He and Jake clasped hands, and with a determined nod, Sam moved to the trapdoor. One more kiss with Kate and he was head first through the trapdoor. Everyone was poised and ready, waiting for his signal. The three knocks came quickly, and they sprang into action. Emily and Jake put down the cover fire. Sam sprinted to the jeep and turned the engine over. Keeping his head down, he jammed it into first and slammed his foot down on the accelerator, aiming for the shooters taking cover behind the SUV. When Kate heard the collision, she rocketed out the back door and ran.

****

Carlos had been watching from the ridge. His was the shot that drove the foursome to run for the cabin in the first place. He'd continued to fire, keeping them pinned down until his men arrived. Then he sat back and watched the fun. His position offered an unobstructed view of the back of the cabin, so he saw Kate burst out the door. He was stunned by his good luck. This is too perfect. The gazelle comes to the lion. "The hell with the other three." He laughed. His men can finish them. Failing that, they will keep them busy long enough for him to accomplish his ultimate goal. *I will have Kate.*

Carlos ran down the slope toward the path Kate was rushing headlong down. As she rounded the curve, he barreled right into her, knocking her to the ground. At the rate at which she was running, Kate took a hard fall, knocking the wind out of her. As she curled into a ball and fought for breath, Carlos dealt her a hard right, knocking her unconscious. The gunshots were slowing and Carlos felt confident his men were finishing what they had started. He picked Kate up and carried her to his car, dumping her unceremoniously into the trunk.

****

Sam punched the accelerator, aiming the jeep toward the men taking cover behind the SUV. They turned their weapons on him and began firing at the windshield. Sam lay on the seat and prayed. He felt the impact as the jeep hit a body and saw one shooter bounce off the hood and over the roof. The other three jumped back out of the way, two into the open. Jake and Emily opened up. They scrambled for cover, returning shots. Sam jumped out of the jeep and dove into the brush, looking for the third guy. He had crawled under the SUV and was laying down a hail of bullets in Sam's direction. The brush didn't provide much cover, so Sam scrambled backward behind a tree. The two exchanged gunshots off and on until the bad guy's gun jammed. Sam could hear the distinctive ratcheting of the clip being pulled and rammed back into the magazine. He sprang forward, diving toward his adversary, firing all the way. It was over quickly.

Sam heard shots from the cabin and, checking his ammo, realized he only had five shots remaining. He circled to the back, where the other two had taken cover. One was down with a shot to the gut and the other was looking at the SUV. Sam didn't give him the opportunity to flee. He shouted out, causing the fourth guy to turn around. Sam fired two shots into his forehead.

"Combatants down. All clear." Sam shouted and ran to the house. Helping Jake, the three made their way to the SUV. Sam looked at the crumpled front end and smoking radiator on his Gladiator. "Damn, I really liked that jeep." With Jake and Emily settled in the back seat of the SUV, Sam climbed behind the wheel. "How nice. They left us the keys. Emily, check your cell. As soon as you get a signal, call an ambulance and John. We need the cavalry." Engaging the motor, Sam drove off to intercept Kate and get Jake to the hospital.

Sam figured she would just be coming out of the woods at the river trail cut-off on the north end. When he didn't see her, he got worried. They passed a gray Honda driving sedately. Sam glanced over at the driver. It was coming on dark and visibility was lousy, but he could have sworn it was Ramirez.

"Sam, Jake is fading in and out of consciousness. There is so much blood. I'm scared. Please hurry." Emily cried from the back seat. There wasn't time to waste. Sam hit the gas. He ran into the trading post to call for help and look for Kate. She hadn't made it and he hadn't seen her on the road. His worry was growing and his sixth sense was kicking in. Could that have been Ramirez? Just then, the gray Honda passed the trading post. Sam watched the car pass by. Ramirez *was* the driver.

****

When Carlos saw the SUV in his rear-view mirror, he slowed, thinking it was his men. As the bullet-riddled vehicle made to pass him, Carlos raised his hand in acknowledgement. Realizing at the last moment it was Slater behind the wheel, he used that hand to obscure his face and kept driving. Damn it! The man is like a cat with nine lives. *Slater must have neutralized my men. Too bad. Good men were hard to find, and I liked my team.* Still smiling, Carlos knew that revenge was just around the corner, literally around the corner. Holding to the speed limit, he continued down the highway, passing the trading post on his left. He saw Sam standing there, looking back the way he had come. He could read the worry in the slump of Sam's shoulders. Kate wasn't there. But then she wouldn't be because she was in the trunk of his car. Carlos turned on the radio, beating out the rhythm on the steering wheel to a Tejano song, imagining all the fun he was going to have.

****

Jake was sitting in the back of the ambulance. The

shot had gone straight through the fleshy part of his shoulder, just missing the lung as Sam had feared or any other vital organs or the collar bone. He'd lost more blood than they liked and they wanted to transport him, but Jake refused to go to the hospital. He was adamant, so the paramedics patched him up, set up a saline drip, and were monitoring his vitals. Sam shared his concerns with them regarding Kate, Carlos, and the Honda.

"It looks as if Ramirez was watching the whole time. In fact, it was probably him that made the initial shot that drove us to the cabin. The whole thing was well orchestrated. He probably saw Kate leave and took advantage of the situation that presented itself, grabbing her as she ran by. The authorities closed down the area and haven't seen the car yet, so that means he might still be within the confines of the reserve. Jake, fill in the team when they get here and let them know I'm out there. I don't want them shooting me by mistake. I've got to find her."

Sam laid two fifties on the counter, picking up a flashlight and ammunition for his Glock. As an afterthought, he grabbed a skinning knife, just in case. Jake and Emily watched as he got into the SUV and drove off in search of Ramirez and Kate. They prayed he'd find her and kill him.

****

Carlos turned down the old hunting trail, stopping to lay brush over his path to obscure its view from the road. Driving through heavy undergrowth, he made his way to a shack standing in a small clearing about a mile in. It was crude but had power and running water. The shack was lit by a single bare and dusty bulb hanging from the overhead beam. There was also a lamp on a dining table flanked by two ladder-back chairs. A couple of bunk beds tucked next to a small all-inclusive 'kitchenette' with stove, sink and small refrigerator completed the 'fine décor'. Dust covered the surface of the furniture and rose from the bunk beds when Carlos patted the ratty bedding. It had all the comforts of home.

Carlos lifted Kate out of the trunk. She was still out, so it was simple to carry her to the cabin and hang her by her wrists to the crossbeam overhead. As she came around, he tightened the ropes and raised her just high enough so she had to stand on her tiptoes to keep the strain off her wrists. He secured her feet so she couldn't kick him and lastly put a gag in her mouth. No sense in alerting any visitors earlier than necessary. Carlos had selected the cabin for its remoteness. It would serve his plan well. He knew Sam would come. He looked forward to the opportunity to watch his face as he witnessed the degradation Carlos would inflict on Kate. Then he'd cut her just deep enough to bleed out and slowly die as Sam looked on helplessly. Carlos imagined the last moments the two lovers would share and laughed out loud.

****

Sam checked with the local authorities and confirmed the Honda had never made it past the roadblock they'd set up. That limited the search grid to the only highway going into the reserve. Sam turned around and slowly drove back, looking for any point where Carlos could have left the road. He found it easily. Almost too easily. Stopping the SUV a hundred feet off the road and along the dirt trail, Sam checked his gun, the extra clip, and grabbed the flashlight. The quarter moon had risen three hours earlier, so there was enough ambient light that he didn't really need the flashlight to make his way, but it was drizzling. Visibility would deteriorate quickly, along with any trail he might find. After walking about three-quarters of a mile, Sam saw light coming from a rundown shack about a hundred yards in front of him. He stepped off the trail and carefully made his way toward the building, hiding behind trees. Sam didn't see any movement or hear any sound. He approached cautiously. He spied Kate through the dirt-encrusted window hanging from the rafter with half her blouse ripped open and her eyes closed. After another round of the shack and, not seeing anyone, he entered.

Kate's eyes flew open at the sound of the door. She slumped in relief as Sam rushed to her and took the gag from her mouth. "Are you all right?" he asked.

Kate nodded.

Sam was cutting the ropes from her feet when she cried out a warning. Sam turned in time to have the butt of Carlos' gun smash down on his temple. He crumpled to the floor.

Dragging Sam's body to the post of the bunk bed was no effortless task, but Carlos slid him up into a seated position, securing his hands behind him to the post of the built-in bunk bed with zip ties.

The earlier drizzle had turned into a full-blown Texas thunderstorm with rain lashing at the grimy windows. Carlos patiently sat on one of the rickety chairs, waiting for Sam to regain consciousness. He was cleaning his nails with the knife Sam had picked up at the trading post when Sam came to.

"Ah, welcome, my friend. It's nice to have you join our little party. We've missed you, haven't we, Kate?" Carlos smirked, flipping the knife end over end. "This is a nice knife, Sam." Carlos noted admiringly. "Well-balanced for the work at hand."

Sam turned his gaze to Kate. She was still tied, but it didn't look like Ramirez had touched her. He let his gaze take in the rest of the room, realizing how stupid he'd been, letting his guard down. It was like the dream, not being able to move, feeling helpless. Pushing down a rising tide of inadequacy, Sam breathed steadily in and out, reviewing his options. Their lives depended on his clear thinking. He shifted his weight and pulled on his wrists to gauge the tightness of his bonds. The zip ties were tight enough to cut off his circulation.

"So, my friend," Carlos said, grinning, "you are quite helpless. It must be frustrating. The big, strong Sam Slater, retired Navy Seal, hero, Homeland Security officer. You must feel so powerless. So inadequate. I will enjoy watching you suffer." Sam's eyes cut to Kate. "Ah, yes. She is the love of your life, is she not? And she is lovely to look at. I enjoy it very much."

Carlos rose and walked toward Kate. Using the skinning knife, he cut the rest of her blouse, baring her breasts. "You have enjoyed these lovely breasts, have you not, my friend?" Carlos asked, his hands reaching toward Kate's chest.

Sam growled deep in his throat.

"Ah, do you anticipate my plan? Perhaps you will enjoy watching? Because you will see everything as I take my pleasure with her." Carlos used the knife again to cut away Kate's shorts, leaving only her panties in place. "These panties are so delicate; don't you think, Sam? How many times did you slide them down her long legs so you could touch her? Moist and inviting, just for you?"

"Ramirez, I'm the one who killed your brother. This is between you and me. Let Kate go. She had nothing to do with it. If she meant anything to you at one time, let her go. You want me. You want to kill me!" Sam endeavored to reason with Carlos and buy time.

"Yes, she meant something to me, a future that promised success. I envisioned her as my first lady of Mexico, but now, that is no longer possible because you have ruined everything. You have destroyed my family and my future." Carlos' fury sizzled like grease on a hot pan. "So, you see, my friend, killing you isn't enough. I want you to live and always remember." As he laid his lips and hands on Kate, he watched Sam's eyes flare up with hatred and helplessness. "I want you to know that you could do nothing to save the woman you love, just like I had to sit and watch as you killed one brother and crippled the other while I could do nothing. Revenge is sweet, is it not, my friend?"

As panic rose in Sam's gorge, he felt something else—a loose nail in the floorboard and hope. Using his fingernail, he worked to pry the nail from the board. He felt his fingernail on his index finger tear away. There was warmth from the flow of blood from the torn nail. He used his middle finger. He'd go through everyone if necessary to pull that damn nail out.

Sam's gaze continued to fixate on Carlos as the man fondled Kate, watching her eyes widen in horror. With each cry escaping her mouth, Sam's rage grew, vowing he'd kill Ramirez. Carlos skirted around to Kate's back and, looking over her shoulder at Sam, ran a hand across her abdomen, all the while smiling. Sam spit with rage. The nail was loosening, but not coming out quickly enough.

Sam listened as Carlos hummed softly to himself in a crazed high-pitched voice. Suddenly, the interior of the cabin filled with the brilliance of a bolt of lightning and the sound of a tree crashing down somewhere in the woods. Thunder shook the old building and dust drifted down from the rafters as Carlos assaulted Kate. Tears seeped from her eyes as Carlos held her hips against his, enjoying the feel of her body and her degradation.

"You see, my friend, she likes it, wants it. Don't you, *carino?*"

Carlos turned a smug and satisfied smile to Sam after nibbling along her neck. "She is such a wanton, isn't she, Sam?"

"You are a sick bastard, Ramirez!" Sam snarled, struggling at the zip ties. His one hand was growing numb. The nail was no closer to coming loose. Sam was dying inside. His rage was volcanic. Ignoring Carlos, Sam turned his gaze to Kate. She had her eyes tightly closed, and the color had drained from her face, leaving dark smudges of purple shadows under her eyes. He tried to send her his thoughts, willing her to fight and focusing all his energy on the nail.

When Kate finally opened her eyes, Sam was surprised, yet thankful, to see a ferocity in Kate's eyes. He gave her the smallest nod in silent communication to hold on, to fight. They'd survive.

Kate twisted and turned as far as her bonds allowed, calling Carlos every insulting name she could come up with. Carlos just stood there laughing at her. Spitting in his face and trying to bite him, she distracted him enough for Sam to work the nail loose. Pulling it out, he used it to compress the tongue of the zip tie and loosen it enough to slip his hands free.

Carlos had dropped the knife close to Kate to continue his assault on her. Sam took this opportunity and launched himself at Carlos, reaching for the knife. Tackling Carlos at the waist, he took him to the floor, but Carlos was fast and turned on the way down so they were face to face. He had a grip on Sam's hand holding the knife. Using the momentum of the fall, Carlos rolled on top of Sam. Straddling him, Carlos used his free hand to punch Sam several times in the face, breaking his lips and bloodying his nose.

But a thunderous fury that matched the raging storm outside gripped Sam. His savagery overcame any blows Carlos landed. Still, Carlos was able to wrench the knife out of Sam's grip, plunging the blade into Sam's right shoulder. Sam seized Carlos' wrist, using a brute force that only anger and fear can muster. They rolled back and forth several times, trading places.

Sam ended on top. He felt the warmth of blood from his shoulder gash flowing down his chest. He was weakening. Then he heard Kate whisper his name.

Grasping Carlos' hand, he turned it until the blade pointed at Carlos' throat. With a roar of hatred and savagery, Sam drove the knife home through Carlos' throat, so hard that it stuck in the wood plank floor, pinning him to it. Carlos' eyes bulged, staring unbelievingly at Sam, drowning in his own blood. Sam held the knife in place until Carlos' eyes glazed over in death. Wrenching the knife out, Sam stumbled to Kate, cutting her bonds. He held her while she watched emotionlessly as Carlos' blood seeped into the rotting planks of the floor.

Sam retrieved his cell phone and called Jake, letting him know they were safe and where they were. The brunt of the storm had passed over them. Sam used Kate's blouse to staunch his bleeding and used his shirt to cover her nakedness. He carried her to the SUV. By the time they got there, Jake and Emily were pulling up, followed by an ambulance and John with the HSI team. Sam reluctantly handed Kate over to the paramedics, who wrapped her in a blanket. She had cuts and bruises, but no major physical injuries. No, her wounds were emotional. The EMTs cleaned her up and gave her a sedative. Emily insisted Sam get checked over, too. The EMTs bandaged his hands and cleaned up the cuts on his face. They put a butterfly bandage on the cut over his brow and Steri-Strips on the shoulder gash. By this time, Sam had had enough.

"That gash will need stitches. The Steri-Strips are only a temporary fix," the paramedic cautioned.

Sam grunted an acknowledgement and checked on Kate. She was staring at nothing, dry-eyed. When Sam reached out to her, she simply stared at his hand on hers. In the meantime, John and the team walked to the shack and found Carlos. They confirmed the kill and called in the crime scene folks.

****

John and the team squeezed into one SUV leaving the second one for Sam to take. The four of them headed home. Emily sat in the back of the vehicle cradling Kate in her arms. Kate hadn't said anything since Sam had killed Carlos. All three were growing concerned. She rested her head on Emily's shoulder and stared out the window at the darkness. Finally, the sedative took effect, and she slept.

Jake rode up front with Sam. Debriefing would wait until they got home and put Kate to bed. When they arrived, Sam carried Kate to his room and tucked her in. She didn't wake. Emily offered to sit with her while Sam and Jake talked.

Jake was waiting downstairs with four fingers of Sam's best scotch. Handing the glass to Sam, they went out into the garden. Walking to the fountain, Sam ran his hand under the falling water and breathed in the scent of the Formosa tree blossoms. The recent storm had cleansed the air. Everything felt fresh, but he still smelled the damp wood of the cabin and the coppery scent of Carlos' blood. He relived the terror of Ramirez hurting Kate and the satisfaction he felt killing him. Taking a sip of scotch, he stared into the darkness, seeing Kate's dull expression as she'd sat in the ambulance. Sam followed the garden path past the lilies and ginger, jasmine, and gardenia, ending at the vacant chair next to Jake. Jake refilled Sam's glass and waited.

Sighing, Sam put his face in his hands and said, "Just like the dream, Jake. Once again, I failed. I promised to keep her safe and Ramirez got to her. I watched as he touched her. Will she ever forgive me or be able to respond to my touch?"

They both knew that was the crux of the matter. They'd seen too many women, young girls actually, in Afghanistan after being taken and used by the Taliban for their pleasure. They were considered damaged goods, and many chose to commit suicide rather than live with the shame.

Jake reached out, placing his hand on Sam's arm. "She's stronger than that,Sam, and she knows you love her. Don't borrow trouble."

They sat in silence for another hour, then Jake went in, leaving Sam to self-heal. It was midnight when Sam went upstairs and sent Emily to bed. He sat down and slid to his knees. For the first time in years, Sam clasped his hands in prayer and begged God to heal the woman he loved. Sam fell asleep, still on his knees, his head on the bed. When he awoke in the morning, he reached out to Kate, only to see her stiffen and turn her face away.

For the next few days, Kate didn't speak. Emily would greet Kate each morning and open the blinds, trying her best to infuse a sense of cheerfulness. Kate stared down at her hands or, when Emily got her to move to the chair by the window, stared outside at the wind blowing the branches of the trees. She sat quietly while Emily, trying to keep up cheerful chatter, brushed her hair. The trays of food Emily worked so hard to make appealing, hoping to encourage Kate to eat, went untouched.

Sam paced up and down the hallway like a caged animal during Emily's visits to Kate's room, waiting for some positive sign, but the look Emily gave him when she exited with yet another untouched tray of food only upped Sam's anxiety.

At the end of each day, Emily would help Kate to bed and Sam would come in to take up his vigil. Sitting in a chair by the bedside, Sam would watch the emotions flash across Kate's face as she dreamed, reliving every torturous moment of the abduction. When that happened, he would gently crawl onto the bed, taking her in his arms. Kate would instinctively turn to Sam in her sleep, and when he held her and stroked her hair, she would sigh and relax. He left her side before she woke in the morning. He didn't know if he could bear to see her stiffen and turn away from him like she had before.

By the fourth day, Kate was acknowledging Emily's 'good morning' with a dull expression and drinking the glass of orange juice placed in her hand.

"I think a hot bath will do you a world of good, Kate." Emily filled the tub and poured in some ginger oil. The scent wafted out to the bedroom. Easing Kate into the water, Emily noticed the bruising was fading. She said a silent prayer that her emotional bruises would fade as quickly and went out to straighten the bed.

When the water cooled, Kate stepped out of the tub. The horror of that night reflected at her from the mirror, remembering how each bruise came about. She wrapped Sam's big terry-cloth robe around her body and sat in the chair, looking into the back garden, smelling the fresh gardenias and jasmine Sam had placed on her nightstand. She reached out, picked up a blossom, and brushed it across her cheek. The silky feel of its petals brought her some peace and tranquility. With her face buried in the robe, she inhaled Sam's scent. That evening, Kate met Emily's happy greeting with a wan smile. She had several bites of the meal and said a quiet thank you when Emily took the tray away.

Putting the tray down on the kitchen counter, Emily turned to Sam. "She's coming back to us. It's not fast, but I can see her healing. Go slowly, Sam." Jake squeezed Sam's shoulder and put his arm around Emily as they watched Sam slowly make his way up the stairs.

It was all Sam could do not to rush up to the bedroom and take Kate in his arms, but he knew Emily was right. Standing by the bedroom door, he saw Kate wrapped in his robe, fast asleep. He took up his usual place by her side. When her dreams came again, they were less violent. This time, Sam got under the covers with Kate and took her in his arms. She woke and, looking trustingly at him, snuggled closer. They slept.

Sam woke to Kate's fingers running through his hair, looking at him. With fear and anguish, he desperately tried to interpret her expression.

Sighing, Kate took Sam's hand. "It was a horrible experience, Sam. I betrayed you. Betrayed our love. I was frightened beyond belief, but I knew in my heart that you'd come for me, Sam. I knew without a doubt you'd save me no matter what. I love you, Sam. I love you." Laying her hand on his cheek, Kate closed her eyes and fell back asleep.

Sam kissed the top of her head and drew her closer. She turned toward him in her sleep, snuggling under his arm and against his heart. Sam brushed the hair away from her face, stroking her hair, taking comfort in her steady breathing.

Emily came upstairs later that morning and quietly woke Sam, informing him John and Commander Collins had arrived and were waiting downstairs to speak with him and Jake. Rising softly and tucking the blanket around Kate, Sam made his way downstairs expecting the worse.

"Sometimes all it takes is one mistake and Carlos made it." Commander Collins paced to the window and looked out at the empty street. Turning to face Sam and

Jake, he punched his fist into his hand. "Our legal team did one hell of a job. They found the workaround and were able to get us a search warrant for the consulate's residence. Carlos and his cronies forgot to take into account that the official consulate office in Dallas is off-limits, enjoying diplomatic immunity. The residence, however, because they chose a private home, isn't. We found a flash drive with all the transactions, money, weapons, drugs; everything outlined. Dates, dollars, buyers, the whole works. It's a gold mine and will put what remains of the Ramirez cartel out of business. Probably boot a few Mexican politicians and police out of office too. Sam, the government has exonerated you and your team. You can return to work whenever you want."

Sam looked from Jake to his boss and shook his head. "No. Thank you, Commander, not now at least."

Sam watched out the window as his second in command and his commanding officer climbed into their government-issued sedan and drove away. Without Kate in his life, he didn't have one. He turned his head toward the stairs and wondered how he'd survive without her.

His feet felt like lead weights as he slowly climbed the stairs. He found Kate curled up in the chair by the window. Emily had opened the window for her and he could hear the splashing of the fountain and the birds singing. Walking across the room, he dropped to his knees. Kate traced the dark shadows under his eyes from his nightly vigils. She ran her fingers over the bruises along his jawline and cheekbone where Carlos had pummeled him. Sam looked at her, trying to fathom the emotions so clearly battling under the surface.

"Sam, you are the bravest, kindest man I've ever known. I know this is the love my mom felt for my dad." Kate's voice faltered and the tears welling up in her eyes cascaded down her cheeks. "But, my mom—she was worthy of his love. After what Carlos did…how he…his touch…Can you forgive me?"

Sam's throat was so tight with emotion that it hurt to speak. He rose and sat on the chair, shifting Kate onto his lap and into his embrace. He cupped Kate's chin in his hand, turning her face toward him. He wasn't sure there were words to express what he was feeling. "Kate, there is nothing to forgive. What happened was horrific and it will be a shadow over us for a while, but it won't overshadow what is in our hearts. You fought. You survived. You didn't betray me."

Kate shook her head. "But it's more than that. When Carlos died, I felt no remorse. I hated him so much I wanted to kill him, to drive that knife home. He died, and I enjoyed watching it. I rejoiced in it. I embraced the darkness. You must be so ashamed of me. You deserve better, Sam, so much better." Kate lowered her face onto his shoulder, tears tumbling freely.

Sam touched her cheek, and she turned guilt-ridden eyes to him. "Ashamed of you? No, Kate, I'm proud of you. And I thank God for you. When I was fighting Ramirez, my strength was flagging. Kate, we both survived. Remember when you shared your thoughts about windmills? How fragile they appear and yet how strong? Able to survive violent and tempestuous winds to provide life-giving water. You are like that, Kate, fragile looking, yet so strong. Kate, I need you. I was so broken before I met you. With your love, I conquered my demons. You saved me. Your love is my life-giving water. My soul thirsts for you. Let me be the light that leads you out of your darkness. It isn't a question of my deserving better. It's a matter of my being deserving enough of you. Never doubt how much I love you and always will. Please, Kate, don't give up on our love." Sam's voice broke as he fiercely hugged her and buried his face in her hair.

They held each other, finding comfort and strength until the moon rose, casting its light across the bedroom. A single silver moonbeam walked its way across the room, lighting on a painting of a woman in a field of wildflowers with a windmill standing as sentinel. Kate saw the beauty in the scene and the light. She had listened with her heart to what Sam said. There were still shadows falling across her emotions, and she knew the darkness would take time to be conquered, but even in that single beam of moonlight, she saw everything she needed to see. Reaching a tentative hand, she stroked Sam's hair. There was so much pleading in his eyes, so much hope. Yes, she thought, you are my light.

"Sam, wash my hair"

Printed in the USA
CPSIA information can be obtained
at www.ICGtesting.com
LVHW022322270923
759269LV00012B/375